The Seven Cozy Shorts

A story a day for
every day of the week:

Ancient ghost
Mysterious omen
Jealous acolyte
Christmas magic
Small town mystery
Soulmates across time
Love conquers fear

Copyright © Erika M Szabo, 2020

The Seven Cozy Shorts:

Bedtime Stories for Grownups

ISBN: 978-1-943962-83-9

Published by Golden Box Books Publishing, New York, U.S.A.

Editing by: Tricia Drammeh

Book cover, illustrations, book formatting and book interior design by the Erika M Szabo

The seven stories in this bundle:

The Ghost of Prince Akhmose
Messenger
The Potion
Bittersweet Memories
The Worthless Painting
Alone
Fake It Till You Make It

ANCIENT GHOST

The Ghost of Prince Akhmose

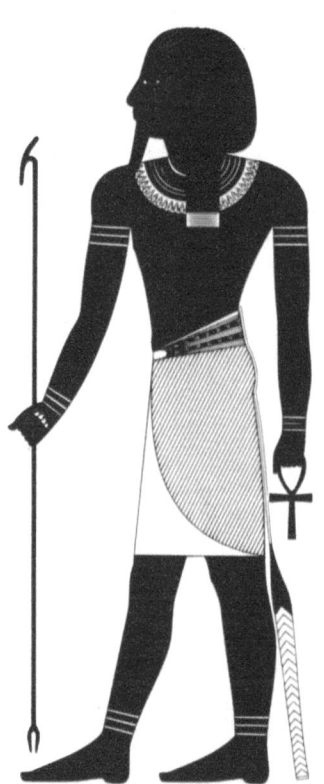

Fate and Destiny

Fate and destiny intertwine
Fulfilling a curse lost in the sands of time
Two lovers destroyed in a jealous rage
Are rejoined in a new day and age
The evil magician returns as well
Assured he'll keep them in his curse's hell
The passing years reveal a way to defend
Proving love conquers all in the end
© Cindy J. Smith

Prologue

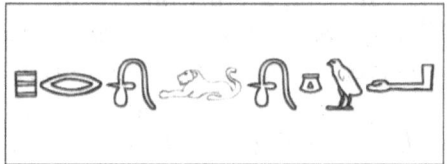

Egypt, 1198 BC

The scorching sun was high in the sky, but Tanakhmet relaxed in the shade fanned by his servants. He watched the builder slaves trudging along in the hot sun, carrying rocks upon their backs, building the pharaoh's final resting place.

Tanakhmet was the closest to the pharaoh, who was on his sickbed, and there was no question that he would be the Grand Vizier of the next pharaoh. The pharaoh's son had been groomed from birth to take his father's place, but he was too young to rule. The pharaoh's younger brother, Prince Akhmose, would be his regent until he'd come of age. But because Akhmose cared more about art and sports than learning how to rule, Tanakhmet made sure that the prince needed him and couldn't rule without him.

Tanakhmet gazed upon the land that would be under his rule. His soon to be wife would elevate his and his future children's status, being of royal blood. She was a princess of a land Egypt had conquered, and she was sent to appease him and secure the alliance. Although he was the second most powerful man of Egypt, the thorn of resentment burrowed deeper and deeper into his heart every time he was reminded that royal blood didn't flow in his veins.

When his future wife arrived and Tanakhmet gazed upon her the first time, he didn't hide his disappointment. The princess was petite and average looking. Breasts barely lifting the light tunic and hips narrow as that of a young boy's, she lacked the beauty he so desired. She was nothing but an obligation, a means to an alliance. Tanakhmet assigned her a luxurious living quarters in the palace with a beautiful lotus pond in the courtyard, far away from his quarters, and he provided an adequate number of servants to fit her high status. He would see her again on their wedding day.

Glancing at the beautiful young slave kneeling at his feet, his loins immediately stirred with desire. Her skin had a sun-kissed glow and a pleasantly round body, which was soft in just the right places. Her shaved head downcast as she held out a cup of wine. He loved to see the look of defiance in her eyes, wondering what words would tumble from her lips if she was allowed to speak. She would be killed on the spot for her insolence if those words that clearly showed in her eyes ever left her lips. She was but a slave, a possession. She obeyed him, yet her gaze only held hate and disgust.

Why can't she accept her fate? He often questioned, but deep down, he enjoyed the absolute power he had over her. Even after she bore his child, she remained obedient, but cold and distant toward him.

"I want you in my room tonight. It's time to give your meowing pup to the wet nurse and return to my bed," he said, watching the daggers in her eyes that clearly reflected her feelings.

She bowed her head in submission at his sharp gaze, stood up, and quietly retreated. Tanakhmet reserved a forced, kind expression only to royals, but those of lower status knew his true, savage nature. Having been born to a servant out of wedlock and greedily watching the privileged life of the royal family, he swore he would reach a high status one day. When the old Grand Vizier noticed his eagerness to learn, the aging man began teaching him all he knew. Soon, Tanakhmet made himself indispensable to the pharaoh and the entire court by creating healing potions and casting spells. When there was nothing more he could learn from the Vizier, Tanakhmet added a few deadly herbs to his master's wine. He didn't even feel a twinge of guilt or sorrow. In his mind, the Vizier had served his purpose by elevating his status and became disposable.

A servant approached holding a piece of papyrus. Tanakhmet's eyes narrowed as he read the urgent message. The pharaoh was sending him to negotiate a treaty with not a minute delay. He glanced once more at the retreating slave, stood up and strolled out without another word. He hated that he had to obey the order of the pharaoh, but he knew the time will come when he would give the orders, and everyone will obey—including the pharaoh's successor.

Chapter One

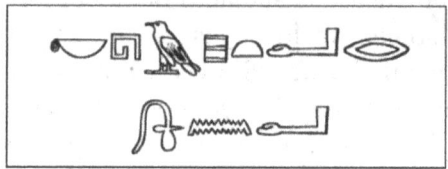

Present time

Layla Lockhart, a petite slender woman, emerged from the bathroom, bare feet slapping against the wooden floor. Teal-blue silk pajamas swished softly on her slender body as she walked toward the kitchen, eyes swollen from sleep and hair messy from the restless night.

The smell of frying bacon filled the air and her stomach rumbled at the scent. The small TV was on in the living room. The cheerful voice of the channel six weather reporter announced, "Another beautiful, sunny morning, the temperature is a balmy seventy degrees."

"How could anyone be so damn cheerful in the morning?" Layla mumbled walking into the kitchen, raking her fingers through her tangled, long, jet-black hair. "Ouch!" she exclaimed as her hand got caught in a snag.

"Top o' the mornin' to you, too!" her roommate called out and smiled at Layla, holding a greasy spatula.

"Sheesh, Mara! You don't have to yell." Layla rubbed the back of her neck as she made her way to the table.

"Here," Mara giggled as she poured steaming coffee into Layla's favorite cup and handed it to her. "This will get you out of the morning fog."

Sighing, Layla plopped down onto the squeaky kitchen chair and lifted the cup to her lips but froze when she heard Mara's shout, "Hey, it's hot! You'll burn your mouth."

"What would I do without you?" Layla's grumpy expression softened looking at the redheaded woman lovingly.

"You'd go hungry, a lot. That's for sure!" Mara laughed as she filled Layla's plate with fried eggs and crispy bacon. She winked before turning her eyes to her own plate, her curly un-tamable mane moving as if it had a mind of its own. Unlike Layla, Mara was a morning person. As soon as her eyes opened and feet touched the floor, she was ready to go. "Eat up! You have a long, busy day ahead of you," she said, handing her friend a slice of toast.

Mornings were always rough for Layla, she needed some time to shake the foggy, morning mood. "Yeah, another boring day at a boring job." Her head fell onto the table. "For all those tedious years studying for my Masters in Egyptology only to get a job cataloging artifacts and restoring broken pottery."

"Oh, don't be such a sourpuss!" Mara whacked her hand playfully with the back of her fork. "Now listen here! Most of the people of your graduation class are either teaching kids with their fancy degrees or shoveling sand in the desert somewhere in Egypt, in a 'going nowhere' job."

Layla lifted her head and sighed. Mara was right... again. Mara was always there to help her to put her mind straight. "You're right, I was lucky to get in. It's just so depressing when I have all this knowledge and I can't use it to discover something new and exciting."

"Let's face it, girlfriend, you're a true introvert. Can you picture yourself living in a tent with ten other people in a hundred and twenty degrees with no AC in sight, or being in a classroom with rowdy, overgrown teenagers?" Mara took a sip of coffee and continued, "This position in the museum suits you. You can work by yourself and have little interaction with others."

Layla paled at her words, neither of the two situations sounded good. She would take cataloging alone in a clean museum any day over having to spend months brushing the sand from broken pottery with a competitive team or being in a crowded classroom giving the same lecture year after year.

"You're right... again." Layla caught Mara's bright grin and hid a frown behind her coffee cup. She wouldn't trade their friendship for anything in the world. Even with just a few words from Mara, she was already feeling better. She winked and flashed a warm smile over her coffee cup, "I don't know how you put up with me for all those years. You're my best friend, you know."

Mara snickered, "Because you're the only person who doesn't annoy the hell out of me." She motioned around the relatively quiet apartment, "I have enough 'peopling' to do at the hospital. When I get home, I love the quietness and knowing you're always there for me."

Layla laughed, "I'm not a chatterbox, that's for sure."

"Definitely not, but that's the way I like it."

Layla loaded her fork and stuffed the food into her mouth, "And your superpower is to make fried eggs and bacon so damn tasty."

"That's for sure!" Mara laughed.

They ate quickly, the hands on the clock seemed to be moving faster as they polished off the food. Layla made a move to clear the plates, but Mara snatched them first. She made a motion with her hands, "Now shoo, get ready for work. I'm off today, I'm going to do some food shopping. We're running low on everything."

Layla stood up, hugging Mara before hurrying back to her room to get ready. "I hope we'll stay best friends, forever," Layla whispered.

"You bet! You're stuck with me for life," Mara said lovingly.

Meeting Mara was probably one of the best things that had ever happened to Layla. Her parents decided to move to the United States after the death of her maternal grandparents. Despite only knowing Egypt as her home, her father wanted to move back to the United States. Her mother, who now had no more ties to Egypt, agreed. Shortly after her ninth birthday, Layla found her home away from home in Boston.

It wasn't easy to fit in. She felt sad leaving her home and friends but as soon as she started the school year in Boston and met Mara, everything fell into place. The red-haired freckled girl inherited her Irish ancestors' cheery mood and positive outlook on life. They became best friends and Mara helped the timid, shy Layla ease into her new life. The two became inseparable.

It was impossible to stay together all the time, but they made a promise that they would always be close. That promise lasted through high school and well into college. The best friends moved to Albany and rented an apartment together. Mara, fulfilling her childhood dream, entered nursing school, and Layla, to her mother's delight, chose to study Egyptology.

Their apartment looked nothing like a usual, uniformly furnished home. Scouring for furniture that they could get at a relatively low price, they collected pieces at yard sales, second-hand shops, and wherever they could find usable chairs, tables, beds, shelves, and anything else they needed. They ended up with an apartment that looked like an antique shop, but they liked it that way. Mara's unique paintings hung on every light-maroon colored wall and Layla's ancient Egyptian style statues, scroll replicas, and vases made the apartment feel like a cozy home, even in Albany style standards.

Chapter Two

Present time

The morning traffic was crazy, as usual. Layla tapped the steering wheel with anxious fingers and kept looking at the dashboard clock. "I'm going to be late... I'm so going to be late," she mumbled, mentally pushing the cars in front of her to move faster.

Finally, she turned her small, secondhand Lyme-green car into a parking space, and the sounds of the noisy street cut off as soon as the heavy door to the museum closed behind her. The thud echoed through the wide corridor across the marble floors. Her shoes clicked rapidly as she hurried toward a large storage room that housed her studio as well.

She had barely thrown her bag onto a chair when her door slammed open. Jerome, her balding, overweight boss in his early fifties, rushed into the studio, exasperated. "Ms. Lockhart! You're not going to believe this!" His face was flushed, his eyes bright with excitement. His voice squeaked, "Guess!"

"What's going on?" Layla asked, as she observed the usually stoic man's exhilarated fidgeting. *He's going to have a heart attack*, she thought observing his red face and shaking hands. She felt concerned.

"We're getting the well-preserved mummy of Prince Akhmose, the son of Queen Takhat. Dr. Wilson just phoned me last night from Cairo." The words continued to spill out of his mouth at an unnaturally fast rate as if he were trying to tell her everything at once. He took a deep breath and continued, "He was at the dig site with no phone, until yesterday," he said. "Finally, his lawyers got the paperwork done a week ago, and because he's the benefactor of our museum, Prince Akhmose's sarcophagus will be displayed here. The crates will arrive today."

Layla's heartbeat quickened. "This is an invaluable treasure that our humble museum could ever hope receiving!" she announced and held her breath. "If I remember correctly, Prince Akhmose, son of Queen Takhat, was the brother of Amenmesse who ruled from 1201 to 1198 BC. He was the fifth pharaoh of the Nineteenth Dynasty. Not much is known about him because he ruled for such a short time, but I remember reading about Prince Akhmose in a scroll. The only mention about him was that Pharaoh Amenmesse mourned his brother who died young."

Jerome let out a nervous laugh, scratched his balding head and replied in a calmer tone, "Well, if he'd been a pharaoh or a well-known prince, I doubt the Egyptian government would've given us the right to transport his mummy out of the country." He smiled brightly and his face started to return to a normal color, "Regardless, I'm happy that they did."

"Yes, me too! I'm looking forward to deciphering the hieroglyphs on his sarcophagus and hopefully, we'll get some scrolls as well." She glanced at the broken pottery pieces on her table. The possibility of working on something great made her excited.

"Oh, yes! You're fluent in the 19th dynasty dialect. I knew hiring you would come in handy someday," Jerome cackled, wringing his chubby fingers. "Let's get busy. Pack away everything you've been working on. Our priority is now Prince Akhmose. You'll catalog everything and start working on decoding while I'll organize the preparation of the green room. Oh, my! I'll get everything we have from the 19th dynasty transferred to the green room. It's going to be a fantastic display." Jerome turned and rushed out of Layla's studio.

Layla hummed as she worked to carefully pack away the broken pottery pieces. There was no rush to restore them, and she had to stop a few times to calm her excitement. *Finally, there will be something I could really enjoy working on.* Her stomach felt like it was tied in knots and could hardly wait for the crates to arrive.

Chapter Three

Present time

The crates arrived in mid-afternoon sending everyone buzzing and into action. The transporting crew carefully unpacked the crates making sure not to get in Layla's way as she took pictures of every single item from different angles. Jerome was at her side, placing handwritten labels on every item the helpers placed on the large table and shelves. The crates were carried out of the room as soon as they were empty and moved into the large storage room.

Jerome kept slipping between the workers and constantly warned them, "Be careful," which resulted in many annoyed eye rolls and sighs.

After hours of hearing him only say those few words and being constantly underfoot, one of the older helpers finally snapped, "We are careful!"

Jerome's face reddened and he muttered an apology, never taking his eyes off the ancient artifacts. "Sorry, I'm just so excited." He was as sincere as he could be given the fact that he was surrounded by one of the greatest treasures ever delivered to the museum. The helpers merely shrugged, they had gotten used to him over the years and went back to unpacking all the crates.

Layla gasped as the beautifully decorated sarcophagus was uncovered. It had stood against the time well, showing little weathering. The colors were still bright and the hieroglyphs easily readable. If she didn't know better, she would have guessed that it was recently painted.

She tore her eyes away from the sarcophagus as they unpacked a smaller crate that revealed the canopic jars. Each jar carved from limestone was about five inches tall, decorated with depictions of the four sons of Horus: Imsety, Hapi, Duamutef, and Qebehsenuef.

His back turned to her; Jerome didn't see Layla's shocked face as she lifted a fifth jar from the crate. It was different, masterfully carved from green marble. The lid depicted a young man's head inlaid with gold. The body of the jar had rows of hieroglyphics carved into it.

She had mastered the hieroglyphs of the 19th dynasty, studied the language and culture, and sometimes longed to be a part of that ancient civilization. *I've never heard of having five canopic jars placed in the tomb with any mummy in any dynasty.* Her eyes glazed over with amazement, there was so much that she could discover. She didn't say anything to Jerome and making a haste decision, she hid the marble jar in her desk. She wanted to start deciphering the fifth jar's writings without Jerome's meddling. She had wished for so long that she could be part of something exciting, and now it was finally happening.

When the crates were empty and everything carefully labeled and cataloged, Jerome looked around with great pride. "This is fantastic! Look at all those funerary items and the sarcophagus! That will be the focus of the tours when we have everything organized and displayed in the green room."

Layla smiled, "Yes, it will be spectacular."

Jerome rubbed his hands. "Okay, let's get busy! You can continue cataloging and then start decoding, and I'll call the company that supplies us with the climate-controlled display cases. I need to order one for the mummy before we open the sarcophagus." He hurried out of the room and Layla sat by her computer to organize and print the photos she took.

Time flew by, and a few hours later Jerome opened her door a crack and poked his head in. "Let's go home and get a good night's sleep. We'll have a busy day tomorrow."

Layla glanced back and forth between her boss and the computer before speaking in a small voice, "I'm not finished yet. I'll stay a bit longer."

He wasn't swayed and took a step further into the room. "No, you're not staying here all by yourself, again! You'll finish it tomorrow. Let's go." He motioned for her to move.

Layla stayed glued to her chair and started to object, "But…" but Jerome's stern expression stopped her.

She hung her head in defeat. She was itching to be alone to take a closer look at the fifth jar, but she knew what that look meant. There was no way he would let her stay, even for a minute because if he did, he knew that she'd get right back to work. He knew her too well. There were mornings in the past when he had found her hunched over her work, unaware that she had spent the entire night in the studio. But then, she was useless the entire day, yawning and dozing off at her desk.

Layla wanted to read the inscription on the marble jar so badly but couldn't say no to Jerome. He was the boss. *I'll get to you first thing tomorrow,* she thought as she reached into the drawer and ran her fingers on the carved symbols of the cool marble jar. She shut down her computer, grabbed her backpack and followed Jerome. On their way out they said goodnight to Joe, the security guard, and walked to the entrance. Joe locked the door behind them.

Jerome looked exhausted, but the expression of the good kind of exhaustion and satisfaction lingered on his face.

Layla quickened her steps and enjoyed the hum of anticipation running through her. "Goodnight Jerome, I can hardly wait until tomorrow!"

He chuckled, "Get some sleep. I'll need you in tip-top shape tomorrow."

Layla unlocked her car and slid into the driver's seat. Thankfully, her work hours usually meant that she avoided the afternoon rush hours, but she couldn't seem to find the motivation to start the car. Her mind was drawn back to the fifth jar that was sitting in her office drawer. *I can't wait until tomorrow; I wouldn't sleep a wink. I want to read the inscription, now. But I can't…* she thought, chewing on her lower lip when suddenly, she remembered. Her fingers wrapped around a cool metal key in her pocket. It was the service door key she forgot to give back to Jerome after she locked the door behind the delivery people. *Should I…* she played with the thought. *The delivery crew accidentally busted the security camera, so I could get in and out without Joe and the other guard seeing me on the monitors.* She contemplated this sneaky but enticing act.

Her decision was made, she waited for Jerome's car to pull out of the parking lot before she got out of her car and walked toward the service entrance. Her legs were a bit shaky. If Joe catches her, she'll lose this amazing opportunity, but she was drawn to the jar. She couldn't wait, she had to know why it was in the tomb. Out of the hundreds of archeological digs she either participated in or learned about, there had never been a fifth canopic jar found.

She quickly unlocked the heavy door and punched in the security code before the alarm could go off and reached her studio without any problems. She grabbed the marble jar with trembling fingers and put it in her backpack.

She tiptoed by the sarcophagus in the eerie, dark room clutching her backpack that held the precious canopic jar. The fear of getting caught made her palm sweaty and she could hear the blood rushing through her head, but the desire to decrypt the ancient hieroglyphics was stronger than any rational thought she had at the moment. She held her backpack tightly as she crept toward the door.

Suddenly, a bright, narrow light beam swept the floor a few feet from her, and then she heard the light footstep and soft humming of the night guard. Layla quickly crouched down behind a large Anubis statue trying to hold her breath. Luckily, Joe, the stocky, middle-aged man, was too lazy to walk through every single room. He just shined his flashlight around looking for any movement. Not that he was expecting ancient mummies or statues to suddenly walk around at night in the museum, but he had to be watchful for artifact thieves. *Just like myself,* Layla thought.

As soon as she heard Joe walking down the corridor toward the guards' room, she crept to the door and peeked. She watched Joe disappear at the corner and hurried toward the service door. Carefully locking the heavy door behind her, she ran to her car.

She could hardly wait to get home. It had taken all her self-control to keep her from taking the jar out of her backpack. She reached in and caressed the carved symbols with her fingertips.

Chapter Four

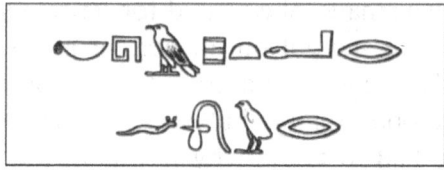

Present time

On the drive home, Layla kept tapping the steering wheel in anticipation. Thankfully, the traffic was light, and it was only a short drive, but every moment that precious artifact rested in her bag, was another moment that delayed her from examining it. She could hardly wait to get home and bury herself into translating the hieroglyphics. She was expecting to find Mara home, and, in her mind, Layla ran through some excuses she would tell Mara so she could lock herself in her room. However, she knew, she wouldn't get past Mara, who'd sense her excitement, and force it out of her. Mara knew she could get herself totally immersed in her projects, but also understood that for Layla, it was like exploring a whole new world, a world that didn't exist anymore.

The moment Layla walked into the apartment; she felt the weight of her actions. She had just taken an exceedingly rare artifact out of the museum. What if something happened to it while it was out of the museum? How was she going to explain what she had discovered? What if someone questioned why she was so late leaving the parking lot? She hung her keys on the hook and cradled her bag. She started to tiptoe to her room, hoping that she could stash the bag before Mara noticed.

Her hopes of getting to the room unnoticed vanished when Mara called out from the kitchen, "Hey, you're late. Want me to make you a sandwich?"

Layla gulped and started to peel her jacket off. She cleared her throat, "Um... yeah, sure, thanks."

Mara appeared at the door. "What's wrong?" she demanded; her brows raised with worry as she leaned against the wall.

Layla took one look at Mara's worried expression and crumbled to the floor. "I'm a thief! I'll be in so much trouble if Jerome finds out." Layla's hands started to shake as she tugged at the zipper of her bag and biting her lip to stop her from crying out. With tender hands, she pulled the canopic jar from her backpack and showed it to her friend.

Mara marveled at the handcrafted piece. "It's beautiful!" she exclaimed, but her awe was quickly replaced with disbelief. "You stole it?" Knowing Layla so well, she couldn't believe that her friend would do such a thing.

Layla picked at her shoelaces, "Um... well... I kind of borrowed it because I couldn't wait until tomorrow." Layla clutched the marble jar to her chest. "I hid and didn't catalog this piece, so Jerome doesn't even know about it." She confessed, bowing her head.

Mara started walking out of the hallway, beckoning Layla to follow. She asked, "Why is this statue, or whatever it is, so important?"

Layla got up on shaky legs and followed her friend to the kitchen. On her way, she carefully placed the jar on the coffee table. Her stomach loudly rumbled as she straightened up, making her realize that she forgot about lunch. She felt famished and slid into the kitchen chair, wincing as it creaked. "Because no one has ever found five canopic jars in any tomb before. She took a deep breath and tried not to rush all the words out, "The four jars contain the organs of the mummy decorated with depictions of the four sons of Horus: Imsety, with a human head, protects and carries the liver to the afterlife. Qebehsenuef, with a falcon's head, carries and protects the intestines. Hapi, with the head of a baboon, carries and protects the lungs. And Duamutef, with the head of a jackal, carries and protects the stomach."

Mara nodded as she opened the fridge door and took out the sliced ham and the mayonnaise jar. "What did they do with the other vital organs? Did they leave them in the mummy?"

"No. According to their beliefs, the brain was just mush and they extracted it through the nose. The Egyptians believed the heart to be the seat of the soul, and so it was left inside the body."

While listening intently, Mara made ham sandwiches and put a plate in front of Layla, a distinct look on her face. "Interesting," she observed and sat across from Layla, "Are you going to decode the hieroglyphics on the jar? Can I watch? There is nothing worth watching on TV."

"Sure," Layla smiled and mouthed thanks as she stood up, picked up the plate and started walking to the living room. "But I warn you, it's a tedious, boring job," she warned. "I might be up half the night."

"You're such a child!" Mara laughed, picked up her plate and followed her friend. "You can't even sit for five minutes to eat your food before you start playing with your favorite toy."

"I'm so excited about this," Layla admitted putting her plate on the coffee table and sat on the carpet crossed legged. "But are you sure you want to stay at home? It's your day off. Go, have some fun."

"It's okay, I have nothing better to do." Mara sighed, "We might be the only single ladies staying home every night without a date."

"What happened to that surgeon, Dave?" Layla inquired as she bit into her sandwich. She swallowed the mouthful of food and glanced at her friend. "You went out with him last night. He didn't ask you on a second date?"

Mara plopped on the couch and Layla nearly dropped her sandwich as she almost knocked the jar to the floor. Layla moved the jar out of the way of her friend.

Mara stared up at the ceiling. "Well, you were sleeping by the time I got home, and I didn't have a chance to tell you in the morning, but he turned out to be a real jerk." she frowned. "We had dinner at Paolo's, and I could hardly wait for the night to be over. It was boring as hell. All he talked about was how successful he is. He wasn't interested in me, he simply wanted to get into my pants for a quicky. I ended up punching him in the mouth when he got too frisky in the car. I had to grab a Taxi to get home."

Layla snorted. Mara rolled her eyes and playfully kicked her thigh. "Ouch!" Layla called out and rubbed her leg. "I meant to say that he was an ass, and I'm sorry that happened to you. I was laughing because I pictured what his face might have looked like when you socked him in the mouth."

Mara laughed, "He looked like he couldn't believe what happened, and then he screamed like a girly girl holding his bloody nose. Ugh, I have no clue what made me think he's an honorable person. He's just another pompous, self-centered ass." Mara chuckled lightly, "Now finish your sandwich so we can get to the good part of this sad evening. By the way, you haven't had a date since... have you heard from Baahir? You haven't mentioned him for months."

"It's been a year already since he left." Layla's expression saddened. "The last time I spoke to him was about three months ago. The dig, he'd found a collector to sponsor, was going well. Anyway, although we went out a few times, we've never become close enough to miss each other."

"Oh, then what were those tears you shed for weeks after he left for Egypt?" Mara teased.

Layla rolled her eyes and took a huge bite while reverting her gaze to the jar that was patiently sitting in front of her. "Yeah, I was sad for a while, but I got over it." She shoved the rest of the sandwich in her mouth and wiped her hands on her pants. Placing the plate to the side, she carefully picked up the jar.

It had taken her but a few minutes to realize that the hieroglyphics didn't make any sense. She had tried to read it as fluently as she always had, when she realized that there were no sentences, only rows of jumbled words. She had paused a bit and tried to decipher them slowly, one by one. When she finished writing down the approximate meanings of the words, she exclaimed, feeling frustrated, "It doesn't make any sense!"

Mara sat up and leaned against her side, studying the small jar, "What doesn't make sense?"

"The human and animal figures face toward the left, so it should be read from left to right. I'm reading the upper symbols and then the lower ones, and it's still just a jumble of words." She tried reading it backward, sideways, grabbing and writing down every other word, and then every third word. "Nothing makes sense!" she cried out in frustration. She flipped the jar and looked at the bottom. "Tanakhmet," she deciphered the name.

"At least you can read something." Mara nudged her friend, "What does it mean?"

"It's a name."

Mara leaned closer to take a better look, "It's not in a cartouche."

Layla impatiently sighed but immediately felt ashamed. *If she'd be talking about how the kidney works, I would ask questions as a layperson, too.* She flashed a warm smile at Mara and replied, "The cartouche was preserved for Kings and Queens." Hoping the explanation would be enough and Mara wouldn't ask more questions, she placed the jar on the table and stood up. She crouched next to the table, eyeing the jar, "What is your secret?"

She stared at the beautiful, ancient piece, squinting her eyes. "What a…" She scrambled to pick up her notepad and pen.

How had she missed that some of the carved symbols and pictures stood higher than others? It was a rookie mistake. Without her professional magnifying glass, she wouldn't be able to accurately gauge the depth by looking at it, so she closed her eyes and ran her fingers over the carved hieroglyphs. Doing so revealed that there were three different heights.

First, she wrote down the meaning of the picture groups that were the highest and read it out loud, "I, Tanakhmet, the Grand Vizier of Pharaoh Amenmesse, curse Prince Akhmose, son of Queen Takhat. I curse him to forget the names of the forty-two underworld judges." Layla sat stunned as she held the small jar in her hands. She whispered, "This is a curse!"

Mara stifled a yawn and asked, "What are those judges?"

Layla smiled and recited a passage from the Book of the Dead: "If the dead can't demonstrate that they know each of the judges' names, they can't prove that they're pure and free of sin. Anubis, the god of death and the afterlife, weighs their hearts against the feather of Maat. If their hearts are heavier than the feather, they will be devoured by the Goddess Ammit, permanently destroying their souls. They will not be presented to Osiris, who could admit them into the Sekhet-Aaru, the Field of Reeds, which is the heavenly paradise where Osiris rules."

Mara seemed to forget how sleepy she was and nudged her friend, "Read more!"

Layla ran her finger over the hieroglyphs again, concentrating on the characters that were carved a little lower than the first group was. She touched the carved vulture with a human head and showed it to Mara, "See this? This is Ba, the symbol of the soul. See this?" Layla touched the circle character with a base. "This means eternity. And this one similar to the Ankh means protection."

Mara's eyes were wide with amazement. "Wow!"

Layla smiled; this was the most awake she'd seen her friend at home at this time of the night. Usually, she would be getting ready to go to bed soon. Layla gnawed on her fingernail. "Okay, I need to concentrate."

"I'll zip up and just listen!" Mara promised. "Pretend I'm not even here."

Layla wrote the decrypted words down one by one and concentrated putting the group of characters in order. "This is the sign of Tether, that one is Feather, but I don't remember this one." Layla stood up to get her books, scouring for the symbol. She let out a gasp when she found it, "Oh, this is the symbol of rope. But what does it mean in the sentence?" she mumbled.

After hours of searching and reading the hieroglyphs over and over, she cried out, feeling excited, "I think I got this part!"

Mara's eyes lit up in anticipation. "What does it say?"

"It says, but mind you, it's just a rough translation. It says, "His heart is heavier than the feather of Maat but will not be devoured by Ammit. This spell will protect it. His soul will be tethered for eternity and never enter Sekhet-Aaru."

"Oh, my! Translate the rest. I can hardly wait to hear it. I'll make a margarita while you work on it."

Layla looked at her friend and quickly diverted her eyes back to the jar, mumbling, "That'll be nice."

The third part proved to be the hardest to decode. After three margaritas and finishing a book she started to read a week ago, Mara dozed off on the couch. Layla covered her softly snoring friend with Grandma's quilt and continued puzzling the words and word groups together to make sense of the pictorial writing.

"Oh, my, God!" Layla shouted as her old grandfather's clock struck midnight. Her blood ran cold as she jumped up and stood frozen, staring at the canopic jar.

Mara's eyes popped open, and she looked around the room with a panicked expression, "Who... what happened?" She sat up and threw the quilt to the floor. "What is it?" she asked. Seeing the terror on Layla's face, Mara stood up and grabbed her friend's shoulders. "Layla! What's wrong? You're scaring me!"

Layla's body trembled as she looked at Mara, and then relaxed a little. She stuttered, "I... finished... the... the translation. You're not going to believe it."

Layla was pale, almost too pale. Mara grabbed her shoulders and shook her. "What is it? Tell me!" she demanded.

They sat down on the couch, side by side, and Layla glanced at her notes. "This is a powerful spell and I'm not sure if I should take this seriously or..." She grabbed Mara's hand and continued. "It says, "My curse will be unlocked when the one who was born at midnight awakens our souls. I Tanakhmet, curse Akhmose to walk the Earth as a restless ghost, forever. I curse him to fall in love with the one who was born at midnight, to never have her. My soul will take a body, and I will possess her, the reincarnated soul of Anakhmun."

Mara, rubbing the last morsel of sleep from her eyes asked, "What does it mean? Who is this 'born at midnight' person?"

"The name Layla means 'born at night' in ancient Egyptian. My mom gave me this name because I was born at midnight, twenty-six years ago. Could I be the reincarnated soul of Anakhmun?"

Chapter Five

Present time

The old church bell chimed twelve times, the sound echoed through the silent museum, weaving its way into Layla's half-dark studio. Akhmose stretched and sat up feeling groggy and disoriented. He looked around the large room that was lit by the full moon through the window. *Where am I? What is this strange place?* he thought, feeling confused. *How did I get here?*

He looked toward the window. The pale moon and the chirping sounds of the night birds and insects spoke of serenity. Akhmose stood up and started walking toward the window but felt as if he was walking on air. Looking down at his legs, he realized that his feet didn't touch the ground. Startled, he concentrated on standing with feet firmly on the ground. When he descended, he felt the floor under his bare feet. *What is going on? Am I dreaming?*

As his eyes adjusted to the moonlight, he looked around and saw a sarcophagus in the middle of the room. *How strange. This place doesn't look like a burial chamber.* He walked back to the sarcophagus and dropped his hand to the surface, only to watch his fingers sink into the solid wood with no resistance. Yanking his hand back, he stared at the large sarcophagus in total confusion. He could see the face painted on the exterior, and at that moment, he realized that the sarcophagus was made for him. *But I'm not dead. I'm dreaming.* He sighed in relief. *That's it! This place is not a burial chamber and can't be the beautiful place of the afterlife, the Sekhet-Aaru. And besides, even if I were dead, the sarcophagus shouldn't be closed, not until my body was placed inside.*

"Where am I?" His voice echoed in the room, but it was only met with silence. Panic started to set in, not knowing why he was brought to this strange place. He buried his face in his hands and felt the smooth skin and muscles beneath. *My body feels solid and real, yet everything around me feels as soft as clouds. Why?*

His steps made no sound as he walked toward the walls. Shelves upon shelves were filled with papyrus rolls but they looked old and faded. He saw strange symbols painted on small paper squares, but he couldn't read them. None of the figures made any sense. He felt anxious and lost.

Then, he saw colorful hieroglyphics. They were so clear and real and beautiful. *Whoever painted them must have been schooled by a really great teacher.* He tried to unroll one of the papyri open, but his hands kept sinking into it. He gave up and turned away.

Suddenly, a bright light beam swept across the floor and then the walls. He froze as his eyes followed the light. Was it a sign? What caused this strange bright light? It looked to be as pure as the sun, but how could it be seen at night? Was he in the realm of the gods? Heavy footsteps approached, and he moved toward the sound. A large man in strange clothes held a torch that didn't burn with flames. *That's no torch with fire!* Akhmose decided. *How could they trap the sunlight in that small cylindrical object the man is holding?* The strange man looked old and worn, paying no attention to him. Akhmose crossed his arms and commanded, "Tell me what this place is!"

His face burned when the man refused to reply, or even glance in his direction. How dare he? He was Akhmose, brother of the Pharaoh of Egypt! He took a step closer to the man trying to avoid the bright light. Standing in front of the man, he shouted, "Can you hear me?"

The stocky looking man didn't even blink. *What's wrong with this man? Those who own this place, why are they employing the blind and deaf?* Akhmose sighed and leaned against the wall. He had given up on trying to get the man's attention. All his life, few dared to ignore him, and even fewer who were not punished for said transgressions.

His gaze was drawn to the moon and smiled. He was in a place where nothing was familiar except the moon staring down at him. He tried to relax and ease the building tension. *A troubled mind attracts confusion, but a level head draws the solution.* His father had told him many times and it had always worked for him. He tried to make it work for him, again.

The bright light from the stranger's torch landed on him briefly, and he wondered if the light was meant to harm him. He jerked backward by instinct, but when the light swept his body, he felt nothing. No heat on his skin, no burns from the light. It was nothing like the sun. Lost in his thoughts, Akhmose didn't notice the man walking in his direction. When the stranger was a foot away from him, he didn't stop. Before he could move, Akhmose felt the man go through his body—it felt like a gust of cold air.

The stranger drew a sharp breath. "A window must be open somewhere. It's drafty in here," he mumbled and shivered. Akhmose watched in horror and couldn't understand a word he was saying. The man shined his flashlight on the shelves and continued his monologue, "This place is giving me the heebie-jeebies. I wish I could get a normal day job." He quickly turned and started walking toward the door.

Surprised, Akhmose reached out and touched the man's arm. "What did you do? How did you do that? How did you walk through me?" He pulled back in horror as his hand and fingers sunk into the man's arm.

The guard yelled in fright, "Who's there? Is there anybody there?" His eyes widened as he looked around the empty room. He turned and ran as fast as he could, his footsteps echoing down the long hall.

Akhmose followed the man who spoke in a strange tongue. He saw another man walking toward them in the long corridor. Sharp light wavered from his torch as he moved his hand.

"Earl! There's a ghost in here! I'm getting the hell out of here." The stocky man pointed at Layla's workshop with shaky fingers.

"Don't be stupid, man!" The taller man shook his head and groaned. "What are you going on about, there's no such thing as ghosts."

The shorter man stuttered, "No? Then you never had one touch you."

The taller man groaned and shivered. "Okay, let's get out of here."

I'm in a strange world and I don't understand what these people are saying. Why am I here? Am I a ghost? Akhmose watched the men flashing their lights everywhere. He wondered who they were. They wore the same black outfit and looked more like watchers than thieves.

Akhmose shook off the uncertain feeling and began wandering. *I must find someone who speaks my language and explain to me what I'm doing here.* He walked from room to room and passage to passage until he came upon a large door. When he tried to grab the doorknob, his hand and arm floated through it. It was a strange experience. *Am I really a ghost? I can feel my body, but everything around me feels as if made of clouds.* Feeling more curious than scared, he pushed his foot through the thick door and when he didn't feel pain or pressure, he rushed his entire body to find himself on wide, stone steps.

It must be a temple, Akhmose looked back at the building with tall pillars. He walked down the stairs and looked around in awe. Everything looked strange. He had never seen anything like it. The buildings were almost as tall as the pyramids and clustered together. He had never seen so many large buildings together. Marveling at the lights, shining from the top of long poles, he wondered. *There are so many people walking about. Why aren't they sleeping? Only watchers and evil people move around after sunset. At least in the world, I knew.* Suddenly, he felt a rush of great power dragging him. Everything turned into a blur.

Chapter Six

Present time

Suddenly, the rushing sensation stopped. Akhmose stood still, listening to sounds, but everything was quiet. He opened his eyes when he felt solid ground under his feet. The floor was different, it felt as soft as the woven carpets of his rooms in the palace, but smoother. He was thankful that his feet were on solid ground, it made the experience that much less awkward. He already felt like he was losing his mind, so he refused to think about how he was suddenly in a strange room. He waited for the panic to set it, but he felt strangely calm. He looked around and tried to make sense of what was happening to him.

The small, crowded room was half-lit by the moon. He shivered, wherever he was, it wasn't his home in his beloved Egypt. He heard a soft moan and when he turned his head, his eyes fell upon a beautiful woman in a lilac colored bed. Her long, black hair spread on the pillow, and in her peaceful sleep, a small smile played at the corner of her shapely lips.

Akhmose stood frozen, mesmerized by the sight of the curve of her dark eyebrows, smooth, sun kissed skin, and the soft rising of her chest with every breath. "Anakhmun, my beloved," he whispered. *Could that be?* He thought and leaned forward to take a closer look. *No, there is only a resemblance.* He realized. *I wonder who she is?*

He took a few steps to reach the bed and gently caressed her face. He cried out in great surprise and yanked his hand away from her face, "I can feel her!" He reached out and touched the pillow, but his hand sunk into it. He then tried to touch the bed and the small nightstand; the result was the same. "Why can I feel her?" he whispered. "I couldn't feel the body of the man who walked through me, and everything around me feels like I'm touching clouds."

Suddenly, he felt a strange pull. *Not again! I want to stay here, with her.* He pleaded, but surprisingly, the rushing feeling never came and he stayed in the room. Instead, he felt the urge to touch the small, marble jar on her nightstand. His hand didn't sink into the green marble, and it felt warm to his touch. He picked up the jar and walked to the window to examine it in the moonlight.

He almost dropped the jar when he recognized his own face on it. *What is happening to me? Why is my face on a jar that resembles a canopic jar?* No answer came and he felt familiar vibration under his fingers as if the pulsing came from the jar. He touched his chest but didn't feel the thudding of his heart. Sudden dizziness swept over him, making him sway on his feet. He steadied himself by grabbing the armrest of the large chair by the window and sat down.

He held the jar to his chest. The vibration of the jar that felt as a rhythmical heartbeat and the sleeping woman's soft, quiet breathing calmed his frayed nerves. The dizziness passed and he took a closer look at the jar. He could read the hieroglyphs by the soft light of the moon and immediately recognized Tanakhmet's style of writing. He quickly read the curse which explained what had happened to him.

The memories of his life rushed back with brutal force. *He killed me. I'm a ghost and I can feel my heart in this jar!* The realization hit him hard. Gazing at the peacefully sleeping woman, a line of thoughts started chasing one after another in his mind. *She must be the one who was 'born at midnight' as the curse says. If I'm a ghost, Tanakhmet must be one too. But where is he?*

Akhmose leaned back in the chair weighing the possibilities. He thought about the men at the place where he woke up. He couldn't understand what they were saying, and when he was on the outside of the building, nothing reminded him of his beloved Egypt. He reasoned that his sarcophagus must have been taken to a foreign land. "But why?" he asked out loud. The woman stirred on the bed and rolled on her side. *Can she hear me?* he thought, alarmed.

He watched her intently but after she moved her legs and pulled the cover up to her chin, her breathing slowed and continued sleeping. Akhmose admired the soft curves of her face and delicate hand clutching the cover. *Anakhmun... I loved her so much. What happened to her? Could she be a ghost or reincarnated as this beautiful woman? The resemblance is uncanny!* Akhmose remembered Anakhmun's sweet lips and velvety skin with tears welling up in his eyes. He touched his face and felt the wetness of a teardrop on his cheek. *How is this possible? Can ghosts cry?* But quickly pushed the thought out of his mind. It was no use thinking about something he couldn't understand or change. Instead, he let himself immerse in memories.

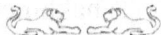

He had a short visit with the Grand Vizier, they were sitting under the palm trees in the vizier's courtyard. Anakhmun served the refreshments and when their eyes met, his heart took a double flip in his chest and the breath got caught in his throat. Tanakhmet sent her away with a wave of his hand, but Akhmose saw her a few times as she stole a glance at his direction from behind a pillar.

It was strictly forbidden to take a slave from anyone in the palace, but Akhmose couldn't get her out of his mind. For months he grabbed every chance to visit Tanakhmet so he could see her. During his visits, he excused himself to use the private rooms and Anakhmun found a way to meet him behind the pillars leading to the back of the courtyard. They talked for a few minutes and later stole sweet kisses whenever they had a chance. Akhmose wanted more but knew it was impossible, unless Tanakhmet would give her to him as a gift.

Tanakhmet didn't seem to pay attention to the main reason for his visits because they had a lot to talk about. The Pharaoh was deathly ill, and it was a matter of time when Akhmose would have to take the responsibilities of a regent to the young prince when he'd be crowned pharaoh.

When Anakhmun's pregnancy started to round her belly, Tanakhmet lost interest in her and made her move to the servants' quarters where she had as much freedom as she wanted. She wasn't given any task, the reason she stayed with the servants was to stay out of Tanakhmet's sight. Those were the happiest months in Anakhmun's life since she was forced to live in the palace.

A few weeks after she gave birth to her daughter, their stolen happiness ended. Tanakhmet ordered her back to his quarters and into his bed. "I can't!" Anakhmun cried on Akhmose's shoulder. "I loathe him. He's a sick man, he will torture me again. I can't… I rather die."

31

Her deep sobs broke Akhmose's heart. "I'll make plans. We'll leave the palace. I'd rather live in a hut and work on the fields than let you suffer."

"No!" Anakhmun cried out. "You can't sacrifice yourself for me. You're a prince and you have obligations. The pharaoh will move to the afterlife soon. What would happen to Egypt without you being the regent of the young prince? Tanakhmet would destroy what your father and brother had built."

"We'll find the solution." Akhmose hugged her.

Anakhmun hurried back to Tanakhmet's quarters, but that night, she snuck back to Akhmose's room and rushed into his arms. "Thank the Gods, the pharaoh ordered him to the border, and he left already. I heard him telling the servants that he'll be away for at least six turn of the moon."

They'd spent every minute together that they could while Tanakhmet was away. They made love under the moonlight, took a night swim in the Nile and long walks in the fields.

And then, Tanakhmet unexpectedly arrived home, three months later. *He killed me!* Akhmose remembered, pure hate rising in his mind filling his entire being. *What did he do with her and her baby?*

Chapter Seven

Egypt, 1198 BC

The riots at the border took less time than Tanakhmet expected, and after three grueling months, he was heading back to the palace. He longed for the comfort of his quarters and the servants who would wait on him every moment of the day. And he longed for his favorite slave. Her beauty was captivating, and he longed to see and possess her again.

He strolled through the palace, his footsteps echoing in the long corridors. How he missed the beautiful wall paintings and magnificent statues of the Gods that lined the wide corridors. He suddenly stopped as he spotted Anakhmun closing the door of Akhmose's quarters behind her. "I'll come back soon after I fed my baby," she called back through the half-open door. Her face was flushed, and a happy smile played in the corner of her lips. She froze as she turned and spotted Tanakhmet and leaned against the wall, shaking in fear.

He walked up to her and grabbed her arm. She winced at his grip but said nothing as he dragged her through the corridors toward his quarters. She knew that it was best to just be quiet and pray the cruel torture she was facing wouldn't last too long.

He threw her onto the floor in his room, shouting, "What were you doing in Akhmose's room? You belong to me!"

She lowered her head and whispered, her lips quivering, "His servant needed help with an embroidery."

He took a step back and observed her. "You're lying!" he accused and hit her across her face. Anakhmun whimpered and shrunk back but her coal eyes flashed with murderous rage hidden by her thick eyelashes.

This is not the sad, lowly slave I left three months ago. She seemed... happy. I must find out who made her cheeks rosy and put a smile on her face. He thought. "Leave! I'll send for you tonight." He dismissed her. He needed time to think of her punishment.

A look of relief crossed her face as she bolted for the door. Her footsteps were light enough that he could hear them, so he waited a few seconds before chasing after her. He was a warrior, and he knew how to lighten his steps and stay concealed behind the pillars. He watched as she rushed down the corridors back to the quarters of Prince Akhmose, opened the door and slid inside.

Tanakhmet stepped up to the slightly open door in time to catch her say, "I was almost caught earlier. I can't come here as often now that Tanakhmet is back. He must have exhausted himself on the way back, I was sure that I would have been trapped in his room for the rest of the day. You can't even imagine how much I loathe him."

"My Anakhmun, I wish..."

Tanakhmet slammed the door open, causing the slave to rush away from Akhmose who stepped in front of Anakhmun, shouting, "Get out of my room!"

Seething in rage, Tanakhmet drew his sword and sliced Akhmose's throat, roaring, "She's mine!"

The sudden attack left Akhmose defenseless. He fell to the floor blood gurgling in his throat. With one final breath, life left his body. Anakhmun let out a blood-curdling scream and knelt beside him. She looked up at Tanakhmet with pain and hate in her eyes. "I curse you!" she shouted. "I curse you to never find happiness and forever crave what you can't have."

The realization of what he did hit Tanakhmet like a ton of bricks. "You are mine!" he growled as he touched her chest with the bloody sword. "You could have whatever you wanted, but instead, you gave yourself to him. You will die knowing that you were the reason for his death."

"I have no reason to live anymore," Anakhmun whispered. "I gave my heart to him, and he gave me more than you could ever give. Not even if you lived thousands of years."

His wounded pride bathed his brain in a red fog of anger and raised his sword to plunge into her chest. Anakhmun dropped to her knees beside Akhmose and her hand stretched out to touch Akhmose. She looked up at the murderer of her beloved with deep determination in her eyes. "Kill me!" she shouted.

Tanakhmet shrunk back and lowered his sword. The sheer hate shining from her eyes burned into his soul. "No!" he said calmly, and a calculating, cruel grin spread on his face. "You will be mine!"

Anakhmun let out a heart-breaking cry and crawled on her knees to Akhmose's body to embrace him.

Tanakhmet laughed out loud drawing pleasure from the sight of the woman's agony. He reached out, grabbed her arm, and yanked her to her feet. Anakhmun resisted, and he threw her to the floor, kicking her side. She felt and heard the cracking of her ribs and passed out.

Tanakhmet's jealous fury calmed and his calculating, cold nature took over. "Akhmose had given his heart to a lowly woman I own and grew to love in my way, so it's only fair that he would go into the afterlife without his heart." He drew his dagger from its sheath, kneeled by Akhmose's lifeless body and carved out his heart. It was still warm. He pulled the cloth off a table and wrapped the heart in it.

Anakhmun moaned and cried out in pain when she tried to move. Tanakhmet yanked her up and dragged her by the arm locking the door behind them, leaving the body of the prince lay on the floor in a puddle of blood.

Hurrying to his quarters he kept thinking. *Akhmose would have been the perfect regent to the child pharaoh. The child listened to his every word and trusted him, and yet, Akhmose had betrayed me.*

He had to hurry. Nobody saw him in his room; therefore, nobody will suspect him. The servants would soon discover Akhmose's body and he will look over the burial preparations.

When they reached his quarters, he threw Anakhmun into a water closet and locked her in. He called for his servants and ordered one to stand guard by the door. "Nobody opens this door other than me! Understand?"

The scared servant nodded, afraid to utter a sound and stood by the door on shaky legs.

Chapter Eight

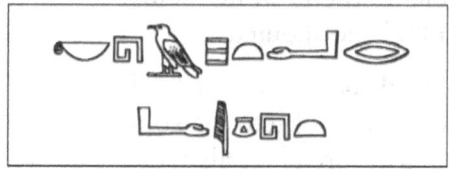

Present time

Akhmose tore his eyes away from the woman who looked so much like his beloved Anakhmun. Rapid thoughts ran through his mind. What had become of his brother? Of his nephew? Of his beloved? Was she cursed as he was? Did she spend the rest of her days tortured by him? Or was she killed for her transgressions? Why had the Grand Vizier gotten so mad? Did he love her in his own sick way? Akhmose loved Anakhmun, and even though she was a slave, it wasn't like he could make her his wife. He knew that he had an obligation to his country, or at least until his brother's son would be old enough to take the throne. He would not give up on his country when they needed him most, and even Anakhmun understood that.

Layla shifted in her sleep, and her eyes shot open. Her gaze locked on the man sitting in her chair, and her scream echoed through the small room.

Akhmose startled by her ear-piercing scream and stood up. "You can see me? How's that possible?"

The second scream froze in Layla's throat and curiosity took over fear when she realized that the man was speaking the language that hadn't been spoken for thousands of years.

They heard running footsteps and Mara burst through the door with a baseball bat in her hand. "What? What's wrong?" she shouted looking around the room like a madwoman.

Layla pointed in the direction where Akhmose stood. "There's a man in my room!"

"Where?" Mara turned around, bat raised, ready to hit the intruder.

"Don't you see? He's standing right there!"

Mara stared at the empty chair Layla was pointing at, but then she looked back at her in confusion. "There's nobody there."

"Are you blind? There's a man standing by the chair dressed in... What bloody hell is this?" She stood up and stared at the man. "He's dressed in a tunic and he has the headdress of the Princes of Egypt on his head!"

Akhmose stood still with his hands up, trying to back away from Mara. His eyes glanced back and forth between them. Although the place didn't look at all like a palace, he was sure by the self-assured, authoritative manner of the two young women that they were definitely no servants.

Mara lowered her bat assured that nobody was in the room besides Layla and her. She stared at her friend and asked, "What's wrong? Are you okay? You're scaring me!"

Layla ignored Mara whose face displayed worry and confusion, clearly not impressed that her best friend had woken her up in the middle of the night with a blood-curdling scream and was claiming to see a man that was not there.

Layla knew that she sounded crazy, but not in a million years could she have imagined the sound that had passed through the man's lips. It was a language that she never thought she would be able to hear with such fluidity.

He shivered when she took a few steps toward him and touched his bare arm. Her touch made his skin tighten into goosebumps. "I can feel your touch," he whispered.

"Why wouldn't you?" Layla spoke the words of the ancient language.

He touched her hand rejoicing. "You understand me. Anakhmun, is that you? Did the Gods grant us to be together in the afterlife?" His voice was smooth and while she didn't understand every word he spoke; she got the gist of it. The strange man in front of her that only she could see thought she was someone else. Someone who he probably loved. She backed away toward Mara, "My name is Layla, and as far as I know, this is no afterlife. Who are you?"

Mara wrapped her arms around Layla's shoulders and helped her to sit down on the bed. "You're scaring me. What's going on? Who are you talking to?" she asked while frantic thoughts ran through her mind. *Schizophrenia usually manifests in the early twenties, but it can start in the late twenties as well. I know she speaks Arabic but sees a man in the room. I must find a way to talk her into going to the hospital and be admitted to get a proper diagnosis.*

Layla stared at the man. "Who are you and why are you here?"

"My name is Akhmose, son of Takhat and brother of Pharaoh Amenmesse," he answered.

"Are you a ghost? Is that why my friend can't see you? But why can I see you and touch you?"

"Yes, it seems like I'm a ghost. I remember my life now. Tanakhmet killed me and cursed me to walk the Earth as a restless ghost forever." He bowed his head, but after he recalled the curse he read on the jar, he looked into Layla's eyes. "You must be the one who broke the curse. The one who was born at midnight."

Mara touched Layla's chin and turned her head. "Stop looking at that chair, look at me! We need to go to the hospital. You're having auditory and visual hallucinations. Let's get dressed and go."

Layla yanked Mara's hand away. "I'm not crazy! Have you ever heard that anyone who hallucinates seeing a man could touch his body too?"

"No, but..." Mara hesitated.

"He's the ghost of Akhmose. I think his heart is in the jar that has the curse carved into it. I don't know why, but for some reason, I can see and hear him, and I've touched his arm. He feels like a flesh and blood person to me."

"Wait just a minute! This is a nightmare. It can't be true," Mara stuttered.

Akhmose looked back and forth between the women. He didn't understand the strange language and the woman with the curly red hair seemed to doubt what Layla was telling her. "Could you please tell her who I am?" he spoke to Layla.

"I'm trying! She thinks I'm crazy," she snapped.

38

Mara looked at her wide-eyed, shaking her head. "I can't believe this! You're talking to a ghost whom I can't see, but you can."

"Please, just bear with me. We'll figure this out." Layla begged.

Akhmose raised his hand to get Layla's attention. "I see your friend has doubts. I have an idea of how we can make her believe that I'm here."

"I'm listening. Her name is Mara," Layla said. She looked at Mara who was shaking her head and looked worried.

Akhmose sat down on the chair and explained his idea, "Tell Mara to stand behind you in the corner, over there, so you can't see what she's doing." He pointed. "Tell her to show me something with her hand, make a face, or pick up any object, and then I'll tell you what she's doing."

Layla's eyes lit up. "That's a great idea!" Feeling excited, Layla told Mara what the prince said.

"Okay, let's do it." Mara agreed and thought, *she's going to see that she has a psychological problem and will let me take her to the hospital.* She stood up and reached the corner behind Layla with a few short steps. "What do you want me to do?" she asked.

"Do whatever you want, but make sure I don't see you." Layla slid on the bed facing Akhmose.

Mara raised her arms. "What am I doing?"

"She'd raised both her arms," Akhmose told Layla.

"The prince says you're raising both your arms," Layla said to Mara in English.

Mara's jaw dropped. "Okay, what am I doing now?" she asked and picked up Layla's phone from the charger on the nightstand.

"She picked up something from that stand and holding it in her hand," Akhmose hesitated. "I don't know what it is, but it's a small, white, shiny box and on one side, it seems like a bright, blue light coming from it."

"He said you've picked up my phone. Well, he didn't say exactly like that, he doesn't know what a cellphone is. He described it as a small, white, shiny box with a bright blue light."

Mara almost dropped the phone and opened her mouth to say something but closed it again. *What the bloody hell is going on here?*

"Well, did he get it right?" Layla questioned.

"Um… yeah, he did. One more time to make sure. You might have just guessed or heard the click when I picked up your phone. What am I doing now?" Mara lifted her pajama top to her chin.

Akhmose looked at her and averted his gaze with a shy smile. "She showed me her beautiful, ample breasts," he told Layla.

"Maraa!" Layla shouted turning toward Mara who just let her pajama fall to cover her chest. "Have you no decency?"

"I can't believe this! I mean, I believe you now, but I can't believe this. There is a ghost of an Egyptian prince in your room, in the middle of the night."

Layla sighed in relief. "See? I'm not crazy."

Mara pinched her arm and cried out in pain. "It's really true! I'm not dreaming, for sure."

Chapter Nine

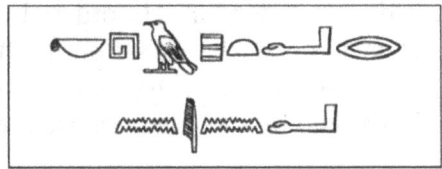

Egypt, 1198 BC

Tanakhmet found the jar he carved from green marble. "This will be perfect." He had it made as a present for Akhmose and planned to carve the protection spell on it. The lid of the jar had Akhmose's bust carved into it and covered with a thin, gold layer. He took the lid off, placed the bloody heart inside and poured vine, honey, and herb-infused oil over it. He sealed the lid with resin and picked up a fine chisel and hammer. He carved his name into the bottom of the jar, wanting Osiris, the Lord of the afterlife to know who had cursed Prince Akhmose to this fate.

Satisfied with his name in the marble, he begun to carve the curse at the side of the jar:

I, Tanakhmet, the Grand Vizier of Pharaoh Amenmesse, curse Prince Akhmose, son of Queen Takhat. I curse him to forget the names of the forty-two underworld judges. His heart is heavier than the feather of Maat but will not be devoured by Ammit. This spell will protect it. His soul will be tethered for eternity and never enter Sekhet-Aaru. My curse will be unlocked when the one who was born at midnight awakens our souls. I Tanakhmet, curse Akhmose to walk the Earth as a restless ghost, forever. I curse him to fall in love with she, who was born at midnight, but to never have her. I will take a body and possess her, the reincarnated soul of Anakhmun.

Tanakhmet felt the power rush through him as he made the preparations.

The incantation and the ceremony to seal the curse took a lot of Tanakhmet's mental and physical strength but he had no time to waste. There was a lot more to be done before Akhmose's body was discovered.

He grabbed a fruit bowl and cloth, hurried to the water closet where Anakhmun had been locked in. He ordered the guard to open the door and stepped inside. Anakhmun sat on the floor in the corner of the room, her face soaked with tears, waiting for her fate. She looked up at Tanakhmet with hate and pain in her eyes.

"You gave your heart to Akhmose, so it's only fitting that your heart would be in his chest forever." He reached the trembling woman with a few strides, grabbed her shoulder, and forced her to the floor. Anakhmun screamed and fought to slip out of his strong grip, but she was powerless. Tanakhmet, looking into her eyes, whispered, "Without your heart, you will not enter Sekhet-Aaru. You will reincarnate in the far future, in the body of your daughter's descendant, who shall be born at midnight. She will break my curse and I *will* find you. You will be mine, again."

"Never! No matter what you do to me, I will never be yours!" Anakhmun screamed.

"You will!" Tanakhmet laughed and plunged the dagger deep into her chest. He cut her heart from her body before she took her last breath. Tanakhmet placed the warm heart into the bowl as it quivered its last beat. He covered the bowl and hurried out of the room. "Nobody goes in there!" he instructed the guard as he headed back to Akhmose's quarters.

The corridors were deserted. Tanakhmet slipped into the room without being seen. He took Anakhmun's heart from the bowl and placed it into the gaping hole in Akhmose's chest. Satisfied, he wiped the blood from his hands and hurried back to his quarters to wait.

Tanakhmet pretended to be shocked by the news that Prince Akhmose's body was found. He rushed to Amanmesse's bed and assured the dying pharaoh that his bloodline will continue to rule, and he will take the role of the regent of his young son.

He proceeded to Akhmose's quarters to give instructions to start the seventy days long mummification process and funeral preparations.

Chapter Ten

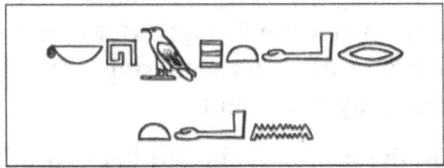

Present time, Egypt

Tanakhmet opened his eyes. He was in a dark place. His ghostly body moved through his sarcophagus with ease. "I'm awake, and I'm a ghost, which means, Anakhmun had been reincarnated! The curse must be broken!"

He floated through the wall of the tomb. The land was covered in sand and no slaves or servants were patrolling the area. "This is not my beloved Egypt! This is a wasteland!" he shouted. As he floated over the sand dunes, he saw people carrying objects from an open tomb. "That is sacrilege! Why are they emptying that tomb, and how much time has passed since my death?"

He watched people moving around speaking strange words. He understood some words, but most sounded foreign to him. Their garbs were nothing he had ever seen, and a sense of dread washed through him as he realized a great amount of time must have passed. He wondered if they'd ever heard of him.

Hoping he didn't lose his powers in the underworld, he glanced around, looking for the right man to possess. Tanakhmet was on a crunch for time, but that did not mean he would possess a man who would not be able to get him where he needed to go. He could already feel the pull in his chest to where the curse had been broken, and it was farther than he had ever traveled before. The man would need to be able to move that far.

He spotted a handsome young man who seemed to be in charge. He seemed to be ordering the workers around with ease, and they obeyed him. Tanakhmet watched him for a while and satisfied with the manner of the man, he started the incantation to possess his body.

The bright sun charged Tanakhmet's ghostly body, and when he felt his full powers, he touched the chest of the young man. His heart stopped in an instant, and his body collapsed to the sandy ground. The workers gathered around his body as Tanakhmet watched his soul floating above. The man's soul lingered for a moment, and then Tanakhmet saw a group of souls gathering around him. A moment later his soul floated away with them.

He called upon the power again and his ghost descended into the body of the young man. The man's memories flashed through Tanakhmet and the body convulsed as his heart started beating again.

Tanakhmet drew a deep breath in the man's body and sat up. "I'm fine. I just need some water and rest in the shade," he said waving away the worried workers. The strange words poured out of his mouth with ease, and because he adapted the man's memory, he understood every word now. He stood up and walked to a tent not far from the tomb. He sat on a cot allowing his mind to explore the young man's memories.

A wave of anger passed through him at how little was known about his home when Egypt was the greatest. His name was not in any of the books this young man studied. This man claimed to be an expert in Tanakhmet's culture and history, but they had only scratched the surface. There were so many princes and pharaohs that were never discovered.

He searched for Prince Akhmose and found in the man's memory that his sarcophagus had been discovered and sent to the United States. "Thank you Baahir for providing me with such a strong body and all your knowledge of your world. Soon Prince Akhmose will be forever roaming this world as a ghost, and Anakhmun will be mine again."

Sitting on the cot, Tanakhmet smirked, feeling satisfied. It was easier than he thought. He had the memories and identifications of the man whose body he occupied. It would be simple to travel to Albany.

He called for Baahir's assistant and instructed the young man. "I got an urgent call, and I have to go to Albany on family business. Continue working, and I'll be back in a few days."

The man nodded, and without questions, hurried out of the tent. Tanakhmet found Baahir's jeep and having his memories, easily drove to Baahir's apartment. He called the airline and booked a seat on the 2 PM flight to New York with a connection flight to Albany.

During the long flight, Tanakhmet felt the pull of his curse growing stronger and stronger. He closed his eyes and relived the day he took revenge on the slave and Akhmose for betraying him. *In the end, there was nothing special about the blood of a royal. It had flown as freely as the blood of the slave.*

Chapter Eleven

Present time

Akhmose watched as the two women conversed in the strange language. Things would be so much easier if Mara could see or hear him. He scanned the paintings on the wall and was drawn to the pieces that looked the most like the ones he would see at home, but these were different. Instead of being painted on the walls, the pictures were painted on smooth papyrus. He watched as Mara paced in the narrow space between the wall and Layla's bed, anxiously wringing her fingers.

Mara stopped and turned pale. "I can't tell if I'm more excited or more scared. What will happen now? What will happen to him? Is he going to stay here? A ghost! We're in a nightmare."

"I don't know. We'll figure it out." Layla bowed her head. "I've never met a ghost before, let alone touched one."

"I know, right?" Mara let out a nervous laugh. "

"Why don't you get some sleep?" Layla held Mara's hand. "I'll be fine, don't you worry. I have so many questions for the prince. Can you imagine how much I could learn from him about the 19th dynasty?"

"I still can't wrap my mind around this, but unbelievable as it is, he did live back then. Okay, I'm going to shut my eyes for a few hours, but if anything happens, call me."

"Nothing will happen. He's a ghost, what could he do to me?"

"True." Mara nodded, stood up and walked to the door. "Don't you dare hurt my best friend," she warned looking at the empty chair. "If you do anything, I'll find a way to kick your ghostly butt!"

Layla laughed and Akhmose arched his brown silently questioning.

As Mara walked out and left the door ajar, Layla told Akhmose what Mara said. He smiled, and that moment seemed to be the icebreaker between them.

"I'll be right back," Layla announced, putting her robe on. "I'm going to... what do you call the room where you do your private business?"

"Water closet." Akhmose smiled. "I'll stay here."

He leaned back in the chair and closed his eyes, thinking. He longed to run his hand through her silky hair, especially now that he knew he could touch her. She was so different from his beloved. Her eyes were softer, and her gaze a lot more confident. This was not the same woman who struggled to survive as a slave. This was not the same woman who was forced to serve a man who was twice her age. Nor was she the same woman who shaved her head as a sign of obedience. She wasn't the Anakhmun he had once loved. He loved how Layla was able to hold his gaze. He could tell that he was interested in knowing how he lived, how different his life was from her own. He loved her laugh, she looked so carefree in those moments, not bound by fear and worry, as Anakhmun was. Would she help him? Could she have been the reincarnation of his beloved? Would she have memories of him and her past life hidden inside her soul? She may not be Anakhmun, but he wanted to find out more about her.

Layla came back to the room and sat on the bed. "This has been a strikingly odd experience. I want to know everything you remember," she stated.

"The last thing I remember is my death. I died quickly. I could see the jealous rage in Tanakhmet's eyes, but before I could move or defend myself, he struck with his sword and cut my throat. I don't know what became of Anakhmun."

"Tell me about your life."

Akhmose talked about the palace where he grew up in comfort and luxury. He was surrounded by beauty and loyal servants who waited on him day and night. But he also talked about the constant intrigue and fear for his life. He couldn't eat a bite without his servants tasting it first and couldn't walk the streets without being surrounded by bodyguards. The only carefree and happy time in his life was when Tanakhmet was away and he spent all his time with Anakhmun. "Please, tell me about your life," he begged.

Layla talked about life in modern Egypt where she grew up, and about her life, after she moved to Boston, and when she entered college in Albany. She had difficulties understanding and pronouncing words, but the prince helped her. He understood that his language hadn't been spoken for thousands of years.

"According to the curse…" Akhmose wondered. "You could be the reincarnation of Anakhmun."

"Perhaps. That would explain my fascination with the 19th dynasty. My mom traced her family tree back for five generations but couldn't find any older documents. But other than that… it's all me. I don't have any memories of my past life, if I ever existed before."

"You don't have any feelings or perhaps dreams?"

"No." Layla yawned looking at the clock and realized how tired she was. "We've been talking for hours. I need to sleep a little, I'm tired." She looked at Akhmose, "Do you sleep?"

He shrugged and laughed. "I don't know. This is my first experience as a ghost."

"Well, if you find out you can sleep, lay down on the couch in the living room." Layla patted her pillow, pulled the blanket up to her chin, and laid on her side looking at Akhmose.

Akhmose left the room and sat on the couch in the dark living room.

Layla closed her eyes. *Maybe this will all be a dream and he'll be gone in the morning.* She smiled. *But I don't want him to go.*

Chapter Twelve

Present time

Layla opened her eyes and was suddenly aware of a warm body pressing against her back. She tried to sit up, but a man's masculine arm reached out and pulled her to his chest and nuzzled her neck. The events of the night rushed back. *That sneak! He didn't like the couch.* She should have been scared, angry, or at least greatly surprised, but she wasn't. To her amazement, she accepted everything, curse, having a ghost in her bed, and all.

His closeness was comforting, but something was off. She was about to doze off when she realized why. She couldn't hear the sound of his heartbeat or feel his breath on her neck. She turned to face him and traced his chin with her finger. Why was she so comfortable in his arms? All her life, she never was able to get totally comfortable with a man, although they spent a lot of time together as a couple in college, not even with Baahir. Yet she could feel herself getting comfortable and cozy next to a ghost whose body she could feel.

Mara knocked on the door and opened it, "Please tell me that last night was a nightmare from listening to you decode that jar."

Layla shook her head laughing, "It wasn't a dream. I seem to have attracted a heavy sleeping ghost and his arm is pinning me down."

Mara groaned, "Great. And I thought it couldn't get any weirder. How come he can touch you?" She snickered, "What's it like to cuddle with a ghost?"

"Everything should seem strange, but it doesn't," Layla mumbled rolling on her side and pushing Akhmose away.

Mara skipped out of the room. "I'll make breakfast. Does your guest like scrambled eggs?"

"Very funny!" Layla grumbled, getting out of bed.

Akhmose stirred and watched Layla with desire. "You're so beautiful," he whispered leaning on his elbow.

"Right!" Layla blushed. "Morning breath and messy hair... I must warn you, I'm not a morning person and I can be pretty grumpy. I have to go to work so..."

"Can I come with you?" Akhmose inquired, standing up.

"Sure. You're invisible to everyone but me. Just... don't talk too much before I have my coffee. Okay?"

Akhmose didn't say a word—he didn't need to. He gazed at her admiring her beauty. *What a woman! She's nothing like the obedient, quiet women of my Egypt.* He smiled and followed her to the kitchen.

"Eat up." Mara handed a bowl of oatmeal with blueberries to Layla and grinned.

Before she could utter a sound, Layla cut her off. "He's not going to eat your oatmeal!" she grumbled.

"Grouchy head!" Mara snickered and poured coffee for Layla. "What are you going to do with the canopic jar?"

"For now, I will leave it at home. Nobody paid attention to it, and it's not cataloged, so it won't be missed. I'll figure out later what to do with it."

Akhmose watched from the corner admiring the two women's playful bickering.

Mara stared at Layla noticing that her morning mood lifted. "I hope you're taking him with you to the museum. I'm not ready to be alone with a ghost."

"Of course." Layla assured her friend. "It's new to me, too. He's a good person, though. Back then people had different morals and customs. I always wished I could time travel back there to see how people lived. Now I have a chance to learn about their lives."

"How does he look? You didn't tell me last night."

"He's handsome," Layla said, blushing. "He's not much taller than me. He has the distinctive Egyptian nose, just like Baahir, and his skin has that sun kissed glow as well…" Looking at the clock Layla stood up. "I have to go, I'll be late."

Walking toward her room Layla called over her shoulder, "Akhmose, stay here until I change. You're coming with me to the museum."

"I will not leave your sight." Akhmose promised. "I've been thinking about the curse. Tanakhmet will do anything to find you. And he will."

"Then we'll find a way to stop him and send him back to the underworld."

Chapter Thirteen

Present time

Layla opened the passenger door for Akhmose, and he hesitantly got into the car. He wondered where the horses were or at least slaves to pull the carriage. He startled when Layla started the engine and suddenly the ugly green carriage moved on its own. The dizzying speed scared him but after a few minutes of watching the tall buildings staying behind, his curiosity took over.

Layla parked the car and walked to the front entrance with Akhmose in tow. He commented on everything that he saw, which made her smile. He was trying to understand the world he was thrown into, and he was taking it in stride.

After they reached her studio and Layla closed the door behind them, she asked him about what might have happened to Anakhmun. He shook his head. "She would not be mentioned history. Slaves were not given even the same respect in death as of people of the lowest class. Slaves were property. She would be buried in the desert without mummification. Although she would enter the afterlife, she would not have anything placed in her tomb and would remain a slave in the afterlife."

"You miss her."

He turned and grasped her hand, "I remember her and miss her, but when I'm close to you, it seems that my worries disappear and my memories of her are starting to fade. I'm not as lonely and confused in this strange world as when I first woke up."

She nodded. Her mind was occupied by the strange man whose heart she held—literally. He was kind and compassionate. She had learned of how even though he loved Anakhmun, he had a duty to his land and his people. How he wouldn't run from his duties and sacrifice his happiness until the young pharaoh was able to take the throne.

After watching Layla work for a few hours and asking hundreds of questions, Akhmose had a better understanding of how the world worked, and he was learning quickly.

Layla's thoughts kept returning to Tanakhmet and the curse. "What will happen when he finds me?" she asked.

"I'm not sure," Akhmose admitted. "As much as I know about the magic he practiced, if he could possess a living person's body, the soul of that person would enter the afterlife and Tanakhmet would own his body and memory."

"Uhm... that would make it easier for him to find me." She immersed in deep thoughts for a minute. "Wait! I remember reading about a spell couple of years ago when I started working here... it sounded like a superstitious tale but now... let me find it. It must be on the shelves somewhere. I didn't think it was worth putting on display in the museum." Layla walked to the shelves loaded with scrolls and started rummaging. "I remember it had a black, wax-like seal. Help me find it," she called over her shoulder.

The door slammed open as Jerome stormed in. "Who're you talking to?" he asked, looking around.

"Nobody," Layla replied. *Phew... he doesn't see the prince either. Now that would be interesting if he did.*

"I heard you talking, it sounded like Arabic," Jerome commented.

"Oh, I was just practicing the ancient Egyptian language." She lied, but Jerome was satisfied with her answer.

"Maybe we should have a lecture, and you could introduce the old language. It would attract new benefactors, I'm sure." He speculated, and turning around, he left the room without telling Layla why he came.

"I think this is the one." Getting Layla's attention, Akhmose pointed at a yellowed papyrus scroll with a black seal.

Layla picked up the papyrus and carefully rolled it open. They read the hieroglyphics together, Akhmose leaning over Layla's shoulder.

53

"It might work, don't you think?" Layla turned and her nose accidentally touched his cheek.

"I think so," he whispered reading the list of ingredients they would need for the spell. He slightly turned his head and moved closer to Layla.

Layla didn't pull back. He felt her warm breath as her lips slightly parted. Their lips met in a sweet, electrifying kiss.

Heat rising to her face, Layla turned away trying to sort her feelings. *What am I doing? Kissing a ghost! But it felt so good... no man ever kissed me like that before.*

Akhmose took a step back in shock. *She might resemble Anakhmun, but she's not her. I loved her, but I've never felt like this when I kissed her. Every fiber in my body craves being close to this woman.*

Layla cleared her throat breaking the awkward silence. "We... we have some of the ingredients at home, Mara loves using exotic spices and aromatic oils. I know she has frankincense and sandalwood, and she uses sage all the time."

"Pink sea salt." Akhmose read the list written on the papyrus. "Do you have that, too?" Layla seemed to pretend the kiss never happened. Although he ached to hold her in his arms, he concentrated on the spell.

"We can pick that up along with myrrh at the health food store. We must prepare everything as soon as possible. If Tanakhmet woke up in Egypt the same time you did and feels the pull of the jar that contains your heart, it wouldn't take him too long to possess a body and find the way to find us."

"We need a place to set up the barrier and when he arrives to perform the incantation."

"I think the best place would be the large living room in our apartment. Mara leaves around 6 PM for her nightshift, and if my calculations are correct, we should expect Tanakhmet to arrive, in someone's body, sometime in the hours of early morning."

"Can we go now?"

"It's almost 5 PM, my workday ended. I'll let Jerome know that I'm leaving." Layla grabbed her backpack, stuffed the scroll inside and moved toward the door quickly with Akhmose at her heels.

Jerome just nodded when Layla knocked on his door and told him that she's leaving for the day. "See you tomorrow," he said and went back to his paperwork.

Chapter Fourteen

Present time

Layla stopped at the health food store and picked up everything they needed for the spell. By the time they got home, Mara was in her uniform, ready to leave for work. "Where's your ghost friend?" she asked mockingly.

"He's right there." Layla pointed, giving her friend an unapproving look.

"Alright!" Mara raised her hands and frowned. "I didn't mean to hurt your feelings. But you have to give me credit for not freaking out."

"I should be the one freaking out, but surprisingly, I'm not. I kissed him, and it felt absolutely wonderful."

"You did what?" Mara shouted. "You kissed a ghost. Seriously!?"

"He looks and feels real to me, except I can't feel his breath or hear his heartbeat."

"This is… this is out of a fantasy movie. But it's not. It's really happening, right? I'm not just having a freaky dream with you, am I?"

"Nope, it's not a dream." Layla opened her arms for a hug, and Mara wrapped her arms around her. "There's so much more to life and afterlife than what we can see and touch. Past and present are connected in ways that I could ever imagine in my wildest dreams."

"One day I might be able to comprehend all this, but for now, I'm working hard to wrap my mind around what's been happening." Mara's arms dropped as she looked at the clock. "I gotta run! I'll be late." She picked up her bag from the coffee table and hurried to the door, walking right into Akhmose, who didn't have time to get out of her way. "What a…" Mara yelled out and shivered. "I feel like I walked through an ice-cold wind."

Layla laughed. "You just walked through Akhmose."

"I did what?" Mara shrunk back in fright, but within a few seconds, her easy-going nature took over and laughed. "You know, if anyone would be telling me about this, I would say they're crazy. But now, experiencing it myself, if I don't want to lose my marbles, I'll just go with it. But there are a lot of things you have to explain to me."

"I will, promise." Layla smiled at her friend. "I'll tell you everything I know, tomorrow. Go, save some lives. I'll be okay."

"Okay, we'll talk tomorrow. Bye Akhmose, sorry for walking through you," she let out a nervous laugh opening the door.

"I'll tell him," Layla promised watching Mara closing the door behind her.

Akhmose smiled at Layla, "I don't understand what she's saying, but I like her."

"She's a great person. She's my best friend." Layla nodded walking to the kitchen. She put her backpack on the table and started taking out the jars she picked up at the store. "We have plenty of time until Tanakhmet arrives, but let's start preparing the spell."

"I can't do much, my hands go through everything as if everything were made of soft clouds. Except you, I can feel you."

Layla blushed and turned to the cabinet to take the needed spices off the shelves. "Oh, I have the frankincense oil in my room." She walked out of the kitchen. "Akhmose, come in here!" she shouted a minute later.

He rushed to her room in a panic and looked at Layla pointing at the canopic jar on the small table. "Is it supposed to glow like that?" Layla asked, her lips trembling.

The jar emitted an eerie, green glow in the dark room. Layla turned the light on, and the glow disappeared. When she turned the switch and the room was dark, they saw the eerie glow again.

"It must be the curse." Akhmose observed. "That's what pulled me to you and that's what pulling Tanakhmet to find you."

"I'm not sure if we would need it for the spell, but just in case, I'll bring it out to the living room." She found the frankincense bottle in her drawer and picked up the canopic jar. On the way to the kitchen, Layla placed the green jar on the coffee table.

She unrolled the papyrus and secured the curling edges with the heavy ceramic salt and pepper shaker. "Here, you read the instructions and I'll prepare the ingredients."

Akhmose leaned over the yellowed papyrus, "We need a ceremonial bowl to mix everything." He looked up.

"This will do," Layla said, reaching up to the shelves and lifted a bowl decorated with paintings of Anubis. "My mom gave this to me; it's been passed down in my family for generations."

Layla poured the pink sea salt crystals into the bowl and added frankincense and sandalwood oils. "How much lotus flower should I put in there?" she asked.

"It says a handful," Akhmose read. "Don't add the myrrh and sage, we'll need to burn them during the spell."

"Okay, I'll pour them into this small glass bowl."

"Now you need to prick your finger with the ceremonial dagger you've brought from the museum. Let the blood drip into the salt and herb oils, and then the preparation will be complete." Akhmose instructed.

"No. With my blood, the spell will only protect me. What about you?"

"My blood can't be spilled. The dagger would go right through me. Remember? My ghostly body feels solid only to me and to you." Akhmose bowed his head. "Whatever happens to me, it's of no importance. I'm already cursed to walk the Earth as a ghost. We must protect you from that monster!"

Layla shook her head as she picked up her backpack and held the jeweled dagger. She frantically searched her mind for a solution. "I got it!" she exclaimed, feeling excited. Tanakhmet must have sealed your heart in the jar shortly after he cut it out of your chest, right?"

"Yes, I guess so," Akhmose replied, a slight flash of hope playing on his face.

"So, your blood must have been mixed with the wine and honey he poured over it, to preserve it. Honey doesn't dry out for thousands of years, it just thickens."

He scratched his chin, thinking. "You... do you think? But then you'll need to break the resin seal on the jar."

"How hard could that be?"

"He might have sealed it with a spell."

"Well, we won't know until we try." Layla decided and went out to the living room to pick up the canopic jar.

She placed it on the table and examined the seal. The resin felt smooth as glass and just as solid. Layla tried to insert a small knife between the seal and the cool marble, to no avail. She rummaged through the drawers to find a suitable tool, but nothing worked until her eyes fell on the electric jar opener. "What if..." Placing the jar in the opener, she pulled down the handle. It hugged the lid of the jar snugly. Akhmose watched her with interest peaking. When Layla turned on the machine, they heard cracking and buzzing sounds for a second, and then the lid broke loose.

"Phew!" Layla shouted, holding her breath. She covered her nose and mouth with her arm and looked into the jar. She saw dark, thick goo and Akhmose's shriveled, decayed heart inside the jar. She quickly poured a few drops of the thick liquid into the bowl, grabbed a tube of glue from the junk drawer and sealed the lid back on. The putrid smell subsided when the liquid mixed with the aromatic herbal oils.

Akhmose shook his head in disbelief. "I doubt there were too many in history who looked down at their own heart."

"Ha-ha," Layla let out a nervous laugh. "I doubt it." She picked up the dagger and bracing herself mentally, pricked her finger. The blood started to flow, and she let it drip into the bowl.

"Mix everything with the dagger," he instructed.

As Layla stirred the salt, herbs, and blood, the mixture seemed to boil but she felt no heat coming from the bowl. "It seems to be working," she announced. "I think it's ready to form the protective circle. Akhmose nodded as she put the dagger on the table and held the bowl walking to the living room.

"Try to pour the mixture evenly on the floor, in a circle."

Layla tilted the bowl and poured the salt mixture around the coffee table and couch in a fifteen-foot circle. When she was done, on a hunch, she turned the light off. The salt cast an eerie green glow that formed a see-through, shimmering wall around them. She turned the light back on and the wall became invisible.

Akhmose leaned over the papyrus and said, "Now you need to burn a small amount of the myrrh and sage. The rest must be burned when we recite the spell."

Layla hurried to the kitchen and brought the glass bowl with the herbs as well as a small plate. She shook a small amount of the herbs on the plate and lit it with the gas stove lighter. "It smells nice." She sniffed the air.

"We have everything ready. Now, we'll wait."

"Come, sit with me on the couch." Layla invited Akhmose who gladly complied.

Chapter Fifteen

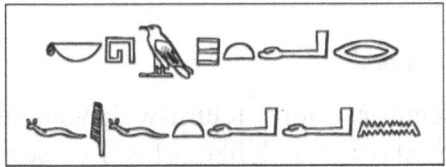

Present time

Despite the danger and uncertainty, they faced, Layla felt serene calmness as Akhmose caressed her cheek and gently kissed her forehead, eyelids, and lips. She nestled to his side, and they talked for hours. Layla felt drowsy but was afraid to fall asleep, the time was near when Tanakhmet could be arriving. "What will happen to you if the spell sends him to the afterlife?" she asked, worried.

"I'm not sure," he whispered bowing his head. "But his curse made me wake up as a ghost when you read it, so I assume, I will remain a ghost. Maybe if my heart would be returned to my body, I could face Anubis and the judges."

"I've grown rather fond of you," Layla said, blushing. "I don't want to lose you, but this is no life for you in a limbo where nobody can see or feel you but me."

"I would stay like this for a thousand years if I could stay close to you." Akhmose hugged her close.

Layla pulled back and looked into his eyes. "We'll figure this out." She promised.

Huddled together on the comfy couch, they dozed off.

A sudden noise made them jump at dawn. They stared at the front door that flew open. A man appeared and with a few short steps through the hallway, he stood in the living room entrance.

"Baahir?" Layla stood up. "What... how...?"

"That generous young man gave me his body and memories," Tanakhmet said with a cruel laugh.

"You monster!" Layla spat. "Why him?"

Tanakhmet shrugged. "I needed a body to come to you, and he was conveniently there. Anakhmun, my love, you will be mine, like it or not."

"My name is Layla."

"Oh, your memories didn't return with your rebirth, I see. You were just a lowly slave. But I like what I'm seeing." He scanned Layla's body with the hungry, cruel look of a predator.

Akhmose held Layla in his arms. "Anakhmun never loved you. She feared you and hated you. Layla is strong, you could never gain power over her."

"Ha-ha!" Tanakhmet let out a shrieking laugh. "I can make her love me. She loved the man in this body once, she could learn to love this body again. This time, with me in it."

"Never!" Layla shot a murderous look at him. "He was a good man and you killed him. You'll pay for it!"

"You'll be mine and nothing you and your ghost prince could do about it." The cruel smile faded from Tanakhmet's face when taking a step closer, he was suddenly thrown back and fell on his back. "What is this?" he yelled, scrambling to get up.

Layla lit the herbs in the bowl and picked up the scroll. She started reciting the spell and Akhmose joined her as if they were in a trance. "The sky quivers and the earth shakes before me, for I am a mighty magician. Retreat! Get back, you savage soul! Do not come against me, do not use your magic against me. Thoth is the protection of all my flesh. Anubis is the protection of my soul. Doorkeepers who guard afterlife, swallow the soul who wishes to harm me."

Layla blinked and came to her senses as the room filled with an unholy shriek. Baahir's body lay on the floor, wildly convulsing. She grabbed Akhmose's hand as they watched a group of dark, ghostly forms dragging Tanakhmet's flailing, screaming soul from Baahir's body to disappear into thin air.

Layla dropped on her knees by Baahir's body. "He didn't deserve to get pulled into this curse. Can we save him?" she asked, looking up at Akhmose with hopes in her eyes.

"I'm afraid not." Akhmose knelt beside her. "I can sense that his spirit is long gone. Tanakhmet made sure of that. His body is but an empty shell now."

"If his spirit is gone, can you enter his body as Tanakhmet did? You could live a normal life instead of being a ghost visible only to me."

"I think it's possible. Tanakhmet was a ghost when he entered this body, I think I could do it too. I would never kill a person as Tanakhmet did, but this body is empty now..." he speculated.

"What if it doesn't work? I'd rather have you as a ghost than lose you forever."

"I'll be alright. I assume it would take some time getting used to being in another man's body, but it will be me inside."

Okay, do it then." Layla nodded.

Akhmose floated over Baahir's body, closed his eyes, and slowly descended. When his ghostly body merged with the lifeless body of Baahir, Layla placed her hand on his chest, wishing she could feel the subtle beat of his heart. The body remained motionless. A painful sob broke free from Layla's chest. "Please make Baahir's body live or come back as a ghost. I can't lose you!"

Akhmose gasped in Baahir's body and his eyes fluttered open. He reached out and tucked a strand of dark hair behind Layla's ear, smiling. "You'll never lose me."

Her face paled, "Akhmose?"

"Yes, it's me." Sitting up, he stretched his arms and reached out to hold her. "I will stay in this body until you get bored with me and put my decayed heart into my decayed body in the sarcophagus. Until my heart stays in the jar, my spirit will stay in this body."

Layla pulled back and stood up. "I need some time to wrap my mind around what happened. Everything feels like a dream."

He smiled, "Layla, my beloved, take as long as you need."

"Do you have Baahir's memory?"

"No. Baahir is gone and Tanakhmet took his memory with him. Only this body remains. It's all me inside this body."

Mara opened the door to find the apartment quiet. As she walked to Layla's room to check on her, something crunched under her shoes. *What a ... why did she pour salt on the floor?* Looking at the bowl on the coffee table, new questions popped into her mind as she smelled the faint scent of burnt myrrh and sage. *Why did she burn those herbs?* Shaking her head, she peeked in through a slightly opened door. "Bloody hell!" she screamed, staring at Layla and Baahir snuggled close to each other under the blanket.

Layla's eyes flew open and sat up. "Sheesh! Must you scream?"

"What's he doing here?" Mara demanded. "Where's your ghost?"

"I'm here, in this body," Akhmose said in the ancient Egyptian language. He sat up hugging Layla.

"We'll have to teach him English." Layla smiled at Akhmose and turned to Mara. "Akhmose said it's him in Baahir's body."

Eyes wide as saucers, Mara shook her head. "Um... come again!"

Layla sent her a warm smile. "It's a long story. We'll tell you everything, promise. But you need to sleep first, you're tired after the long night shift."

"Sleep? How could I sleep?" Mara grumbled. "First, I kinda accepted that my best friend broke a curse that's been cast thousands of years ago. Second, I believed you and accepted that you can see and touch a ghost. But this? Now the long-dead prince is not a ghost anymore and somehow got into your ex-boyfriend's body? I draw the line here. You must tell me everything right now."

"I promise we'll tell you everything later. Let's just sleep a few hours," Layla begged stifling a yawn.

"Not later— now!" Mara shouted. "I'm going to make breakfast, and I want you two in the kitchen in ten minutes." Not waiting for a reply, Mara turned, stormed out of the room, grumbling, "You two have a whole lot of explaining to do. And after that, I'll need a whole lot of therapy."

Layla looked at the handsome man beside her. "I think we better get up and tell her everything. She's mad as hell, and I can imagine how confused she must feel. I'm confused too. It will take some time to get used to... I miss seeing you, Akhmose. It feels weird talking to you and seeing Baahir's face and hearing his voice."

Akhmose smiled and pressed a gentle kiss to Layla's soft lips. "It's me. It feels wonderful to have a flesh and blood body." He reached for Layla's hand and lifted it to his lips.

Layla sighed, "I feel you in there. When Baahir kissed me, it felt different. But my eyes have to get used to seeing him and think of you."

"So, when he kissed you, it didn't feel like this?" Akhmose embraced the trembling woman. Their kiss was sweet and long, making Layla blush. Akhmose started breathing deeper and his new body burned with desire. Their lips parted and Akhmose leaned back whispering, "Layla, you have my heart. Take good care of it."

"I will."

MYSTERIOUS OMEN

Messenger

When the Raven calls, listen!

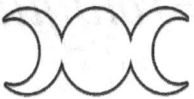

"Harbinger of danger, the Raven calls
Omen of perils that will befall
Ignoring its warning does not bode well
Time of the essence, cast protection spell
Kraa from the oak, flapping black feather wings
Her heart knows the message it brings"
~Cindy J. Smith

Prologue

Lauren had a happy childhood, but the tragedy of losing her parents and brother caused her to grow up too fast. She was eight years old on that stormy morning when the Raven appeared on her windowsill the first time. She was curious and stood up to take a closer look at the bird, but it quickly disappeared.

That night the Raven came back and pecked on her window. This time the black bird seemed menacing, ruffled its feathers and let out a loud *kraa* sound. Its coal-black eyes reflected the light of the room, and it let out another eerie *"kraa"*. Lauren was frightened and ran to her grandmother who was watching TV in the living room. "Grandma, there's a huge black bird pecking on my window and it squawked at me. I'm scared!" Lauren grabbed her grandma's hand. "Come, I'll show you!" she cried.

Her grandmother stood up and followed her.

"There! See?" Lauren pointed at the window.

"I don't see it, but you can. Don't be scared, munchkin," her grandmother cooed gently and hugged her tight.

"Why can't you see it, Grandma?"

"Because it's your spirit guide, only you can see it."

"Do you have a spirit guide too that only you can see?"

"Yes. In our family, everyone has a Raven messenger."

"But why? What does it want?"

"It warns you that something bad is about to happen that will change your life." The old woman sighed and hugged Lauren even tighter.

"But this morning it didn't scare me. Why is it so mean to me now?"

"You saw your Raven this morning?" her grandmother questioned, feeling alarmed.

"Yes, but it didn't scare me then."

"Goddesses help us! I hope I'm not too late." She whispered reaching for Lauren's hand. "Let's go munchkin, we'll light some pretty candles."

"Why, grandma?" Lauren asked wide-eyed.

"Because… it will keep everyone we love, safe."

Chapter 1

Lauren met Luke when she did her surgical rotation in the Presbyterian Hospital. Luke was working for a law firm that handled medical negligence cases and questioned her about a surgery.

He was well-groomed, charming, handsome, and his friendly smile lit up the room. He made her feel at ease and there was an instant attraction between them. After a few dates, their relationship bloomed into a passionate romance and on Valentine's Day, he proposed. Lauren was happy and counted her blessings to have found the perfect man. Although her grandmother asked her numerous times if she was sure about marrying him, she assured her that he's a good man, and he makes her happy.

"His aura is unclear, and his vibes feel off," she told Lauren.

"But why Grandma? What did he do?"

"My intuition tells me not to trust him, and I can't control how I feel. Just think it over carefully, and don't rush into marriage. How do you feel about him?"

"I love him, Grandma. I trust him, and I want to marry him."

Despite the bitter feelings her grandmother's warning left, Lauren didn't change her mind. Her grandmother gave in but insisted on having a prenuptial drawn up by her lawyer which Lauren hesitantly and Luke happily signed. He moved into her penthouse apartment, and they settled into living a seemingly idyllic married life. Soon, he started talking about how stressful it was to work for the law firm and made plans for the time when he'd have enough money to start his own law firm. Lauren laughed and took out her checkbook, "How much do you need?"

Luke seemed to be surprised and at first, he protested against using his wife's money, but soon, happily gave in and rented an office space in a high-rise building on 84th Street in Manhattan. Lauren chose Internal Medicine and opened her office five blocks from Luke's office.

Everything seemed fine for the first few years. Luke was ambitious, and to make valuable connections, he organized parties every other month or so in Lauren's lavish loft and invited influential people. Lauren didn't like the mingling, forced smiles and the endless, nauseatingly boring pleasantries, which seemed to be the same at every party. Her statuesque figure drew admiring glances from men and jealous stares from the trophy wives. She was bored and sometimes disgusted by the business deals they made between cocktails, but she couldn't say no to Luke and put up with it to please him. However, she put her foot down when Luke wanted to spice up the parties with cocaine and other popular party drugs.

Later Luke started to become reckless and confessed to Lauren about the bad investments he made and the tens of thousands he lost at his monthly poker games with his friends. Lauren bailed him out every time, paid his debts and forgave him often recalling her grandmother's wise words. "Every time you forgive a man, he'll love you more, but you'll love him a little less. The time will come when you'll see who he truly is."

The past six months or so Lauren felt a deep coldness slowly seeping into their relationship. He was attentive and loving as usual during the short times in the mornings and evenings they managed to spend together, but numerous times she caught the anxious flash of his eyes or noticed him staring at nothing. At first, she thought it was because she kept bringing up the idea of starting a family, but lately, she sensed something else. He became anxious and sometimes snapped at her when she asked about his company. "Everything is fine," he would say ending the conversation.

She couldn't shake the feeling of uncertainty that crept between them and tried to force some assurance out of Luke. After a nice dinner, she mentioned, again, that it's time to start a family. He clammed up and his expression turned frigid, but knowing how materialistic he was, she kept listing her reasons. "We're happy and we have everything we've ever wanted. My inheritance provides us with financial security and besides, we both have great jobs. I believe we need a child to tie our family together."

"We have plenty of time, we're both young. We don't need to hurry. Let's just enjoy our life and freedom together. Aren't you happy?"

Defiance and anger washed over Lauren and before she could stop herself, she blurted out in a hurry, "My thirty-fifth birthday is approaching, and it's time, but you seem to be so against the idea of having a child. Maybe we're not meant to be together. This is not enough for me. Perhaps we should divorce and go on with our separate lives."

Luke shrunk back with fear flashing through his handsome face. "No, honey. I love you and I'll do anything to make you happy." He stood up and rushed over to Lauren, hugging her tightly. "You're right. Let's start a family, but let's wait a little longer. Maybe until next year."

Although Lauren felt the distance between them deepening as the weeks and months passed by, she quieted her growing concerns and worries. *It's going to be okay when the baby comes. Children tie couples together.*

When her IUD fell out, she took it as a sign and didn't have it replaced. She couldn't help hoping and wondering. *Maybe I'm just late,* she thought, still not willing to believe even after the positive home pregnancy test, but this morning the Lab confirmed it. The happy feeling suppressed her anxiety about what Luke will say. *I'm going to have a baby!*

Chapter 2

Lauren stood by the open window of her second-story office. The sun was about to set and painted the top of the trees in the park across the street with golden light. Shaking her long auburn hair from the constricting ponytail, she enjoyed the beautiful view after the hectic day of treating patients with all kinds of problems. She sipped her tea, leaned on the window frame and watched people hurrying about their business on the sidewalk. A noisy group of teenagers were shooting hoops in the park's playground as a flock of pigeons fought with a pesky squirrel that was about to steal the tasty seeds, courtesy of Mrs. Wilkins. The old lady fed the birds every day, rain or shine.

"Lauren, Marcia and I are leaving. Should I call you a cab?" Kathy, her attractive redhead receptionist with freckled skin knocked on the open door. Her curly, long hair flipped as she turned toward Marcia, her plump blond nurse, who appeared beside her.

Lauren turned to look at her best friends since high school. When Lauren applied to medical school, she tried to talk Marcia into applying as well. She had the credits and her SAT score was even higher than Lauren's, but Marcia said becoming a doctor was not what she wanted. Her dream was to become a nurse. After graduation, she worked at a hospital and when Lauren started her practice, she joined her. Kathy never had any ambition to go to college. She was a member of a coven and enjoyed being a practicing witch. She worked at the Presbyterian Hospital with Marcia as a receptionist, and as soon as Lauren opened her practice, she joined her as well.

"No, thanks. Luke is picking me up."

"Okay, then. I'm exhausted, it was a busy day." Kathy sighed. "I need a hot bath and a tall margarita."

"Me too," Marcia laughed.

"Yes, it's been a long, tiring day." Lauren smiled feeling drained. "But you two made the day go smoothly, as usual."

"Of course," Marcia giggled. "You pay us well to do our best."

"Shoo, get out of here and enjoy your night. See you tomorrow."

"Goodnight," she heard the women say in unison as they turned and walked toward the reception area through the hall. "I'll lock the door," Kathy yelled back.

"I'm so glad it's Dave's night to cook," Lauren heard Marcia's voice.

"You're so lucky!" Kathy replied. "I only have my cat to keep me company on lonely nights."

Lauren heard the front door open and Marcia's voice again. "Why don't you date? It's been six months since you got rid of that leech. You should cast a love spell or something and snag a nice man."

"Marcia, I told you many times." Kathy raised her voice in anger. "Spells are powerful, you can't just go and cast a love spell."

"Alright! I was just saying. You can unruffle your feathers."

The door closed with a thud and click. Lauren smiled and turned back toward the window. *I'm glad, she got rid of that loser. He was draining her dry for years, but she clung to him. Marcia helped her to realize that he was just using her.* The sharp ringtone of her phone snapped her out of her thoughts.

"Sorry, honey, I'll be a little late. I'm stuck in traffic." She heard her husband's voice, muffled by the sounds of honking and the loud purr of the car engine.

"It's okay, I have some charts and lab results to go through. I'll order Chinese when you get here, and we'll pick it up on the way home."

"Sounds good, see you in a bit."

Lauren didn't really feel like doing paperwork and looked out the window dreamily. *I'll tell him tonight, after dinner.*

Across the road in the park, there was a group of mothers with their young children. It seemed as if they were all friends, spending an afternoon together, something Lauren imagined doing herself. Being out there with her son or daughter, pushing them on the swing after she'd spent her day at work seemed so rewarding. She wouldn't want to give up her career to be a stay at home mom, and she knew Luke wouldn't give up work either. Coming to a compromise now must be a priority, as their child was growing within her, so maybe he'd agree to hire a full-time nanny. *Finally. I'll be a mom.* Lauren put her hand on her belly and couldn't stop smiling.

Suddenly, she heard a deep, throaty *kraa* sound. Lauren took a deep breath. She knew what the all too familiar sound meant. Her eyes shot toward the tall oak tree across the street where the eerie sound came from. The Raven's shiny, black eyes fixated on her and let out another loud screechy sound. Lauren's stomach shrunk into a knot and a dreadful feeling washed over her. *No! Please not again!* She screamed in her mind. "Shoo!" she yelled out loud. "Nothing bad is going to happen."

The Raven flapped its wings, called again even louder, which sent sheer terror through Lauren's nerves as she remembered her grandmother's warning. "The Raven is your messenger, and it warns you that something bad is about to happen which will change your life. You must perform a protection ritual and call on the Wolf spirit to protect you from harm."

A sign of something bad coming wasn't what she needed. Not with the happy news confirmed this morning. Lauren rushed to her desk and yanked the bottom drawer open. In there was a box with her grandmother's spellbook, candles, and herbs.

She looked up feeling anxious when she heard the front door of her office opening. *It's too early for Luke to get here, maybe one of the girls must have forgotten something.* She called out, "Is that you, Marcia, or Kathy?" Closing the drawer, not wanting anyone else to know about the family secret, Lauren stood, walking over to the door. Just before she got there someone rocketed through the door. A gloved fist in front of her face grew large and the next thing she knew she was falling backward and hit the carpet with a thud. Darkness began to envelop her when she felt an excruciatingly painful blow to the side of her head before she lost consciousness.

Chapter 3

Lauren slowly opened her eyes. The white ceiling tiles with fluorescent light fixtures told her exactly where she was. *I'm in the hospital, but why? What happened to me?* Slowly, she tried to move. Every part of her body ached. Her head throbbed, and when she slowly turned her head, she was able to see the IV pole with a pump attached by her bed. *My throat hurts. Was I intubated? My belly hurts as if I had surgery. Why can't I remember?* She touched the side of her head and felt a large, painful lump but no wetness in her matted hair. *No open wound, I must have fallen and hit my head. But why does my abdomen feel like it's on fire on the inside? Is my baby okay?* She screamed in her mind but knew it was safer for her not to make sudden movements or sit up, but she needed to know why she was in the hospital and what happened to her.

Before she could reach the call button, Marcia rushed into the room and called out to her with worry in her voice, "You must stay in bed! You've lost a lot of blood."

"What happened?" Lauren managed to croak out her question. She felt a sharp pain in her throat when she made sounds and could barely manage to move her swollen lips.

"I'm just glad you're okay!" Marcia embraced her in a careful hug. "I went back to the office because I forgot my phone, and I found you on the floor unconscious and bleeding."

"Is my baby alright? Please tell me I didn't lose the baby!" Lauren cried out tears welling up in her eyes.

"The baby's fine. By the way, I didn't even know you're pregnant." Marcia looked at her accusingly. "You didn't tell us."

"No, I didn't tell anyone yet, I wanted to tell Luke first. I just got the lab result back this morning."

"Luckily, the knife missed the uterus when the attacker stabbed you, but the doctor said she had to take out one of your ovaries because it was badly damaged. I'm so sorry."

"It's fine—I'll be okay. The baby is stable and nothing else matters." Lauren sobbed.

"You'll be okay. I'm here for you, and I'll always be here for you, you know that." Marcia whispered, stroking her shoulder.

"I know," she whispered and tried to smile. "Is Luke here?"

"I called him while you were in surgery, he's on his way. He knew about the baby…" Marcia's voice trailed off into silence as she looked away.

Lauren looked up at her and was surprised to see the angry flash in her eyes. "What is it, Marcia? Tell me!" she demanded.

Hesitantly, Marcia replied, "It's just… he just… his first question was, 'Is she alive?' which took me by surprise. Usually, when people get bad news like that, they worry and ask, 'Is she okay?' or something. And then he asked, 'What about the pregnancy?' and when I told him that the baby is fine, he just said, 'I'm on my way' and hung up on me. He just sounded so cold…"

"Everything will work out. He's just in shock." Lauren defended her husband. A tear trickled down Lauren's cheek as she touched her belly. The baby she'd wanted more than she could put into words, was safe. "My side hurts when I breathe. Do I have broken ribs?"

"Yes, the doctor said you have two broken ribs and you're lucky it didn't pierce your lung. Also, your face is swollen, and you have a concussion from the blow to your head. You must stay in bed." She warned.

"But what happened to me? All I can remember is falling and then blackness."

"When I got back to the office, the door was ajar. I called the ambulance and police right away. The cleaning crew was working on the first floor and they didn't see anyone. But the officer said the lock wasn't broken."

Lauren struggled to talk. "But only you, Kathy, and I have keys to the office."

"The attacker might have picked the lock. The detective thought they were probably looking for drugs, but the keypad on the med room was intact and the lock on the crash cart wasn't broken either."

"I don't understand. For whatever reason they broke in, they didn't need to beat me unconscious and stab me," Lauren whispered and then remembered that she was about to do a protection spell when the attacker stopped her.

"What can I do for you? I'll stay with you."

"No, go home. I'm sure Luke will stay with me. I'll try to sleep. Maybe when I wake up, I'll find this was nothing more than a horrible dream."

Marcia stroked some strands of hair off Lauren's forehead. "Anything I can do, call me right away. I'll be here first thing in the morning." She looked at Lauren with concern when she winced in pain. "I'm calling the nurse. You need pain medication."

"I'll be fine, don't worry. I'll take as much painkiller as I can take safely. I can't hurt the baby with strong narcotics." Lauren managed a weak smile and changed the subject. "I'm glad you forgot your phone and found me."

"You're my best friend, Lauren. I love you."

"I love you too."

Soon after Marcia walked out of the room, Luke stormed in and rushed to Lauren's side. "Are you okay? Oh, my God! Your face looks all bruised and swollen." He reached for her hand and lifted it to his lips.

"How did you find out about the baby?" Lauren managed to ask. "I was going to tell you tonight after dinner."

"I saw the home pregnancy test in the bathroom, but I didn't say anything. I waited for you to tell me when you were ready." He stroked her arm gently.

"Are you happy about the baby?"

Before Luke could reply, they heard a man clearing his throat in the doorway. "Excuse me for the interruption, but I need to ask a few questions," The lean man dressed in a dark blue suit wearing a gray tie, spoke. "I'm detective O'Connor." He walked in and stood beside Lauren's bed. "What do you remember about the attack, Dr. Bailey?"

"I don't remember anything," Lauren replied feeling a bit annoyed for the interruption. "It happened so fast. Oh, I remember a fist coming at my face and that I was falling. Everything turned dark and I don't know what happened."

"Did you see the face of the attacker? Do you remember the clothes they wore or any mark on their skin such as tattoos or birthmarks?"

"No. All I can remember is what I just told you. All I saw was a gloved fist as I turned. I fell and everything turned dark."

"Can you think of anyone who'd want to hurt you?"

Lauren shook her head. "I don't think so… wait, there was a man a few months ago who accused me of not doing everything possible for his wife. She had an inoperable, malignant brain tumor and passed away. He was bitter and angry but stopped the threatening calls a few weeks ago. I think he finally understood that there was nothing anyone could do to save her.

"Can you give me his name? I'll look into it. Is there anyone else you can think of?"

"No."

"Okay, thank you. If you do remember anything else, please call me. Feel better." He placed a card on the bedside stand and walked out of the room.

Just as Lauren turned to Luke again, the surgeon and pulmonary specialist walked in. They spent over an hour talking about her condition and treatment plan. Both doctors assured her of a full recovery. By the time they left, Lauren felt exhausted and she was in pain, she didn't feel like talking and sent Luke home.

Her belly and side hurt so much that it brought tears to her eyes. She rang for the nurse. After the pain medication kicked in, she fell into a welcomed sleep.

Chapter 4

After a restless night, the usual hospital noises woke Lauren. Her mouth was chalk dry, but the pain was more bearable. Being a patient and depending on the nurses to help her with every move, was a horrible feeling. Yet Lauren let her nurse, Tammy, help her to the recliner chair.

"Let me know when you're ready to go back to bed." Tammy patted Lauren's shoulder. "Don't go trying to get back by yourself. Marcia will kill me if you fall and add to your injuries."

"I promise I'll call you." Lauren smiled at Tammy. "I appreciate everything you're doing for me."

"Don't mention it."

"Where did you meet Marcia?"

"She used to work here before she abandoned us and went to work for you. She's a great nurse, I enjoyed working with her."

"She is great and a good friend, too."

"Doctors are often the worst patients to deal with, but you're different. At least for now." Tammy laughed and put her hand on Lauren's. "It's a nice change to have a doctor for a patient who doesn't act almighty." She flashed a warm smile and walked toward the door.

Lauren reached for her phone as she glanced over at the clock. *It's nine o'clock and Luke's not here —not even a call.* A sad feeling washed over her. *I knew it. He's not happy about the baby. But I don't care.* She touched her belly. *This little one is more important.*

Lauren watched Tammy walking through the door until she could be certain there was no possible way the nurse would be able to hear the conversation she was about to have. Then she punched in Kathy's cell number.

"How are you feeling?" Came Kathy's worried voice. "Marcia called me an hour ago and told me what happened. I'm so worried. I hate Marcia for not calling me last night. Are you okay? I was about to come to the hospital to see you." Kathy took a noisy breath seemingly running out of air after her long speech.

"Everything is just so wrong!" Lauren touched her swollen, painful lips. It hurt to move her mouth. "Listen. The Raven warned me shortly before I was attacked. I was about to get everything ready for the protection spell when I was knocked unconscious. I must perform the spell, and I need you to bring me the candles and Grandma's spellbook from the office."

Kathy had taken over her grandmother's coven after she passed a year ago, and they often performed protection and cleansing spells together after office hours when Marcia left. Although Marcia was her best friend, her constant making fun of Kathy about being a witch, caused Lauren to keep it a secret from her.

"But I don't have a key to the drawer."

"It's open. I was about to take the spellbook out when…"

"Okay, I'm heading out the door, now. Do you want only the candles and the book? No. After your messenger's visit and what happened to you, I believe you need a powerful protection spell. I'm bringing my herbs too."

"I just… I've got this weird feeling that it's not over."

"We were both taught to listen to those feelings. I'll be there in an hour."

"Thank you. I don't know how, but we must figure out how to perform the protection spell here, in the hospital. We'll find the way—we have to."

"That's easy!" Kathy assured her. "I'll tell your nurse we will be praying in your room and they'll not disturb us. I've done it many times with the sisters of my coven when they were in the hospital."

Lauren ended the call as she heard a knock on the door and saw Luke walking into the room with a flower bouquet. Lauren watched him, mixed emotions sweeping through her when from the corner of her eyes she saw a dark shadow. Turning her head slightly she saw the Raven on the windowsill. *Oh, no. Please, not him!* She cried out in her mind. The black bird fixed its shiny eyes on Luke for a second and then disappeared.

"I'm so sorry I couldn't come earlier." Luke apologized and bent down to kiss her forehead.

"What happened?" Lauren managed to whisper, trying hard to hide the dreadful feeling her premonition triggered. The raw emotion was more painful than her physical injuries.

"A client called. He was arrested and I was with him trying to figure out his defense." He sighed, sitting down on the bed facing Lauren. "Nothing for you to be worried about, though. How are you feeling?"

"Everything hurts, but I'll be okay. More importantly, the baby is fine." She baited him for an answer she didn't get the day before.

"Yes, I'm so glad there's no lasting damage. I spoke to the doctor on my way out last night, and she assured me of your full recovery."

Lauren noticed the lack of emotions in his eyes when she mentioned the baby. It made her wonder if her husband even cared. Luke smiled, but it didn't quite reach his eyes, which made Lauren even more suspicious.

She tried hard to hush the bitter feeling. "I don't understand why the person who broke into the office beat me so brutally. I don't even know if it was a man or a woman. Without saying a single word just knocked me unconscious as if wanting to kill me. The detective said the person might have been looking for drugs, but nothing is missing."

"Maybe someone disturbed him, and he got away," Luke speculated.

"But if someone else was there too, why didn't they call for help? I was on the floor, bleeding until Marcia found me."

"I don't know, darling, and we may never find out," Luke announced reaching for his phone, which was ringing in his pocket. He looked at the screen. "It's the office. I must take this call." He looked at his wife for approval.

"Sure, no problem." Lauren nodded and reached for the orange juice on her table to take a sip. She listened to Luke talking to someone in a hushed voice. "Do you have to go?" She asked when Luke ended the call.

"Unfortunately, yes. There's another crisis at the office." He scratched his chin nervously. "I'll stay if you want. To Hell with the office and clients, you're more important."

"No, there's not much you can do here but sit with me. The nurses keep an eye on me, and things could be a lot worse. I'm alive, and I'll recover in time."

Nodding, Luke glanced at his phone. "It's ten o'clock, I hope I can be back in the afternoon to stay with you."

"Sounds good. Go get your work done. We both know what you're like if you've got something still to do."

"Are you sure?"

"I'm sure. Go."

Lauren felt exhausted, every part of her body and mind cried for rest and sleep. *Luke won't be back for a while; I must rest and think.* She rang for Tammy and with her help, she got to her bed. Tucked in and feeling relatively comfortable, she closed her eyes and sunk into a dreamless sleep.

Her phone woke her an hour later. "I'll be in later than I thought." She heard Kathy's voice. "The police put a seal on the office door, I can't get in to pick up the candles and book. We don't really need the book because we know the spell, but I don't have all the herbs and candles we need. I'll have to stop at the magic shop in Brooklyn, so it will take a while."

"Don't worry. Be careful. The traffic is brutal this time of the day." Lauren mumbled.

On the verge of falling asleep but too tired to open her eyes, she felt the nurse checking her vitals and then walking over to the IV pole changing the IV bag. Later she heard Marcia's muffled voice talking to the nurse outside the door, and then she tiptoed into the room and sat down on the chair beside her bed.

Lauren recognized the tune of her phone, but before she contemplated opening her eyes, Marcia answered it on the first ring.

"She's asleep," She whispered. "No, she's fine. She needs as much rest as she could get. When are you going to get here?" She was quiet for a few seconds and said before disconnecting the call, "I have to go home but I'll try to come back later."

Lauren was oblivious to the world for a few hours when a loud noise woke her. Her eyes popped open and saw the Raven on the windowsill. The black bird stared at her with its black pearl eyes and made a loud *"kraa"*. *Not again! Please, what do you want now?* She begged silently, a dreadful feeling flooding her.

Suddenly, Luke's sinister, sneering face swam into her mind as a powerful vision, his eyes glowing with anger and hate. Behind him lurked in a haze, a longhaired figure. Lauren strained to make out the features of the blurry figure, but the vision disappeared within seconds. Lauren had no way of being certain if she was dreaming, or if it was a premonition her grandmother warned her about to pay close attention to. Eyes closed yet wide awake and her nerves on edge, she tried to make sense of her terrifying vision.

A nurse entered her room. Lauren watched her through half-closed eyes, uncertain why that specific nurse gave her a bad feeling. Nurses came and went all the time, but there was something telling her to be wary—most likely her strong intuition. With a syringe in her gloved hand, the nurse made her way over to Lauren's bed, grabbed the IV tube and injected something into it. Lauren watched her eyes open just enough to see under the protection of her eyelashes. *A nurse would never inject anything into the line before wiping it with alcohol. She's not a nurse.* Thoughts were popping in her mind sending her nerves on edge. *If she finds out that I'm awake, who knows what she would do before I can call for help. I can't defend myself, not with broken ribs.*

With eyes still half-closed, Lauren slowly reached over to her left arm under the blanket where the IV needle was taped to her hand, trying to make her movements seem as natural as she could. Ever so slowly she pulled the tape off and pulled the IV needle out and pinched the tubing, not wanting whatever had just been injected into the IV to go into her body or to drip on the bed. Fortunately, the possibly *pretend nurse* didn't seem to notice.

After a few seconds of a heart-pounding wait, the nurse walked away, not checking to make sure the IV was still attached. *I wish I could see her face.* She moved her head slowly and managed to look at the woman's back before she reached the door. Lauren observed the surgical cap on her head and the ribbon of her mask tied over it. *I've never seen a nurse without a stethoscope and she's wearing low heel pumps. Every nurse wear sneakers or clogs. Now I'm sure she came to kill me!* Lauren screamed in her mind and took a deep breath to calm herself. Thanks to her messenger, she knew she had to be suspicious of everything and everyone. She heard the door open and sighed in relief when she saw Marcia walking in.

"What's wrong?" Marcia asked and rushed to her bed.

"Thank God! I'm so glad you're here!" Lauren cried out. "I have to get out of here, now!" She tried to sit up but the sharp pain in her side made her fall back to the pillow.

"Wait! Let me help you. What do you mean you have to get out of here? You're in no condition to go anywhere!"

"I have to. I have a strong feeling that someone is trying to have me killed and it might be Luke."

"What? Why?" Marcia cried out.

"I just had a premonition and I have a strong feeling that it's Luke."

"Luke? I never trusted the guy, but to kill you? A premonition? What did you see? Tell me! You're scaring me."

"I don't know for sure but… he's been distant and cold. He's changed since… I don't… we've been married for so long. I don't know what's really happening and why. I just know I'm in danger and I must get out of here and away from him. A woman dressed as a nurse had injected something into my IV line just now. I'm unsure and confused. I'm scared! I must get away."

"Should we call security or the police?"

"And tell them what? What could they do to protect me based on my suspicion and feeling without any proof? If I'd tell them about my vision, they'd most likely admit me to the psych ward. No, I must leave and go to a safe place. You can help me."

"You might be right. I'll do anything, but how are we going to get you out of here?"

"Find Tammy. I trust her. She'll help us. I'm still not convinced it's Luke, but premonitions never lied to me before. All I know is that I'm not safe here and there's only one place Luke doesn't know about. Now I'm glad I never told him about the summerhouse I inherited from Grandma. It's not too far from here, about a two-hour drive up to the Catskill mountains."

"Right, I'll go find Tammy!" Marcia turned and hurried out the door.

Kathy! She didn't call. Lauren grabbed her phone and dialed. After a few rings, the call went to voicemail. Lauren didn't bother leaving a message, disconnected and sent her a text. *Kathy, where are you? Are you okay?*

Marcia came back trailed by Tammy. Lauren told her everything she knew.

Tammy looked at her wide-eyed, terrified. "You're right. You're in danger here! I'll do anything I can."

Lauren remembered. "I closed the IV line to save what she'd injected in it. Would you put it into an evidence bag and about half an hour after we leave, call this detective." She handed the card to Tammy. "I want to know what she injected into the tube."

Tammy sprang into action right away. "Of course, I'll do as you asked. To get you out of here is easy. I'll get a wheelchair and when you're ready, I'll create a little commotion on the other end of the hall and Marcia can push you to the elevator."

Marcia agreed. "Great! My car is in the ER parking lot. Nobody will pay attention to us if I wear scrubs and Lauren changes her clothes."

Tammy nodded and as she walked toward the door, Lauren's phone rang. "Kathy! Where are you? You said you'd be here hours ago," Lauren asked in a hurry and put the phone on speaker.

"Some idiot stole my car while I was in the Magic Shop and the police just found it. I had to go get it because my bag with my phone and amulet were in there. I'm on my way now, I'm about ten minutes from the hospital."

"Listen. I'm in big trouble and I need to get out of the hospital!"

"What? Goddesses help us! What happened? What's wrong?" Kathy's words came in puffs sounding petrified.

"I'll tell you everything later. Marcia's with me. Meet us in the ER parking lot."

"Okay. I'll be there in ten minutes."

"Magic Shop? Spellbook? What's going on?" Marcia asked as she walked to the closet to get Lauren's clothes.

"It's time for you to know, and I'll tell you everything on the way to the summer house. Sorry, I didn't tell you before, but you've always made fun of Kathy about being part of the coven."

"Yeah, I did… because she's always talked about witchy stuff and drove me crazy with her candles and burning herbs. Are you… are you a witch too?"

Lauren winced in pain trying to untie her hospital gown. Marcia reached the bed with a few quick steps and helped her. Lauren sighed. "No, I'm not a practicing witch but Grandma was. Kathy took over her coven when she passed away last year. I'll tell you everything when we're safely in the car."

Tammy opened the door pushing a wheelchair with a large plastic hospital bag stuffed full. "Here." She patted the bag. "I put gauze, tape, and everything you need to dress your surgical wound, and also an IV starter kit and two bags of Saline and IV antibiotics that will be enough for five days. You'll need IV fluids for at least another day. Here are the scrubs for you, Marcia." She pulled the folded green scrubs from under the bag.

Marcia quickly put the scrubs on over her jeans and T-shirt.

Lauren choking up managed to say, "Thank you, Tammy!"

"Don't get sappy on me now." Reaching into her pocket she sniffed a tear back and handed a medication bottle to Lauren. "I can't take any pain medications out from the Pyxis, I'd lose my license for that, but I got you a bottle of Tylenol." She bent down to put Lauren's socks and shoes on.

All dressed and Lauren sitting in the wheelchair, they were ready to go. "Let me go make some chaos in Mrs. Bentley's room. Good luck with your escape and call me as soon as you can." She winked at the two of them and left.

A few minutes later a code sounded through the loudspeaker and they heard running footsteps. Marcia opened the door wide and when she didn't see anyone in the hall, she pushed Lauren in the wheelchair toward the elevators. They got in undetected and got down to the ground floor. The ER waiting room was full and nobody paid attention to them when they left through the ambulance entrance.

Kathy ran toward them and hugged Lauren, crying. "I'm okay. Give me everything that I need for the spell. I'll tell you everything later. We're going to the Catskills."

"You're not going anywhere without me. I'm coming too!" Kathy announced louder than she should have. A couple walking toward the entrance looked at them suspiciously.

Marcia put the brake on the wheels and helped Lauren stand up. "Great! Let's get into the car," she said opening the side door of her minivan. "We're taking the wheelchair too. You'll need it for a few days."

"You hospital thief, you!" Kathy giggled breaking the anxious mood.

"I'll bring it back!" Marcia protested while she folded the wheelchair and put it in the back. Kathy climbed into the van and lowered the back seat to reclining position for Lauren. Lauren cried out in pain stepping up and climbing in. When she was seated, she fished out a Tylenol from the bottle and swallowed it dry.

"These shoes are killing me," Kathy mumbled taking off her pumps and stuffed them into her duffle bag.

Marcia got in the driver seat and leaving the parking lot, headed over toward the East River Bridge.

Chapter 5

On the long drive after Lauren's pain subsided, she told Kathy everything she knew.

"The bastard!" Marcia yelled. "I never trusted that shifty-eyed mongrel. Didn't I keep telling you, Kathy?"

Kathy nodded. "I never trusted him either, but Lauren loved him and seemed to be treating her well."

"That dirty rat!" Marcia huffed.

Lauren cried out, "I trusted him. Could it really be him behind all this or am I imagining it?" She asked her best friends.

Kathy shifted in her seat turning toward Lauren. "I don't know, there's no proof other than your feelings. What about his secretary? She's an attractive woman and strong enough to knock you unconscious. Did you ever suspect them having an affair?"

Lauren sighed. "I did for a while, but he always acted very professionally with her and sometimes was even rude to her. Once when we threw a party and he invited all his lawyer friends and a few rich clients, I told him to invite Chloe too. He said, 'Why should I invite her? She's just a secretary in my office.' His tone was belittling, and it convinced me that they didn't have an affair."

"Not to defend Luke, but why would he want you dead? Maybe his secretary wants you out of the way and acted alone." Marcia speculated. "Affair or not, or whatever is going on, your intuitions never lied to you. You did the right thing to get away from him."

They spent the rest of the ride in deep thoughts and Lauren finally dozed off. Her phone woke her up. It was Luke. She didn't pick up, letting it go to voice mail. A few minutes later she put the phone on speaker so Kathy and Marcia could listen to the message.

They heard Luke's anxious voice. "Where are you, darling? The hospital just called that you left, and nobody knows where you are. I'm worried! Please call me as soon as you get this."

Lauren turned her GPS tracker and her phone off.

Chapter 6

The summerhouse sat deep in the woods in the outskirt of a small mountain town. The lawn was mowed, and everything seemed to be in order as they turned into the driveaway and the headlights lit up the front yard. Although she hadn't been up here for years, Lauren paid a couple in town to maintain the house and the yard.

Even if she hadn't told Luke about the place, there was no reason to think she was safe. *Luke might somehow know about it.* Breathing in deeply, her heart pounding, Lauren walked to the front door holding onto Kathy's arm. "We must perform the protection spell before we do anything else," she whispered.

"Right. I have everything here." Kathy lifted her duffle bag and winced in pain stepping on a small stone with barefoot.

"Geez! Why didn't you put your shoes back on?" Marcia exclaimed.

"It's new and hurts my toes," Kathy offered.

Lauren unlocked the door and they headed toward the back room that her grandmother used to perform spells. Her grip tightening on Kathy's arm, Lauren tried to slow the pounding of her heart. She'll definitely feel safer once they'd cast the spell, which had always protected her in the past.

Stepping into the room Lauren felt the warm presence of her grandmother. She walked over to the small altar where she placed her family's pictures years ago and lit the candles. Kneeling, Kathy started to pull everything from the bag needed for the spell. Five candles: red, green, blue, black, and grey. She placed them on the points of the pentagram that was carved into the wooden floor.

Lauren recalled the last time she'd been there with her grandmother. They'd talked about the history of the pentagram, how it had been carved into the floor by one of their ancestors, a woman who'd needed to be safe from her abusive lover.

Carefully, Kathy mixed the herbs in a delicately carved wooden bowl. She added ground-up angelica, cinnamon, echinacea, comfrey, and mugwort, not wanting to spill any to the floor. Had there been enough time, she would have planned out the day and the time far better, but Lauren knew the spell had to be done as soon as possible. They couldn't wait for the full moon. The Raven was doing what it could to warn her, but it couldn't protect her.

Marcia stood in the corner in silence and watched every move her best friends made. Kathy sat on the floor crossed legged and lit the candles one by one, red to start and black to end, feeling the power building within her. Lauren eased herself to a sitting position across Kathy. They closed their eyes and gathering their powers as they started the chant that was passed down from mother to daughter in Lauren's family for many generations.

When the spirit guide shall appear
And evil forces sneer
Magical powers surround us
Evil must fail
Doomed to weep and wail
Spirit of the Wolf protect us

Silently they both reached into the bowl and sprinkled the herbs around them. Focused, they let their power sink into the pentagram and let it surround them. They sat in silence absorbing the protective power of the Wolf spirit.

Marcia watched them mesmerized, holding her breath. *It's so beautiful. I can feel a strong power and they seem to be glowing in the candlelight. I'm never going to tease Kathy ever again.*

After they finished the spell Lauren sensed that something was wrong. While Kathy swept the herbs off the floor, she ran through their every move they made in her mind. Lauren recalled Kathy chanting the correct words and used the right herbs. However, she lit the red candle first. Although Lauren never performed this particular protection spell, she knew enough about it from her grandmother to know that when the Wolf spirit is called the black candle must be lit first. *Maybe she was just nervous and forgot. I didn't realize the switch of candles until just now.* Deep in thoughts, she didn't say anything.

Lauren swayed a little walking to the living room. Marcia put her arm around her waist. "You're exhausted. You need to rest."

Lauren agreed and could hardly wait to get into bed. She fell asleep as soon as her head hit the pillow. Tammy called Marcia and told her that she called the detective and gave him the IV bag with the tubing. She told everyone on her shift that she didn't see Lauren leaving, but she called her from the car and asked her to inform the detective about the woman entering her room. Marcia put the phone on the nightstand and curled up on the large bed beside Lauren.

Chapter 7

The next morning Kathy drove to town to pick up groceries and Marcia hooked up Lauren's IV fluids and antibiotic. Lauren felt a little better after Marcia changed her bandages and settled in her grandma's large, comfortable armchair. She turned her phone on and checked her messages. There were ten calls from Luke. She had no desire to listen to the messages.

They spent the next few hours in anxious waiting and planning. "What am I going to do?" Lauren cried in despair.

"It will work itself out, you'll see," Marcia assured her. "I see now how powerful the spell is, I felt it in every cell of my body last night. It will protect you, and the Raven didn't appear since either. You just rest and concentrate on getting well."

"I'm not sure about that. Something is wrong with the spell. I realized afterward that Kathy switched the candles. I'm not sure, though. She's the practicing witch; I'm just an amateur. Well, she knows best, I guess…"

"I'm sure she knows what she's doing. It was amazing. I felt the warmth and a peaceful feeling flooding my body as you guys were chanting." Marcia assured her.

"What am I going to do with the baby?" Lauren sobbed. "Now that I have a strong suspicion and don't trust Luke anymore, I'm alone."

Marcia hugged her tight. "You're not alone as long as we're alive. We're besties and I'm here for you, no matter what."

Marcia was in deep thought for a minute. "What if we hire a private detective? I heard of a good one in Brooklyn. If there's any dirt on Luke at all, he'll sniff it out."

"That's a good idea." Lauren perked up. "At least I'd know something. Right now, I only have a hunch and my intuition. Nothing else."

"I'll Google his number, now."

They heard a car pulling into the driveway and there was a knock on the door a few seconds later. Marcia jumped at the sound. "Who could that be?" she whispered reaching for the loaded rifle she placed on the coffee table after Kathy left. She tiptoed toward the door when she heard a louder knock and a man's voice. "Dr. Bailey? My name is Ben Sims. I'm a private detective and I need to talk to you. It's about your husband, Luke."

Marcia, standing by the door, called out, "Show me your credentials. Hold it up to the small window on the door."

The man did as he was told, he held up his license. "He is who he says he is," Marcia informed Lauren. "Should I open the door?"

Lauren nodded and Marcia opened the door a crack and took a few steps back aiming the rifle at the door. She warned the man, "If you're armed, leave your gun outside. I'll open the door, but any wrong move and you'll be blown to pieces by a hunting rifle."

"I'm unarmed." Came the man's voice. "My gun is in my car." A tall, attractive man opened the door slowly and swept the room with his deep blue eyes. He raked a hand through his blond and slightly shaggy hair, studying the women.

Raising an eyebrow Lauren asked, "What about my husband?"

"He wants you dead. A week ago, one of my homeless informants told me that he was looking for someone to kill his wife. He promised him two hundred thousand dollars to kill you and possibly make it look like an accident."

"Please come in and sit down." Lauren invited him in. Marcia didn't lower the rifle, still suspicious of the man.

Ben took a seat and continued. "I told my informant to take the job to prevent your husband from looking for someone else, and I started looking into his affairs. From what I could find, it's apparent that his business is failing. He lost a lot of money gambling and took a large loan from the mob. He knows they'd kill him if they don't get their money back on time."

Lauren took a deep breath and tears welled up in her eyes. "He didn't tell me anything. He acted like everything was fine, but I knew something was wrong."

"There's more. I've found out from the neighbor of his secretary that they've been having an affair. He has never been seen in her apartment, but she told her neighbor that she's dating a rich man and after he divorces his wife, he'll marry her."

"But he wouldn't get any money if we divorced or his infidelity was proven." Lauren wondered.

"Yes," Ben interjected. "I looked into your prenuptial agreement as well. According to that, in case of your death and if you'd die childless, he'd inherit fifteen million dollars, your total inheritance from your parents and grandmother. If there was a child, the child would inherit everything."

"The bastard!" Marcia cried out in anger. "That's why it was urgent for him to kill Lauren before the baby was born."

Ben continued. "I thought I had more time to dig further when I found out about the attack in your office and in the hospital from a detective friend. I knew the attacker wasn't my informant because I instructed him to ask your husband for details of your schedule so he can make a plan. I know the head of security of the hospital and he let me look at the surveillance tapes. I recognized the woman walking toward the elevator in uniform. It was your secretary, Kathy."

"What are you saying? That my best friend tried to kill me?" Lauren sobbed uncontrollably and Marcia put the rifle down and hugged her tightly with deep shock on her face.

"Are you sure?" Marcia asked her voice shaking. "We've been best friends since high school."

Ben nodded and sighed. "I'm sure. After she closed Dr. Bailey's door, she took her mask and surgical cap off before stepping into the elevator. But let me continue. I had all the evidence I needed, so this morning I gave everything to the police. They've arrested Luke and, on my way here, I spotted your secretary in town. I surprised her as she was putting grocery bags into a minivan. I handcuffed her and took her to the police station. They arrested her and are taking her to New York. They'll be charged with conspiracy to commit murder. You don't have to be afraid anymore. You can go home."

"Marcia asked with suspicion in her tone, "How did you find out that Lauren was here?"

"Oh, that was easy. I have connections and my contact checked the GPS tracking on Lauren's phone. It was turned off, but then I had both of your phone's checked and got the exact location of this house."

"I can't believe it!" Lauren sobbed. "She was our best friend, Marcia. I never suspected anything."

"Me neither." Marcia hugged Lauren and looked at Ben. "You said it was Kathy who tried to kill her in the hospital. Did they find out who attacked her in the office?"

"Yes. It was Luke." He looked at Lauren's grief-stricken face with sympathy and compassion.

Lauren's phone rang; it was detective O'Connor. "Dr. Bailey, I'm calling to inform you that we've arrested your husband. Thanks to a private detective, Ben Sims, we have enough evidence to charge him with attempted murder."

"He's here. He's explaining to me what had happened. Are you sure it was Luke who attacked me in the office?" Lauren asked, sobbing.

"Yes. After the evidence Ben provided, I got a search warrant and we found bloody leather gloves in his car that matches your blood type. Also, I got the result of the substance in the IV tube. It had a fatal dose of Insulin injected into it. After reviewing the security tapes, we've found the discarded mask, cap, Insulin bottle, syringe, and gloves in a garbage bag that was collected from the ER waiting room this morning. On the tape, it's clearly visible as your secretary disposed of the items. The technician was able to lift usable fingerprints from the inside of the gloves. They fingerprinted her before transport and it's a match."

Lauren took a deep breath. "I feel devastated but I'm glad it's over."

Chapter 8

Months went by with nervous waiting. Lauren filed for divorce and given the evidence of his infidelity; the proceeding went smoothly with only their lawyers present. Luckily, Lauren didn't have to be there, and Luke signed everything she needed to divorce him.

Finally, the court date arrived. For Lauren, heavily pregnant, sitting in the courtroom was emotionally and physically hard. Luke hadn't looked at her once, but Lauren hadn't thought he would. He seemed broken sitting by a public defender with hunched shoulders. The proof Ben provided, and the police found, as well as the testimony of the homeless man he tried to hire, making it extremely unlikely he was going to be found innocent.

When they called Lauren to the stand, she told them everything she knew. Before standing up she looked at Luke yelling, "How could you do this to me?"

Luke sat there; eyes fixed on the table before him. He never raised his eyes to look at her.

After he testified, Ben sat with Lauren and Marcia in the courtroom throughout the trial. Without them there, everything would have been much harder. Lauren breathed in deeply as they waited on the head juror to stand.

"Luke Conway, we have found you guilty of all charges."

For a moment Lauren just stared at the man standing there, unable to believe she'd heard those words. It was over. No more waiting to find out what might happen next. Luke would be in jail for a long, long time.

The trial of Kathy was scheduled for the following week and thanks to the overwhelming evidence, her sentence was the same. When the handcuffed Kathy, Lauren couldn't help herself wanting answers. She stood up and yelled, "Why? Why did you do it, Kathy? What did I ever do you to deserve this?"

"What? You stupid, rich bitch," Kathy yelled with so much hate in your face that it shook Lauren to the core. "You had everything, and I had nothing. I took your husband from you, but I wanted everything you had. I hate you! I curse you and the bastard child growing in your belly."

The guards took her away and Lauren collapsed to the chair. Marcia and Ben helped her up and tried to console her.

***

When full moon came, Lauren called on the Wolf spirit for protection. This time she performed the spell correctly with the help of her grandmother's coven. They were devastated by the fact that Kathy betrayed the sisterhood and cleansed Lauren's home and office.

Finally, Lauren could move on with her life.

Ben called her the next day. "The mafia is not satisfied. They'll either have him killed in prison, or they might go after you for the money. My informant says Luke owes them a hundred thousand."

"As much as I hate him, I don't want him dead. I'll give them the money." Lauren decided. "But how would I go about it?"

"Give me a day, I'll try to find out."

The next day Ben met Lauren with a shifty-looking man in a coffee shop. The young man warned her that if she were thinking about involving the police, she'd be in big trouble.

"I won't—just tell me what to do."

"Transfer the money to this account," the man whispered handing her a piece of paper.

"Okay." Lauren opened her Chromebook, signed into her account and punched the numbers in. After double-checking the numbers, she hit transfer.

The man gazed at her phone for a few minutes and then nodded. "All done." He stood up and left.

"Will they leave me alone?" Lauren inquired.

"I'm sure they will," Ben assured her. "The criminal honor and their reputation don't allow them to do otherwise. They didn't have anything against you, and they got their money. They'll leave you and Luke alone."

"Thank you for everything."

"I'd do anything for you," Ben confessed looking into her eyes with warmth and longing.

Epilogue

"I like Ben. I like him, a lot," Marcia told Lauren many times. "I feel his good vibes and the way he looks at you... the guy's in love with you, my friend."

"Right!" Lauren laughed. "I'm as big as a house. I can't even see my toes anymore."

Lauren kept saying she wasn't ready for any relationship, but Ben was special in ways she'd never known a person could be. Maybe she'd never truly loved Luke. Maybe she'd loved the Luke she thought she knew, while the real Luke was hiding from her the whole time.

They spent more and more time together and Lauren felt safe and happy. When she went into labor, she called Ben and asked him if he'd like to be there. Ben rushed to the hospital and with Marcia by his side, held Lauren's hand during labor.

Lauren took time off but paid Marcia her regular salary. She spent the better part of every day at Lauren's apartment taking care of baby Isabelle and Lauren. Ben came to spend the evening with them every day after Marcia left. Lauren trusted him in a way she'd never trusted Luke. Ben was different, and not telling him everything about herself felt wrong in a way it never had with Luke.

One evening they sat by the fireplace sipping wine and watching Isabelle playing on the soft rug. She glanced at him. He was just waiting, not pushing, another sign of who he was, and that was a sign she could be honest with him.

"She's so beautiful." Ben watched Isabelle cooing as she hugged a soft teddy to her chest. "As beautiful as her mother," he announced looking Lauren in the eye and lifted her hand to his lips. "I love you, Lauren. I fell in love with you the first day we met."

Lauren's heart skipped a beat. "You're a good person, Ben. I think I'm falling in love with you too. But there are things I want you to know about me."

"No matter what you're going to tell me, nothing will change the way I feel about you and Isabelle."

Lauren squeezed his hand and began. "When I was eight, I stayed alive when I lost my parents and my brother because... because of who I am." She sighed. "There's a Raven, my spirit animal. It warns me when bad things are going to happen. I didn't know it then, but after the tragedy, I realized that when it appears, I need to cast a protection spell. The morning when I lost my family, the Raven appeared, but I didn't know what it meant. Suddenly, I felt nauseated and mom decided that I shouldn't go on the trip with them and stay home with Grandma. That night the Raven came again, but Grandma was too late with the spell because of me. I should have told her about the Raven when I first saw it. I blamed myself for a long time until finally, I understood. The Raven didn't appear to my mother because it was her destiny to die that day with my Dad and brother."

"So, you're a witch," Ben observed smiling.

"I'm not a practicing witch and because I wasn't interested in becoming one, my grandmother taught me only the protection spell."

"My mother belongs to a coven in Long Island," Ben divulged. "I think it's time you've met my family."

"I think it's time too." Lauren leaned toward Ben. They looked at each other lovingly for a few seconds and shared a gentle kiss.

JEALOUS ACOLYTE

The Potion

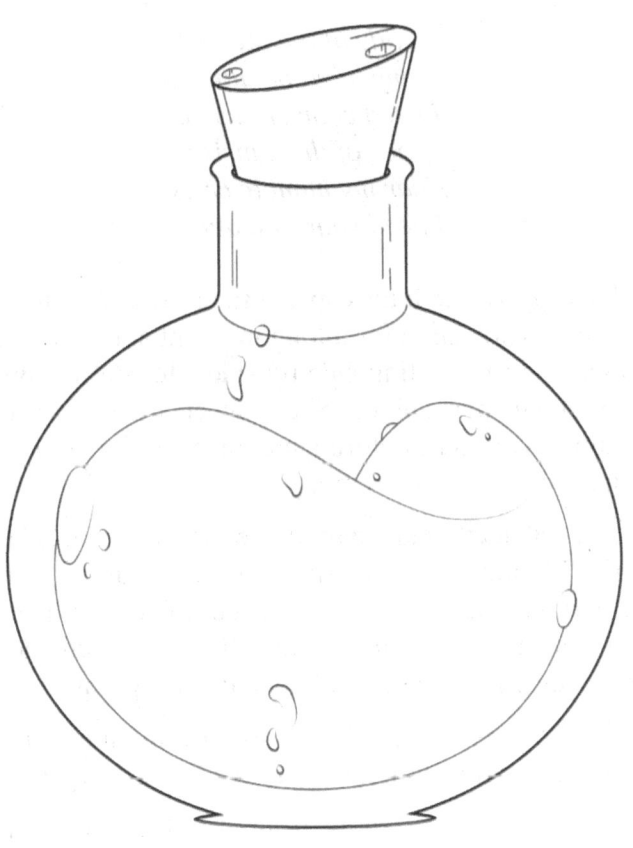

Prologue

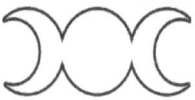

Cordelia, the high priestess of the Ravenwood Coven, stood in front of the altar lighting the candles one by one. The room was dark, and the flickering candlelight cast eerie shadows on the walls. Her hair was pulled into a bun, and her statuesque figure hid under her long, hooded cape. She held her arms high, reciting a prayer.

Lady of the Moon
Let my mind be attuned
I need your guidance
Lord of the Sunrise
Hear my humble cries
I need your guidance.

Cordelia flipped her long cape, turned around with three silver goblets on a tray, and stared for a long moment at the nervous-looking young women and man sitting side by side. Her stern expression sent deep shivers down their spines. She reached them with a few small steps and stood over them before handing them the goblets. "Drink!" Her booming voice filled the room.

Olivia, a slender, dark-haired young woman; Candice, the athletic-built blonde; and Dorian, a dark-haired young man, exchanged nervous glances. They took the goblets with shaky hands, lifted them to their lips and drank the ruby red liquid. Their expressions changed. They seemed to be in a deep trance.

The High Priestess watched the trio for a minute and then asked, "Do you wish to become apprentices of the Ravenwood Coven?

"Yes, I do," came the reply from the three young acolytes in unison.

"Do you promise to follow the Coven rules and promise to practice only white magic?"

"Yes, I do," the three answered.

"Do you promise to be loyal to the coven and its members, and promise not to compete with each other or be jealous of others?"

"Yes, I do," Olivia and Dorian replied without hesitation, but Candice's answer came a second later: "I'll try."

Cordelia drew a sharp breath. *I'll give her a chance because her grandmother is an Elder, but I'll keep a close eye on her.* She clapped her hands, and the young acolytes snapped out of the trance, looking a little dazed and confused.

"Welcome to Ravenwood Coven," Cordelia announced. "You're now apprentices. It will be a long road, and the next months will not be easy. You will study and practice hard before you can become witches and a warlock. Good luck to you all."

Chapter One

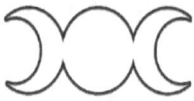

When Olivia passed the entry exam and was accepted as an apprentice into the Coven, it was the best day of her life. Her father and grandmother had been preparing her since she was a little girl, despite the objection of her mother. Her parents were happy together and lived in harmony, except for occasional fights between them about the family tradition.

Her mother, Gloria, objected. "Why does she have to be a witch? I'm not, and we're happy!"

"Because this is our family tradition, and you knew it when you married me. Remember?" Xavier, Olivia's father, patiently replied.

"Why did you marry me? You knew I was different and never wanted anything to do with witchcraft."

"Because the blue butterfly told me," Xavier said.

"A what? Are you losing your mind?" Gloria asked, feeling alarmed and concerned.

"I never told you this…because I never wanted you to look at me the way you're looking at me now." He bowed his head and swallowed hard. He then looked into his wife's eyes and continued, "My family is protected by guardians, and they communicate with us by making different colored butterflies appear to show us the right path. The blue butterfly they sent me the day I met you was to show me that we were soulmates."

"That's so sweet! Scary, but sweet. And yes, we are soulmates, darling. But I don't remember seeing a butterfly," she said, staring at her husband.

"Only we can see them. They function as detectors of people's intentions. You're a good, honest, and loyal person. That's why the guardians showed me the blue butterfly."

"Aw… But still, Olivia doesn't have to be a witch," she protested weakly, folding her arms across her chest.

"I told you before we got married that our children will join the Coven when they turn eighteen, and you agreed," Xavier argued.

"Yes, but…but I was hoping you'd change your mind," his wife replied in a quieter tone of voice. "Okay, okay! It's just… I don't have to like it."

"You should be proud of her, honey. She did very well on the entry exam. She'll be a great witch."

"I'm proud of her, and I know she wants to follow in your footsteps. It's just, I had a different future in mind for her. She loves science, and I was hoping she might want to follow that path."

"And she will. She can be a great scientist or researcher, and a witch, too."

***

Candice enjoyed being popular and never really wanted to become a witch, but because her grandmother insisted, she applied for the apprenticeship. Her mother was absent most of the time, following fleeting dreams and ideas. The only steady person in Candice's life was her grandmother.

Although Candice passed the entry test, which made her grandmother happy, she was more interested in partying than studying spells and potions. The idea of following the strict rules and studying all the time bored her, but her interest flared when she found out Dorian had joined the Coven as well.

She preferred partying with the athletic boys of the football team, but when she noticed that Olivia and Dorian were developing more than a friendship, she grew jealous of their closeness and quiet happiness. She wanted to be happy like them; she wanted him. She tried starting conversations with him, asked him to go to a party with her, and asked him to study potions and spells with her. Dorian gave her a polite excuse every time.

Feeling frustrated, Candice confided in her grandmother. "They're spending all their free time together and started dating! How could he like her? She's so plain and weird. Okay, she's a caring person, but still. I'm a cheerleader and the prettiest girl in school. How could he not like me?"

"You're the prettiest, love," her grandmother cooed, hugging her. "He's interested in her, so leave them be. There are other boys. Looks like the family curse follows you too like a shadow." Her grandmother sighed.

"What curse?" Candice asked.

"We're cursed with always wanting what we can't have."

"No, Grandma! I want him! I want him to go on a date with me, to return my feelings. I want to be his girlfriend, but no, he had to ask Olivia, sweet and boring Olivia. All she cares about is school and being boring. I'm popular and full of zest for life. What does she have that I don't have?"

"Nothing, dear. She's just a plain and boring girl, just like her grandma was. They make a good pair; Dorian is not an interesting person either. Even if he'd have asked you out instead of Olivia, you'd grow bored with him in no time."

"No, Grandma. I want him! I'll find a way to make him fall in love with me."

"And, the family curse continues..." the old lady muttered under her breath, feeling sad and frustrated.

Chapter Two

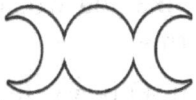

Candice and Olivia were seniors in high school, and both came from a long line of witches and warlocks. They hadn't really spoken to each other before they both became acolytes of the Ravenwood Coven. Candice was a beautiful and popular cheerleader, always wearing colorful clothes. Olivia was a shy loner, always dressed in black. Candice hung out with the cheerleaders and often humiliated Olivia publicly, or sometimes she posted degrading things about Goth people on social sites to make fun of her.

They were warned by the High Priestess not to tell anyone about the Coven. They kept it a secret, and Candice rarely talked to Olivia in school. She spoke to her only when she needed her help. One day, at lunch, Candice surprised Olivia by approaching her at the *geek* table. As Candice sat down, Olivia watched the brown-winged butterfly hovering over her head. *She's a bad person. Dad warned me about the brown butterfly people. I must be cautious*, she thought.

Candice leaned closer to Olivia and said in a hushed tone, "I'm in trouble! I didn't have time to practice, and we'll have to perform a protection spell tonight. You have to help me."

Olivia looked at her in disbelief. "You didn't practice? Studying for school and memorizing the spell and ritual kept me up half the night."

"We had cheerleading practice, and after that, we went to a party. I was too tired. Being a cheerleader is a commitment, and sometimes it's not easy to keep up with the others. You always have to pretend to be chipper and happy, even when you're not. And you always have to do everything as a group. I couldn't just tell the girls that I needed to study a magical protection spell, now could I? Besides, we had so much fun last night. The football team joined us." Candice smiled, and her blonde ponytail bounced as she shifted in her seat impatiently.

"I can imagine. Maybe I should have joined the cheerleading squad instead of the science lab," Olivia said sarcastically.

"You know you wouldn't have made it. You're not flexible enough… and a Plain Jane like you wouldn't be accepted, anyway." Candice turned away, muttering.

Her mocking tone hurt Olivia's feelings. She knew Candice didn't care about her; she just tolerated her and used her, but she couldn't say no. "Okay, I'll help you." She helped Candice memorizing the spell at recess, and the day went by quickly.

***

On the way home Olivia was thinking about her growing feelings for Dorian. She first saw him when his family moved to town to be closer to his ailing grandmother when they were in the ninth grade. She liked him and secretly hoped that one day he'd like her back. But deep down she never thought he would like a girl like her, until recently, when he joined the science club and was accepted into the Coven. He was nice to Olivia and didn't care about how she looked. They had become best friends. He was interested in the genuine person she was.

Her heart warmed every time she saw him, and she fantasized about him a lot. One day when they were in tenth grade, she was going home from the store and saw him in his Grandma's driveway next door. He was working on his car, leaning over the engine, under the hood. Olivia was too busy gawking at him and dropped her bag while taking the paper out of the mailbox. He had looked up, startled by the loud thud.

"Are you okay?" he'd asked, concerned.

"No, I'm fine, just dropped my bag. What are you working on?"

"Changing the oil. Mom and I came over to clean Grandma's house."

"Is she home from the hospital?"

"We're going to bring her home tomorrow. She had a hip replacement."

"Yes, my mom told me."

"Hey, would you like to go for a cup of coffee after I finish the oil change and get cleaned up?" he'd asked.

He'd always been friendly, but Olivia hadn't expected him to ask her out and felt the heat rising to her face. "Are you asking me to go on a date?" She didn't really believe her ears.

He cocked his head. "It's about time, don't you think? Or if you don't want to go out with me…" He left the sentence open and looked at her questioningly.

Olivia had smiled, feeling and looking embarrassed. "Yes… I mean… Okay," she stuttered but quickly came to her senses. "I have a few things to do, but we can go to Karen's shop in about an hour for coffee and cake." She didn't want him to think she was a desperate loner who'd been fantasizing about that moment for a long time.

"She makes the best lemon poppy cupcakes with vanilla frosting." Dorian had smiled and turned back to the car.

Olivia had nodded and hurried inside before she could manage to make herself look foolish.

One date and bonding over cupcakes had led to more dates. They enjoyed each other's company, and they spent as much time together as they could. They took long walks by the river, and he helped her collecting herbs in the woods. Dorian's grandmother, a *retired witch*, as she often called herself, was an Elder of the Ravenwood Coven. She was happy when Dorian decided to follow her. His mother never showed interest in joining the Coven. She divorced Dorian's dad when he was very young, and he rarely visited but once or twice a year.

Dorian knew Olivia's father and grandmother practiced witchcraft. He asked them to help his mother after his grandmother told him it was beyond her knowledge, and the doctors were puzzled by her mysterious illness that left her weak and tired all the time. Olivia's dad and grandma had performed cleansing and healing rituals, making Dorian's mother healthy.

When Olivia told Dorian that she wanted to be an apprentice, he was eager to know more. She told him about white magic, and he decided to apply for apprenticeship in the Coven as well. Their friendship deepened and bloomed. When he confessed his love for her, and they shared their first kiss, Olivia watched as a blue butterfly flapped its wings above them. *I know he's a good person, but could he really be my soulmate? Well, the guardians didn't lie before…*

Chapter Three

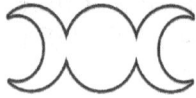

Candice watched Olivia and Dorian for months as their close friendship grew into more. She did everything she could think of to get his attention, yet he didn't show any interest in her. One day she watched them kissing and holding hands as they walked to the parking space at the Coven. *It should be me kissing him!* she screamed in her mind with jealous rage. She couldn't take it anymore. Bitter jealousy gnawed at her insides, and she knew what she was going to do. *I'm going to make him love me!*

She let the jealous thoughts and feelings stew inside her mind as she rushed home in a fury of anger and sorrow. *Why did he have to like her?* In her haste, she opened her grandmother's spellbook and flipped through the pages. She was warned by the High Priestess not to use magic for her own gain, but she didn't care and planned to do it anyway. Although she knew she would be kicked out of the Coven and lose her chance of becoming a Ravenwood witch if they found out, she couldn't care less at this point—she wanted Dorian.

She knew her grandmother would be late, busy with the Witches Council meeting, so she flipped through the pages looking for the love spell that would make Dorian fall in love with her. When she found it, she opened her grandmother's cabinet and gathered the ingredients. *Pink sunrise rose petals*, she read the instructions. *Where are those damned rose petals?* she murmured, rummaging through jars and bottles. *Here it is!* She grabbed the jar hiding behind books on the bottom shelf. She yanked out the glass cork and looked inside. *But these are not pink. They're brownish-colored. Duh, these petals are dry. They lost the original color in the drying process.* She added three petals to the brew and concentrated on Dorian as the potion bubbled.

When it was done, she cast the spell thinking about how he'd fall madly in love with her.

I pray to thee,
O Goddess Aphrodite,
Make him love me.
Make his love strong and true.

She finished reciting the spell and poured the potion into a glass bottle. Next, she made the cupcake batter as the spellbook instructions said and added the potion to the batter. She set the oven, baked the cupcakes, and when they cooled, she piped the prepared frosting on top.

She hid the cupcakes in her room and cleaned up the kitchen. By the time her grandmother got home, she was in bed. All she had to do was make him take a bite the next day. The potion took a night to set, at least that's what the spell book had said.

The next day on her way to school, Candice took a detour over to Dorian's house. She fantasized about after graduation when Dorian would be madly in love with her and ask her to marry him. They would find a charming house in the woods, secluded but not haunted or creepy, unlike her grandma's old Victorian house.

She parked her car further up the street and walked to Dorian's house. She hid behind the oak tree across from his house and waited for him. She imagined his dark hair and blue eyes as he would greet her, and she would hand him the cupcake. *Once he eats it, we'll live happily ever after.*

When Candice saw him closing the front door, she started walking and, casually, as if she'd just noticed him, called out, "Hey, Dorian."

"Oh, hey, Candice. I haven't seen you in a while. You live on the other side of town; what are you doing here? Where is your car?" he asked, surprised.

"Grandma asked me to drop off some cupcakes at her friend's house, and I decided to walk. It's not that far. I saved a few cupcakes; do you want one? It's lemon poppy with vanilla frosting." She smiled at him while opening the box.

"Thanks! Those are my favorites." He picked a cupcake from the box and took a big bite. "This is really good," he mumbled with his mouth full and licked the frosting off his lips.

"Thank you. I made it." Candice smiled with eyebrows raised. She waited impatiently to find out if the potion had worked, but she wasn't prepared for his unexpected reaction.

Suddenly, Dorian swayed on his feet and grabbed her arm, mumbling, "I feel... dizzy." His knees buckled; his body turned limp, and his eyes rolled back as he fell hard onto the sidewalk.

Candice screamed as she knelt beside him and quickly yanked out her cell phone from her back pocket, dialing 911.

"911, what is your emergency?"

"My friend. He passed out!"

"Is he breathing, miss?"

"Dorian? Dorian!" Candice shook his shoulder gently at first and then forcefully. "He's breathing but not responding... He hit his head pretty hard on the sidewalk."

"Where are you located?"

Candice gave the address to the dispatcher and waited on the phone until the ambulance got there. *What have I done? I must've put the wrong ingredient in the potion*, she cried. She sat on the concrete sidewalk beside Dorian, holding his hand in shock. *What the hell have I done?*

She watched as the paramedics loaded him up in the back of the ambulance and started climbing in.

"Miss, you can't come with us!" the EMT warned.

"I'm his girlfriend, and I'm coming with him," Candice blurted out in a hurry and gave the EMT a stern look.

"Okay," the man gave in. "You can sit on the floor, in the corner. I need space to monitor him.

Candice sat down on folded blankets and watched the EMT hook Dorian up to a heart monitor and check his vital signs. Her body trembled with fear as frantic thoughts ran through her mind. *What is wrong with him? The potion wasn't supposed to make him sick! What am I going to do? I have to tell someone, but I can't tell them the truth. I'll text Olivia. She'll know what to do.*

Candice grabbed her phone and texted Olivia with shaky fingers.

Chapter Four

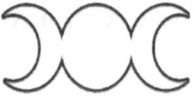

The bright morning sun blinded Olivia as she was driving to school. She put her sunglasses on and turned the volume up a notch on the radio when her favorite song started to play. She was a little nervous about the upcoming history test but was looking forward to working on a science project with Dorian after school. When her phone pinged the arrival of a text message, she pulled over to read it.

Dorian is on the way to the hospital. He passed out. She read the message from Candice and gasped. Time seemed to stand still for a few moments as she stared at the phone.

Is he okay? she texted Candice when she came to her senses. She waited a few seconds, and when Candice didn't reply, she typed quickly, *on my way!* and threw her phone on the passenger seat.

Fighting panic and tears, she stepped on the gas pedal and turned her car with screeching tires. When she stormed through the ER door, the nurse didn't let her in because the doctors were examining him. She had to wait outside his room and heard the commotion and people talking from around his bedside.

She leaned closer to the thick curtain that separated the patient cubicles and heard a man's voice. "I don't understand what's going on with him. He's clearly in a coma, but why? There is no reason for it. The CT scan and bloodwork came back normal. His heart, lungs, and, as a matter of fact, all his organs work properly, and there is no seizure activity."

"This is weird," came a woman's voice. "Look at the EEG! It seems like he's in REM sleep and having a wild dream. It's definitely not a seizure."

"I have no clue!" the man cried out with frustration in his voice. "If he were in REM sleep, we'd see eye movements and involuntary muscle movements. There is nothing, and he's not responding to any stimuli."

"We'll have to wait and do more tests. I'll call neurology for a consultation."

The doctors came out of the room shaking their heads.

"Can I see him?" Olivia asked, anxiously wringing her fingers and biting her lips.

The male doctor gazed at her questioningly. "Miss…"

"Olivia Douglas."

"Miss Douglas. How do you know the patient?" he inquired, tilting his head.

"I'm his girlfriend."

"But his girlfriend came with him; she was here a minute ago." The doctor looked at her, confused.

"Is she a blond girl?" Olivia asked.

"Yes, but…"

"It's okay; she's a friend. She texted me and probably told the EMT that she's the girlfriend, so they'd let her ride with them in the ambulance."

"Oh. Well, you can sit by his bed while we inform his family."

"His mother is out of town, but his grandmother is on her way. I called her when I was parking my car."

"Tell the nurse when she gets here. We need to talk to her."

"What happened to Dorian? Why won't he wake up?"

"I'm sorry I can only discuss medical information with a family member." With that, both doctors side-stepped Olivia, talking amongst each other.

Olivia walked into Dorian's room and made sure she was careful not to disturb any of the wires hooked up to him. She sat down next to his bed, holding his hand, and started to weep. *How could this have had happened to him?* She rested her head on the bedrail, sobbing. She wished for a miracle—but she knew just wishing wouldn't solve anything. She had to wait for Dorian's grandmother so they could find out more.

I'm going to call the High Priestess. The doctors seem clueless; maybe Cordelia can help. She pulled out her cell phone and took several deep breaths to calm herself. Her hands shook as she held the phone, dialing Cordelia's number.

"Hello?" Cordelia's stern voice answered.

"I need your help. I mean Dorian needs your help," Olivia blurted out.

"What's wrong? Where are you?" She sounded worried.

"Dorian is in a coma, at least that's what the doctors are saying, but they can't figure out what's wrong with him."

"What happened?"

"Candice told the nurse he just fell on the sidewalk as they were walking to school. He's now in a coma. I overheard the doctors saying that there is nothing wrong with him physically. I'm so worried!"

"Is Candice there?" Cordelia asked.

"No, the nurse said she came with the ambulance, but as soon as she told the nurse that one minute he was eating a cupcake, and the next he just collapsed, the nurse said she was very upset and told her she had to go home."

"You said he was eating a cupcake?" Her voice sounded distant as she spoke.

"Yes, that's what Candice told the nurse. Could you come to the hospital?" Olivia pleaded and hoped she wouldn't say no.

"If the doctors can't figure it out… Okay, I'll come over. Is his mother there?" She sounded worried.

"No. She's out of town, but his grandma is on her way."

"I'll be over in a few minutes," Cordelia assured her and hung up.

As soon as Olivia put her phone away, Dorian's grandma walked in, her cane clicking against the stark white tile floor. "Olivia! I'm glad you're here." She reached out and hugged the young woman.

"Of course! I wouldn't want to be anywhere else." Olivia pulled out a chair for her to sit by the side of his bed. The older woman held his hand and gently patted it, crying. Olivia held his other hand and had to fight back the tears that threatened to overflow. She had to be strong.

A short time later Dorian's grandmother went to talk to the doctors, and Cordelia showed up. She looked him over while she held a crystal over his third eye, moving it down his body. Olivia waited silently in the corner, deathly afraid. *If it was magic that put him into a coma, could Cordelia break it? If it wasn't a spell, what could the doctors do?*

Cordelia sighed heavily and turned to look at Olivia, her expression grave. "It's a strong spell. You said he was with Candice when he collapsed?"

"Yes, but she wouldn't want to hurt him. I mean, they're friends. She wouldn't hurt a friend. Would she?"

"Maybe, but she's just an apprentice, and she could've been trying to do a spell and messed it up by accident," Cordelia speculated.

"If you're sure it was a spell that caused this, and if it wasn't Candice, maybe she saw something that could help point you in the right direction."

"That's what I was thinking. I want to give her the benefit of the doubt." She placed her hand on Olivia's shoulder. "We'll figure this out."

"Thank you so much, Cordelia."

"We'll see what we can do. I'll call Candice."

Olivia sat back down next to Dorian and listened to his steady breathing. His face looked pale but other than that, he seemed as if he was sleeping.

Chapter Five

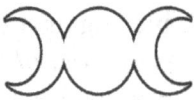

As soon as Candice got home from the hospital, she quickly flipped through her grandmother's spellbook, trying to find the spell she used. Once she found it, she rushed upstairs to the cabinet and looked through the ingredient list. She pulled out the jars and vials one by one and counted the ingredients to make sure she had used the right ones.

Her stomach sank when she found the pink sunrise rose in a jar on the top shelf. *Goddess help me! These petals are pink, but the ones I used had a brownish color. What did I do?*

She panicked as she stared at the jars and bottles. Startled by the doorbell, she shut the cabinet door and made her way down the spiral staircase to the small entryway. When she opened the door, she almost fainted when she saw Cordelia.

"Oh, High Priestess!" Her heart turned to ice as she blocked the doorway in a panic.

"Can I come in? We need to talk about Dorian. He's not doing well." Cordelia looked around to make sure no one could overhear her. "Someone cast spell on him. I was wondering if you know or have seen anything."

"No, I didn't see anything and have no idea who would have done that to him. He's a very likable guy." She felt her legs turning to jelly and shifted her weight.

"Are you sure?"

Candice nodded. "I'm sure. I don't know anything." She raked her fingers through her long hair and shifted her eyes.

"Okay, if you're sure you don't know anything, I'm going back to the Coven to talk to the Elders. We need to find a way to help Dorian." She turned and started to walk back down the drive. "If you do happen to remember something, let me know," she called over her shoulder.

"I will!" Candice promised before retreating into the house.

She shut the door and leaned against it. *I hope she believed me. If not and she finds out, I'll be kicked out of the Coven, and my grandma will be furious with me.* She gulped a lungful of air and let it out slowly. She stood there shaking as she tried to wrap her head around what just happened. *How can I make this right without the High Priestess finding out?* She wasn't sure if it was possible, but she had to try before they caught on.

She went upstairs to try to find out what she put in the potion instead of the pink rose petals. Her heart sank. *He'll never love me know, not ever, and I could end up losing everything because of this.* She sighed and sat down on her grandma's armchair. *How could I be so stupid and not pay attention to what I was grabbing?*

Candice stood up quickly and began to pace back and forth. After she calmed down a little, she pulled out Grandma's old spell book to see if she could figure something out. *Maybe something is written down somewhere in her old notebook that she filled to the brim with tips for anything dealing with witchcraft.*

The more she flipped through the worn pages of her books, the more desperate she felt. She couldn't find anything and pounded her fists against the table. *Why is this happening to me? I haven't done anything wrong before. I've never taken anything that wasn't mine. I just wanted him to love me! Why is the universe out to get me? What can I do? I can't leave him in a coma for the rest of his life.*

Chapter Six

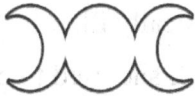

Olivia woke up the next morning even more tired than she was before she fell asleep. Dorian's grandmother stayed with him in the hospital, and Olivia promised she would be back in the morning.

As soon as she sat up in bed, she called his grandmother, and she had only sad news. Dorian's condition didn't change, and the doctors still didn't find the cause. Olivia's body ached and felt heavy. She went down to the kitchen, contemplating skipping school and going to the hospital but changed her mind. *Candice hasn't called me back. I must talk to her.*

Olivia found her father in the kitchen, frying eggs.

"You look awful!" Xavier looked at her with a concerned expression on his face. "Did you sleep at all?"

"Thanks, Dad!" Olivia mumbled sarcastically. "I slept a little but worry kept me up. We were happy. Now he's in a magic-induced coma… and no one knows who did it or why they did it. Maybe he pissed some witch off at some point, and they cursed him."

"Cordelia called a meeting; I'm heading over to the Coven after breakfast. Are you going to school?"

"Yes, Candice is not answering my calls, so I want to catch her at school. As soon as I talk to her, I'll go to the hospital."

"Have some breakfast."

"I can't eat, Dad. My stomach is in a knot." She grabbed a protein bar and left the house.

The town wasn't very big, but she liked living there. Whenever they visited big cities, she felt uncomfortable and hated the crowds. People there seemed disconnected and uncaring. Small town people knew each other and were close. Dorian shared that feeling with her.

She drove toward the high school, her vision blurry from the tears she couldn't hold back. *The witches and warlocks in the Coven will figure something out, I'm sure. He must get better.* She missed their long talks and the walks after school and missing him and worry about him made Olivia physically ill.

Before she got to school, she tried to call Candice one more time. Finally, she picked up.

"Candice, tell me exactly what happened!" Olivia demanded.

"I don't know. Honest! We were talking, and he just collapsed. At first, I thought he was choking on the cupcake I gave him, but he was breathing okay. He just didn't wake up," Candice spoke fast.

"Did you do something to him?" Olivia questioned.

"I didn't, promise!" Candice muttered.

"Liar!" Olivia accused when she saw a yellow winged butterfly hovering over the steering wheel. Her guardians gave her the sign of deception and distrust. "You did something, I know it! Tell me what you did!" she yelled, feeling frustrated.

Candice abruptly ended the call.

Olivia called the school and told the secretary she was sick, and then turned her car and headed toward the Coven, fuming. *I know she gave him something. The butterflies don't lie.* When she got to the ivy-covered gate at the old cottage at the edge of town, she took a deep breath before knocking on the door. She was unsure if she would be allowed to enter when it wasn't the scheduled practice time for apprentices. She wasn't a full-fledged member of the Coven.

The metal knocker felt cool in her hand as she knocked on the front door, even for the unusually warm autumn day. The leaves were falling around her, cascading down onto the beautifully manicured lawn. She could hear footsteps and mumbling voices from inside.

Cordelia opened the door. "I was wondering when you'd get here!" She stepped aside with a smile on her face. "Have you talked to Candice?"

"She answered my call but didn't want to talk to me other than repeating what she told the nurse," Olivia replied as she followed her inside. "But I know she was lying."

Cordelia shut the door behind them. "How do you know? Did she say something?"

"No, but the guardian's butterfly was yellow."

"Oh? Then she must be hiding something," Cordelia acknowledged. She was aware of Olivia's family blessing and the signs their guardians sent. Olivia's father confided in the High Priestess when he traced his bloodline back to the dark ages of Europe when witches were hunted and killed. Some of his ancestors survived when his great-great-great-grandmother summoned the protectors. The powerful spell claimed her life, but the guardians, the invisible entities from a different dimension, had stayed with her descendants and followed Xavier's grandmother to America.

"Did you find out how to help Dorian?" Olivia asked, sniffing her tears back.

"We don't know what spell was used. Therefore, we don't know how to reverse it yet."

"That's bad. Really bad. What can we do?"

"Well, Candice knows more than what she admits." She looked out the window. "I called her, but she hasn't shown up yet, even though she said she'd be here."

"Do you think she'll come?"

"I don't know, to be honest. I hope she does."

Olivia sighed and looked back toward the door. Thinking hard and recalling how Candice looked at Dorian since they started dating, she had a strong feeling she might have done something. "Maybe she cast a spell, but she didn't realize she did it wrong. Maybe she intended for something else to happen."

Cordelia looked at her questioningly. "Do you think she tried doing a spell on him?"

"Maybe, but I'm not sure. I've been sensing her jealousy… the way she looked at him sometimes. Yes, I think she might have tried to do a love spell."

"If she did, then something went terribly wrong. There is always a fine line between a spell and a curse. One ingredient could make a huge difference. Well, we'll find out either way, even if she doesn't confess to it. Before we perform a locator spell, which can be dangerous, we'll wait for a while. And if she doesn't show up, we'll find her." Cordelia sat down on a flower-patterned chair next to a bay window.

"I have to go to the hospital. I'm worried sick."

Cordelia nodded. "Go. Stay with him and call me if there is any change."

***

Olivia drove to the hospital and rushed into Dorian's room. "Is there any change?" she asked Dorian's mother, who was sitting by the bed, wiping her eyes.

"Unfortunately, no," she said, sobbing. "The doctors said everything looks fine, and he's healthy, for now. They did all kinds of tests, but they can't figure out why he's still in this comalike state. The neurologist said he's in a deep sleep, but if he doesn't come out of it soon, it will cause damage to his nervous system and brain."

"Goddess, help him!" Olivia cried out and sat down on Dorian's bed, holding his hand.

"Oh, right, you belong to that cult too! Maybe they did something to him," she accused.

"Or maybe they're trying to help him!" Olivia snapped.

"I don't care who helps him and with what! I just want him better," the distraught mother cried.

Olivia knew Dorian's mother was against anything magic and hated it when Dorian followed his grandmother into the Coven. She sensed that Dorian's mom, feeling desperate and helpless, blamed the Coven and would pick a fight with anyone, especially with those who belonged to the Coven. She had a hunch that's why Dorian's grandmother left when her daughter arrived.

Olivia didn't want to be the target of her fury either. "I have to go back to school," she lied as she stood up. "I'll be back later to check on Dorian.

His mother just nodded, and Olivia bent down to kiss Dorian's forehead. "We'll find out what happened and how to make you better, I promise," she whispered and left the room. She drove back to the Coven.

Chapter Seven

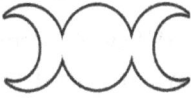

Candice spent the night pacing and sleeping in short fitful periods with vivid dreams. When she heard her grandmother's footsteps on the stairs, she dressed quickly and went down to the kitchen. *I must tell her everything. Maybe she can help.*

"We'll figure it out," her grandmother said after she'd heard the whole story, but Candice wasn't convinced.

They rummaged through the cabinet. Candice recognized the jar. "This is the one I put in the potion." She picked the jar up and showed it to her grandmother.

The old woman shrank back in fear. "Child, what did you do?"

"What? Grandma, you're scaring me!"

"These are pink rose petals laced with diluted nightshade essence. This is used for a curse and not for a love potion!"

"Curse? What kind of curse? Is he going to be okay?" Candice cried out.

"I… I meant to use it once… on your mother. She was a drug addict, and I was angry at her for abandoning you. I changed my mind because the curse is powerful, dangerous, and it's unpredictable," the old woman admitted.

The blood drained from Candice's face. "In my haste, I must not have read the entire label, and my mind only registered the words *pink rose*. I must get to the Coven and tell them what happened. I didn't mean to hurt him. I didn't mean for him to fall into a coma!" she cried.

"I'm coming with you," her grandmother decided, holding her book of shadows. "The curse is almost identical to the love spell except for the rose petals. I'm going to show it to the witches; maybe someone knows the counter curse."

Candice seemed scared but made up her mind. "I must confess to what I did, and we must find out if anyone has ever used the spell before. If they did, on whom, when, and why. Did they feel the same way, or did they suffer the same fate as Dorian?"

They left the house, and Candice drove to the Coven. A small part of her hoped the spell wasn't used on anyone, but the other part made her sick to her stomach at the thought that there could have been some poor soul lying in a hospital bed with family and friends worried sick about whether he or she would ever wake up.

Candice was petrified as they got out of the car and made their way up to the small porch. Her heart pounded as she knocked on the front door. *I didn't want him to get hurt; I just wanted him to love me*, she cried in her mind and only had to wait briefly before Cordelia opened the door with a grim look on her face.

"We've been waiting for you." She turned her back to them and walked inside.

Candice and her grandmother followed after closing the door behind them. "I'm sorry I didn't come sooner."

When Cordelia gave her an expectant look, Candice had a feeling she knew. She wasn't sure how much she knew or how much she suspected. Candice brushed back her hair and chewed on her lower lip as they sat down.

Cordelia motioned to Candice's grandmother to join the witches in the other room and called Olivia to join them. She wanted to talk to the young acolytes alone. She sat down facing Candice. "Are you sure you don't know anything about what happened to Dorian? I know you were there when he collapsed, and you went to the hospital with him."

Candice was contemplating not telling her the whole truth, but her conscience didn't let her lie any longer. "I do have something to confess but please don't be mad."

"What?" Cordelia didn't sound happy. Her nostrils flared, and her gaze urged the young woman to start talking.

"I accidentally, uh, well, I accidentally messed up a potion I was working on."

"Was the potion for Dorian?"

126

"Yes. I was trying to make a love potion, but now I'm sure I put the wrong rose petals into the potion. I am so sorry!"

Olivia drew a sharp, noisy breath and opened her mouth, her face red with anger. Cordelia stopped her with a sharp look.

Candice put the spellbook with the love potion as well as her grandmother's book of shadows on her lap. "I don't know why Grandma had these rose petals I mistook for the pink rose petals I was supposed to use. I don't know what this spell is for either." She opened both books and showed the pages to Cordelia.

Cordelia's face turned pasty white. "Are you telling me you've used the pink rose petals laced with diluted nightshade essence in the love potion?"

"I didn't mean to!" Candice cried out. "Believe me, I didn't mean to. It was a mistake. I don't even know why Grandma had that in her cabinet."

Cordelia sank back into the chair. "No, no. No. This is bad."

"What is it?" Olivia asked, fearing the answer.

"This curse is similar to the love potion except for one ingredient. This is a powerful spell. Even practitioners of black magic use it only as a last resort to break someone's addiction. However, unscrupulous sorcerers of dark magic may also use this potion as a strong love spell. But if it's cast on a person who already has a soulmate, it turns into a curse, putting the person into a deep, unconscious state.

"So, he's in a coma because he's my soulmate?" Olivia asked, her voice shaking and fighting the threatening flow of tears back.

Candice felt devastated. "I am so sorry, I shouldn't have tried to get him to love me, but the jealousy I felt was so strong."

Olivia shook her head. "I... I can't even talk to you right now!" she shouted and turned to Cordelia. "Is there is a way to break the curse?"

"Yes. We need a rare flower, the spotted orchid, to counter the curse. It blooms only at night during the blood moon. It has to be harvested before midnight, and it must be added to the counter potion before dawn. We must give the potion to Dorian before sundown."

Candice's face lit up. "That sounds easy, High Priestess. Tonight is the blood moon. Tell me where to find the orchid, and I'll go to find it," she quickly said.

"It's not that easy, child. The flower is fiercely guarded by Liam and his pack."

"Are they..." Olivia was afraid to hear the answer.

"Yes. Liam is a werewolf." Cordelia sounded distant, and Liam's lovely face swam before her mind's eye. *I broke the Coven rules when I was their age. I met Liam when he was in human form and fell in love with him,* she thought with a heavy heart. *When I made a mistake entering the forest during the full moon because I ached to see him, he almost killed me. It wasn't his fault, but I had to accept that werewolves and witches don't mix. Never did and never will. I truly understand what Candice must have felt. Wanting someone she can't have is thrilling and tempting. The young girl doesn't have the willpower yet to resist her feelings.*

Candice snapped her out of the bitter thoughts. "Cordelia, I know that every member of my family, and unfortunately, including me, can't seem to stop wanting what isn't ours or what we can't have. Why do we have this curse?"

"Because long ago, your great grandmother fell in love with Olivia's great grandfather. She made a love potion, and her great grandfather ran away with her. Olivia's great grandmother cursed her and her descendants to always crave what they can't have."

"Oh. Can this curse be broken?"

"I'm not sure, but I can talk to the Elders about it. But not now. We have a more pressing issue to deal with."

Olivia gasped, "We must find a way to get the flower!"

"It can be done, but it will be hard. I won't lie about that. Liam's pack is unpredictable during the full moon, but the blood moon makes them especially anxious and can trigger a blind rage."

Candice bowed her head, wringing her fingers on her lap. "Are you going to kick me out of the Coven? I'm really sorry about the mistake I made, and I'll do anything to make it right. Please give me a chance!" she begged, looking up.

"I have to tell you now, Candice, you will not become part of my Coven." Cordelia snapped at her.

"I made a mistake, and I said I was sorry."

"If you had come forth right away, I wouldn't be making this decision. Unfortunately, you lied to me, and I can't trust you. Trust is a crucial part of Coven life. Without trust and total honesty of the acolytes, there is no order."

Candice looked down at her feet, tears flooding her eyes. "Before I didn't take it seriously to be part of the coven, but now I want to. I want you to be my family. The damned curse! We always want what we can't have."

Olivia couldn't believe her ears and shouted, "How could you be so selfish, thinking about yourself when Dorian's life is in danger?" She looked at Candice and paused when she saw a brown-winged butterfly hovering over her head. *She's still the good old, self-centered, shifty-natured Candice. But maybe there is hope. Maybe if she's given a chance, she could change.*

She cleared her throat and started talking, "Cordelia, can you give her a second chance? I understand loyalty and all, but she made a mistake. I don't think she did what she did out of malice. She made a mistake."

"Are you sure, Olivia?" Cordelia looked baffled as she glanced back and forth between the two of them.

"I seriously doubt she'll make the same mistake again. She's aware of the family curse, and maybe you could help her break it. She came forth with what she knew; yes, maybe a little too late, but she did."

Cordelia sat quietly for a minute. *Olivia seems different. She was upset, and nobody can blame her for that. I would have been too if I were in her shoes. But there's something else. Normally she's quiet and timid. Now she seems to be strong, self-assured, and compassionate. She will make a great leader someday.*

"I am so sorry. I won't ever lie again. I promise I will be open and honest from now on," Candice said quickly, hoping that Cordelia would give her another chance.

Cordelia sighed. "Fine, but only because Olivia is willing to forgive you."

"Thank you!" Candice sobbed, looking sincere. "I'll do anything to make it right."

"We must obtain the flower to make the potion, but unfortunately, witches and warlocks are forbidden to enter werewolf territory. The peace treaty was made long ago when I was your age to prevent a tragedy… If one of us enters the werewolf territory, they will kill us."

Olivia, anxiously wringing her fingers, asked, "I'm not a witch yet. Can I go to the forest to find the flower?"

Cordelia sighed with a heavy heart. "Yes, you can. Any other time I would forbid you to go there, but in this case, we don't have a choice. Dorian will fade away if we can't cast the counter curse in time."

"I'm going too!" Candice volunteered.

"Well, let's go to talk to the Elders. They might have suggestions on how we can protect you."

The Elders couldn't offer much. The only thing they could do was cast a general protection spell, hoping it might provide at least some protection against the werewolves.

Before the young acolytes left the Coven at sundown, Cordelia pulled Olivia aside and handed her an amulet. "This will protect you. It always protected me when… Well, when I met Liam in secret," she hesitantly admitted. "Are you sure about Candice?"

"No," Olivia said, bowing her head, sighing. "Her butterfly is still brown. But everyone deserves a chance. Maybe she could change."

"I'm just curious," Cordelia hesitated, "what color is my butterfly?"

"Yours has always been pink. The sign of sincerity, honor, and loyalty."

Chapter Eight

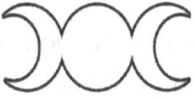

Olivia watched from the edge of the forest as the orange sun dipped behind the mountain tops. "The moon will be up soon; I think we should start going. We have a long way to go."

As they entered the forest, the owls hooted in greeting or maybe warning. Candice shivered out of either fear or from the cold breeze that whipped around them.

"Are you okay?" Olivia asked.

"Doing great! Just peachy…" Her voice wavered, and she shied away as a wolf, or perhaps a werewolf, howled in the distance.

"They must smell us and are getting their guard up."

"I doubt the spell can protect us from them," Candice squeaked and slowed her steps, falling in behind Olivia.

An owl hooted above them on the tree branch, and Olivia heard running footsteps, breaking branches, and a stifled scream behind her. She looked back and saw Candice running toward the clearing where they had parked their cars. *I knew it! She's just a big mouth coward,* Olivia fumed. *Well, she doesn't know that Cordelia gave me an amulet. I just have to find Liam and show it to him. I must save Dorian. I can do this.*

Although scared out of her mind, Olivia crept deeper into the forest, slowly pushing ahead. She followed the path for about an hour, her body tensing at every sound and her nerves on edge. She heard faint footsteps and heavy breathing around her. She whimpered as her body urged her to run, but when she saw Dorian's face in her mind's eye, she kept going.

Finally, she got to the clearing where the rare flowers bloomed and stood gazing at the beautiful orchids. Their fragrance was mesmerizing. She inhaled the sweet scent and froze when she heard low rumbling from behind her. She turned slowly and saw the dark black fur of the alpha werewolf standing close to her and the pack of seven or eight werewolves crouching behind him. She gasped and took a step back. Her breathing became heavy, and she could feel her heart thudding hard against her ribs.

The alpha took a step toward her, and a menacing low growl escaped his throat. He pulled up his upper lip, showing a row of sharp teeth. His yellow eyes glowed in the moonlight. Olivia couldn't move; his eyes held her captive. She inhaled sharply and, with shaky fingers, pulled Cordelia's crystal amulet hanging around her neck on a string and held it up in the moonlight.

The moon shone through the crystal, casting an eerie amber glow onto the werewolves, which made them back up and growl deeper from inside their chests. They kept retreating into the forest. Olivia quickly picked one flower, not wanting to keep her back turned to them for long, in case they were waiting for their moment to strike.

She ran through the forest, clutching the flower firmly to her chest, back to her car as fast as she could.

She panted heavily as she leaned against her car and held the flower tightly. She fished her keys out of her pocket with shaky fingers when she heard a throaty growl and loud ripping, breaking sounds behind her. She was petrified but slowly turned her head.

She saw a naked man crouching behind a low bush, his face contorted in pain. "Thank you... for taking... only one flower." His words came in short puffs. "I can't hold my human form for long— you must leave. Tell Cordelia... tell her... I love her and miss her... so much." He howled, and his body started to contort and change.

"I'm... I will," Olivia managed to say and quickly got into her car. She drove off on the dirt road and sighed with relief when she reached the paved road. Finally, she made it to the Coven and yanked the knocker on the door. Cordelia let her in and led her into the small room in the back where the Elders were waiting.

"I got it," she said, breathing heavily. She held up the still-glowing flower.

The Elders gasped and broke out in cheers. It was a beautiful flower, one that most would never see.

"It's beautiful!" exclaimed Olivia's father. "I knew my girl could do it!" He looked around proudly.

Cordelia smiled, held the precious flower and looked at the others. "Let's make the potion."

The Elders gathered and started to work on the potion.

Olivia motioned to Cordelia, and they left the room. Safely out of earshot of the others, Olivia told the High Priestess what had happened and gave her Liam's message.

Cordelia sat down. "I'm extremely disappointed with Candice. I had a feeling she couldn't be trusted and would flee at the first sign of danger; that's why I gave you the amulet. You're a brave soul, my dear."

"I'm far from being brave," Olivia admitted. "I've never been so scared in my whole life, but your amulet saved me. Thank you!" She pulled the crystal from her shirt and handed it to Cordelia.

The High Priestess hugged Olivia. "Try to take a short nap. It will take until sunrise to brew the potion and to perform the spell. I'll call you when it's ready."

Cordelia left the room, and Olivia curled up on the inviting sofa. She fell into a fitful sleep.

"Olivia," the High Priestess called softly.

"I'm up!" Olivia mumbled and, rubbing her eyes, followed Cordelia to the room where the Elders stood in a circle over the pentagram etched into the wooden floor. One of the Elders held a bottle and offered it to her. The liquid glowed an iridescent red color.

Olivia looked around the circle with tears at her lash line. "Thank you all so much for everything! I think I'd better get this to the hospital."

"Olivia," Dorian's grandmother called out to her as she turned to leave. "I'm coming with you. Although I told the hospital staff you can visit and stay with Dorian even after visiting hours, they might object, and I want to be there when he wakes up."

"Oh, thank you!" Olivia replied. "Then I don't have to worry about how to sneak into his room."

Chapter Nine

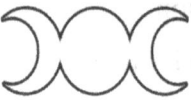

Olivia and Dorian's grandmother hurried out to the parking space. While Olivia drove as quickly as she could to the hospital, they planned how to give the potion to Dorian without the staff noticing. She had the valet park her car, and they hurried up to his room to give him the potion before the sun rose too high.

They waved to the nurses, stepped into Dorian's room and closed the door behind them.

"I'm going to give you something to make you feel better, okay, Dorian? You must swallow it, love," Olivia whispered into Dorian's ear before kissing him on the forehead.

Dorian's grandmother held his head, and Olivia slipped the small bottle between his lips. She tipped it enough so it could trickle into his mouth. He coughed, and some of the potion spilled onto his chest, but he swallowed a few drops too. Olivia lowered the bottle and gave him the rest of the potion drop by drop.

Olivia sat on his bed, holding his hand, and his grandmother silently prayed from her chair.

"Please, Goddess! Let it work," Olivia cried.

"Olivia?" Dorian's fingers fluttered in her hand, and his voice sounded gruff and hoarse.

"Thank you, Goddess!" Olivia whispered.

"Where are we? What happened?" He looked around the room, confused, as he took everything in.

"Shh… you're okay now. You had a nasty fall, and you're in the hospital. Do you remember?"

"No… what happened?"

"You felt dizzy and fell when you walked to school with Candice. You hit your head hard on the sidewalk and fell into a comalike state."

"I did? I don't remember." He touched his bandaged head. "Ouch! It hurts."

"You have stitches in the back of your head. Don't touch it."

"But why was I walking to school with Candice? She lives on the other side of town, and honestly, I can't even stand that girl."

"Well, she gave you a love potion—at least she thought she made a love potion."

"Are you serious?" Dorian looked at Olivia with raised eyebrows and anger in his tone.

"Yes." She sighed. "It's a long story. I'll tell you everything later."

"Okay, but that love potion didn't work," he laughed softly. "I'm in love with you, more than ever." He caressed her fingers.

"I love you, too. More than ever. The most important thing now is, how do you feel?"

"I'm starving!" He chuckled.

"I'll get you the biggest burger I can find." Olivia gave out an anxious laugh.

His grandmother cried with joy, "I'm so glad you're back." She bent to kiss his forehead and quickly straightened up when they heard a knock on the door.

The doctor walked in, and his jaw dropped when he saw Dorian sitting up in bed. "Wha... Wow! You're awake. What happened?"

Dorian chuckled. "I don't know. You tell me!"

"I'm... Honestly? I have no clue, young man. How do you feel?"

"I feel fine; I just don't remember what happened."

"Can I examine you?"

"Sure."

Olivia sat in the corner while the doctor did his examination. "You seem to be fine. This is truly a miracle. To tell you the truth, I have no idea why you were in such a deep sleep state and what made you wake up."

"I feel fine. Can I go home." He looked at the doctor, pleading.

"Not so fast, young man!" The doctor gave out a nervous laugh. "You gave us a scare, and we still don't know what happened to you. We need to do some tests to make sure everything is okay. We'll take the stitches out tomorrow, and then we'll talk about discharge."

"Okay, I'll stay for a day, but not a minute longer," Dorian agreed.

The doctor left, and Olivia called the Coven. "He woke up! Everything seems fine," she announced happily as soon as she heard Cordelia's voice.

"Thank you, Goddess!" she cried out. "I'll be there shortly, and I'll call his Mom too."

"Could you pick up a cheeseburger on your way? He's starving."

"And a pizza and cupcakes, lots of cupcakes," Dorian yelled.

Olivia gasped. *I doubt you'll love cupcakes so much after I tell you everything*, she thought but didn't say anything.

"I heard," Cordelia laughed. "It's a good sign."

Olivia hung up and walked back to Dorian's bed. "I missed you, and I was so worried." She hugged him tightly. "Do you remember anything? The doctor said you were in REM sleep."

"I can't recall what happened, but I remember dreams… I was in a deep hole and couldn't crawl out, and then something chased me, and I couldn't run. It was awful." He shivered. It must have been hard for you seeing me here like this." He sounded distant.

"It was. Don't tell anyone, but I bawled like a baby." Olivia held on to his hand. "I'm just so glad you're better now."

"Me too."

The nurse and the neurologist came in. "I see our sleeping beauty is awake," the nurse said with a nervous laugh. "We were worried about you, young man."

"And I got my wakeup kiss too." Dorian laughed, winking at Olivia.

After a short examination, they left as Cordelia walked in with armloads of takeout bags.

"A feast!" Dorian reached for a bag, opening it with haste. "I'm famished." He took the first bite and then wolfed down the burger in no time. "Yum…"

Olivia's stomach growled, and Cordelia quickly handed her a burger. "You haven't eaten for days either. Eat."

After they finished eating and Dorian leaned back on his pillow, Cordelia whispered to Olivia, "Can we have a word?"

"Of course!" Olivia stood up. "I'll be right back." She caressed Dorian's hand.

"Take your time. I'm going to rest my eyes a little."

Olivia followed Cordelia outside the room. "Have you heard from Candice?"

"No, not yet. I haven't seen her since she left me high and dry in the woods." Her voice sounded bitter and disappointed.

"Well, she'll come around, and she will find out from her grandmother that Dorian is okay."

"I'm not going to call her."

"I understand. We'll find out why she left you in the forest. Maybe she has a good explanation."

Chapter Ten

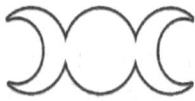

After Candice left Olivia in the woods, she drove home and lay in bed looking up at the ceiling. *How could I be such a coward? What if the werewolves killed her?*

She was worried but decided to wait for Olivia to call her. *When Grandma gets home, I'll find out what happened, anyway.*

Hours went by with anxious waiting, and then she heard the opening of the front door. "Grandma?" she called out, her voice trembling, and jumped off the bed.

"Yes, it's me!"

Candice ran downstairs as her grandmother locked the door. "Where were you? I was so worried!"

"What happened? Is Olivia okay?"

"She's okay. She brought back the flower, and we made the potion. It worked. Dorian is okay." The old woman looked at her, and sadness spread on her face. "What happened? Why didn't you come back to the Coven with her?"

"Did she say anything?"

"No, and we were busy making the potion, and then she took it to the hospital. I didn't have a chance to ask her."

"Grandma, I made a huge mistake," Candice admitted. "I was so scared that I left her in the woods and drove home."

"You left her there all alone?" her grandmother asked in shock.

"Go ahead, make me feel even worse than I already feel!" Candice snapped, sobbing.

Her grandmother's expression softened as she hugged Candice. "I'm sorry! I didn't mean to. Besides, I wouldn't have had the courage to go into werewolf territory either. I was worried sick when you volunteered. It's going to be alright, child."

"Grandma, I don't want to be a witch. I should never have asked to join your Coven. I don't belong there."

"Maybe it's for the best." The old woman sighed.

Epilogue

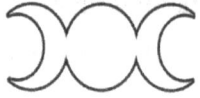

Two days later Dorian was discharged, and the potion didn't seem to have any side effects. He felt great but still didn't remember anything besides the vivid dreams.

Finally, Olivia had a good night's sleep, and being Saturday, she drove over to Dorian's house in the morning. After she told him every detail of what happened, they kissed, and he wrapped his arms around her waist and looked into her eyes. "I love you, Olivia; I always have. And not only because you saved my life."

He let her go, stepped back and held out a small ring box. Seeing Olivia's shocked expression, he quickly said, "No, it's not an engagement ring. Not yet. It's a promise ring. I'll always be yours, and one day when the time is right, I'll ask you the question."

Olivia smiled as a tear rolled down her cheek. "I'll always be yours. You're my soulmate." He put the ring on her finger and kissed her.

After a long minute, Olivia pulled away. "We have to go. The Elders are waiting for us. Today is our initiation day."

They drove to the Coven and knocked on the door. Cordelia opened it and hugged them both. "Follow me."

Olivia and Dorian followed her through a long corridor to the back garden. They'd never been back to the sacred garden before because apprentices weren't allowed there.

The small garden was beautiful. The mums were in full bloom, and they could see a greenhouse filled with herbs. There was a little koi pond next to the greenhouse with a waterfall. The sound of the water trickling down the stones was relaxing and peaceful.

They sat down on overstuffed floor pillows laid on the ground. Olivia took a deep breath and looked around. "Where's Candice? Is she coming?"

Cordelia sighed. "No. She proved with her actions that she doesn't belong here. She knew it in her heart and withdrew her request to join us."

Olivia and Dorian looked at each other, both relieved. "I can't say I'm sad about that," Dorian said, and Olivia nodded in agreement.

Cordelia reached into a lacquered box beside her pillow and handed both Olivia and Dorian a silver key. "Welcome to Ravenwood Coven. From now on, you're full members. Dorian, you've shown dedication and loyalty throughout your apprenticeship months. Olivia, you've proved your loyalty, dedication, and shown great courage even in the worst situations."

The young witch and warlock accepted the keys with happy smiles on their faces. Olivia sighed heavily. "I feel sorry for Candice. Although she's not really an honest and good person, maybe the family curse made her this way."

Dorian nodded. "I never liked her, but I agree."

Cordelia's warm smile seemed to light up her face. "I didn't expect anything less from either of you. Feeling compassion, trying to find a reason to forgive, and wanting to help even those who hurt us is what being a valuable member of the Coven is about. Candice doesn't deserve to be a witch, but that doesn't mean we can't try to help her. Therefore, your first assignment as a witch and a warlock is to find the cure for Candice's family curse."

Bittersweet Memories

Winter vacation

The hallways of NYU School of Medicine were buzzing with the chatter and shuffling of hundreds of students all eager to start their winter vacation. Most would be traveling to different states or abroad to visit family and loved ones for the holiday. But not Elana. She had a tradition of her own.

Ashley, noticing the not-so cheerful look on Elana's usually happy face, gently touched her arm. "Are you okay, Elana? You don't really look like you're in the Christmas spirit."

Elana's lips curled into a faint smile. "I'm fine. Just tired from studying for the big exam. I'll see you after Christmas break, okay?" The two hugged briefly before parting ways into the busy stream of traffic.

Suddenly, Elana heard Ashley yell her name from the other side of the hallway. "I forgot to wish you Merry Christmas!" Elana only smiled in return, waving at Ashley before turning the corner and heading outside.

Bracing herself against the bitter cold, Elana hailed a cab and headed uptown to her lonely Manhattan apartment. The driver whizzed through clusters of traffic, singing along to the radio. His raspy voice was way out of tune. *I wouldn't dare sing in public if I had a voice like you,* Elana thought as she watched small tufts of snow starting to accumulate on the parked cars and sidewalk. The sight opened a flood of painful memories: a broken dam of faded smells, faces, and words that were lost in the moving sands of time.

This was a bittersweet holiday season for Elana. Though there were good memories attached to Christmas, there were also many in her past that she wished she could forget.

Twenty-two Years Ago

On that stormy Christmas Eve twenty-two years ago, a young woman trudged through the unforgivingly cold winds of downtown New York City with a bundle of rags held tightly to her chest. Glass beads of frozen tears clung to the exposed skin of her face. The woman, slightly dazed and clearly distraught, shuffled aimlessly through the snow that clotted the empty sidewalk.

She was uncertain how long she had been pushing her way through the whirling snow, but her raw cheeks were evidence of the stretch of time and the ferocity of the wind. To anyone driving by, she appeared to be just another homeless person: one of the city's many untouchables caught in the fierce weather, trying to find shelter. They'd give her a callous look and go about their business.

The woman, guided by her numb feet, walked and walked until the dim light of a steeple shone through the flittering blankets of falling snowflakes. Slowly, she approached the steps leading up to the door and stopped.

"I'm so sorry," she sobbed, lightly rocking the bundle of rags from side to side. "I'm alone, and I have nowhere to go. You'll be better off without me." Her soft crying was captured in the air as tufts of tiny ice beads—dissipating clouds of unfathomable despair. They would momentarily hover about her face like a thin mask before being swallowed up by the passing gusts of wind from the barren street.

Slowly, she knelt and set the bundle of rags carefully onto the cathedral step. With warm tears running cold as soon as they leaked down her trembling cheeks, she traced her footsteps back down the street and disappeared into the storm. Never to return.

A few minutes later, a priest of the church stepped out onto the front steps. "Good Lord! It's cold tonight," Father Brown, a tall, middle aged man murmured while tossing his long scarf over his shoulder. He shoved his boney hands into the pockets of his long coat and took a moment to silently view the whitewashed buildings with awe. They stood like monolithic snowdrifts, rows of naked windows gleaming with ice, like the eyes of a frozen spider.

Father Brown was on his way to a homeless shelter across town to help with the preparation of Christmas Day dinner. Having no family of his own, it brought him more joy to be surrounded by those in need than to be cooped up in the church all night watching old movies on the ancient black and white TV set in his bedroom. Though he rather enjoyed Jimmy Stewart's performance in the classic film *It's a Wonderful Life*, he'd seen the movie at least fifty times by now, and serving the unfortunate souls would be a better use of his time. The smiles on their faces, as warm and inviting as the turkey and mashed potatoes he was lucky enough to serve, was more than he ever could have asked for on this holiest of days. Pulling his hand out of his jacket to check his wristwatch, he realized that if he wanted to catch the late bus to the shelter, he'd have to get a move on.

Hurrying down the church steps, he nearly stumbled. He looked down and saw the bundle of rags resting on the bottom step. At first thought to be trash, the priest sidestepped to walk around the heap of clothing when, suddenly, he heard a weak moan emanating from the bundle of rags, muffled by the layers. Curiously kneeling to get a better look, he nearly screamed when the rags began to shiver and move at his touch.

That's when he realized something living was wrapped up inside. Fearing the worst, he quickly scooped up the bundle and brought it into the protective walls of the cathedral. Clutching the rag bundle to his chest, he made his way to the nearest pew and slowly set it down, whispering a prayer. Under the glow of various lit candles and assisted by the borrowed white light of the full moon leaking through the stained windows, the priest quickly undid the bundle of cloths.

Lying inside the cocoon of dirty rags was a newborn baby. Still pruned, with dried blood covering her skin and matted hair, her blue eyes rolled listlessly, and dry lips slightly parted to expose purple gums and a swollen tongue.

"Sweet Mother Mary!" Father Brown gasped, reflexively tracing the holy symbol of the cross on his body as he raced his way back to his office. Once inside, his shaking hands grasped the phone on his desk and dialed 9-1-1.

"Yes, I need an ambulance sent to St. Patrick's Cathedral immediately," the priest begged, cold sweat breaking out across his forehead. "I have a dying newborn here. Please, hurry!" Abruptly ending the call, he raced back out to the pew and held the baby in his arms. It hurt his soul to look at the child, shriveled and clinging to life, but he forced his eyes to meet hers.

"Don't worry, little one," he said, cradling the dying baby tightly in his arms to keep her warm. "God is watching over you now."

The ambulance arrived at the church not ten minutes later, and the newborn was immediately rushed to a local hospital. The baby was at the brink of death. She was severely dehydrated, and hypothermia had set in, making her breathing shallow and heartbeat slow.

Unable to trace the parents or relatives of the baby, the hospital contacted child services and arranged for the little girl to be placed in foster care, once she was in better health.

Under the watchful care of doctors and nurses, after fighting a series of infections and neonatal abstinence syndrome because of the drugs she was exposed to in the womb, she slowly recovered. The nurses adored the tiny baby and held her in their arms, cooing to her as much as their busy schedule allowed. By the hospital rules her name was Baby Girl, but the nurses named her Elana.

She was cleared by the hospital a little more than three months later and was assigned a social worker and given an official name: Elana Smith.

Twelve Years Ago

Elana spent the first ten years of her life in the foster care system, bouncing from temporary housing to temporary housing. She'd spent the first two years of her life in and out of hospitals when she'd have a chance to be adopted. Her tiny body fought the addiction to drugs she'd been fed in the womb by her mother, and her weakened immune system couldn't handle the series of infections without antibiotics and supportive treatments. Nobody wanted a sickly child and even most foster parents couldn't cope with the constant care she required.

Later, when she got stronger and healthier, even at a very young age, Elana learned the drill. She'd been through the system so many times by then that she got used to sleeping in different places every couple of months or so. New rooms, new families. Her life felt like a revolving door of shattered hopes and hidden disappointments. None of the families Elana was paired with were bad, and neither was she a bad child, but by the time either of them could make an emotional connection, unfortunate circumstances made her move on to the next foster home.

Her chance of being adopted by a loving family got slimmer and slimmer as she got older. Most couples who wished to adopt wanted newborns or children only a few months old.

When she was ten years old, she was paired with her foster parents, Mr. and Mrs. Whelk. They were loving and caring people and had opened their home for many other children in the past. The older couple whose love knew no bounds, after long years of trying to have a child of their own, gave up and decided to help unwanted and unfortunate children.

"Welcome to our home, Elana." Mrs. Whelk greeted the young girl with a big hug at the door when Elana was dropped off at their midtown apartment with the weathered solitary suitcase of her few belongings. Foster kids moved frequently from home to home; it was best to be a minimalist and have only a few necessary items.

Mr. Whelk stood close by with a warm smile on his wrinkled face. "We're very pleased to have you stay with us," he said, subtly cueing Mrs. Whelk to let go and give the new girl some space. "Please, make yourself at home. Your room is down the hall to the right. Dinner is at six." Elana forced a smile, trying not to seem rude, and quietly carried her suitcase to her new room.

It was a modest sized room; a single twin mattress and rosewood dresser were pushed to one wall. The bed was furnished with several pillows and blankets that looked to be brand new. Elana had seen many rooms like this throughout the ten years of her life, bouncing from home to home, and knew better than to get too comfortable. She knew she was only a visitor—a temporary guest. The Whelks seemed nice, but so did the other families who eventually brought her back to the center. Setting her suitcase on the bed, Elana opened it up and solemnly picked through her few belongings.

"Hey, how's it going?" A young boy's voice suddenly came from the open doorway. Startled, Elana turned from her suitcase to see a boy standing just outside her room. He looked to be around her age, maybe a little older. His narrow cheekbones and short brown hair struck a certain chord somewhere inside Elana, as if she'd met the boy before. This odd feeling stunted any outward reaction that Elana was supposed to have. Leaning against the doorframe, the boy smiled patiently at her and waited for a response.

"I'm fine," Elana finally said after clearing her throat. Sensing her shyness, the boy entered the room and extended one hand.

"My name's Luca. What's yours?"

Elana hesitantly took Luca's hand, shaking it feebly while getting lost in the deep blue of his eyes. She felt a sudden warmth that she'd never felt before, like a flower had just blossomed in the pit of her stomach. But, the foster kid in her quickly pushed the feeling away. The last thing Elana wanted to do was get close to someone she would probably never see again. It was a hard choice, but a necessary emotional defense mechanism that had served her well throughout her short, yet unpredictable life.

After extinguishing the feeling of wanting to connect, she pulled her hand back to her side. "Elana." Tense silence followed, until Elana not so casually asked, "So… are you the Whelks' son?"

Luca laughed heartily. "Nah, I'm a foster kid too. Been living here for a couple months now." He capped the remark with another light smile to assure Elana that he wasn't putting her down. "The Whelks are good people; just follow their rules, don't cause any trouble, and you'll stick around. The last kid who stayed in this room was kind of an oddball."

Elana laughed nervously, unsure of whether Luca was being sincere. "Was the kid crazy or something?"

Luca shrugged. "Probably. You know how it goes sometimes. He threw a fit whenever someone touched him, and even when the food on his plate touched. He just sat on his bed rocking and humming. The Whelks tried everything, but when he hit Mrs. Whelk, they sent him back and Mr. Whelk said he was placed in a special home."

Elana understood; she'd met plenty of kids in the system with mental illness and severe emotional problems. Growing up knowing you were thrown away by the only people who were supposed to love you unconditionally took a great toll on growing children. Some, like Elana, developed a coping mechanism by distancing themselves from the harsh truth; others couldn't. The reality hit them hard and broke their spirit by crushing their hopes every time they moved to the next foster home.

"Don't worry. I'm no troublemaker," Elana said, brushing a strand of dark hair away from her eyes as she looked up at Luca. Eyes locked in youthful wonderment, they gazed at each other without speaking for several moments before Mrs. Whelk's voice echoed up the hallway.

"Supper's done, kids!"

Luca leaned out the door and yelled back, "Coming, Mrs. Whelk!" Before he left the room, Luca turned and nodded assuredly at Elana. "I think you'll be okay. You seem like a tough kid and not a wimp."

As she listened to his footsteps disappear down the hall, Elana let out a deep sigh of relief. For the first time in her life, she felt she could trust another human being. It was a feeling she'd had yet to experience.

Ten Years Ago

In almost total bliss, Elana and Luca spent the next two years together at the Whelks' house. The elderly couple were strict, but fair parents. Each child was expected to make their beds and clean their rooms every morning. After school, they took turns taking the garbage out, clearing the table, and washing dishes after dinner. They were also expected to get good grades in school, which both did with incredible ease. Mr. and Mrs. Whelk treated the two kids as if they were their own children, never making them feel like anything but. Elana had never experienced such stability—such incredible emotional support. Not only did Elana have the loving parents she always wanted, but she'd found a best friend as well. Life finally took a turn for the better.

Elana and Luca started calling their foster parents Mom and Dad after living for about a year in their loving home that provided stability and security for both. Although they would pretend to hate being doted on, they secretly loved all the affection they received, and both felt close to and loved the old couple.

***

Only a year older than Elana, Luca was the product of an alcoholic miner and a battered stay-at-home mother. It was a natural occurrence in the home that his father came home drunk from the bar, as he did on most nights after his shift at the mill. Always a mean drunk, Luca's father would find any excuse to beat his wife. Any reason. He took all his bottled-up anger and frustration out on his wife, as he'd learned from his father and grandfather.

Luca's mother, a petite woman, took the beatings in stride. Never did she speak about the bruises she kept hidden beneath her scarves and turtlenecks. She had many chances to leave or run to the police and get him thrown in jail, but never did. Luca's mother was raised to believe that divorce was a sin, a boy needed his father, and the family had to stay together. No matter what.

Luca's father went too far in his drunken rage, and on a humid July night after a ten-hour shift, beat her hard and fractured her skull. The fracture caused a severe brain hemorrhage that, despite emergency surgery, killed her that night. Luca's father was arrested the next day at work and sent straight to jail until his court hearing for one count of first-degree murder. At the trial, he testified on the stand that he didn't mean to kill his wife, begging desperately for the court's sympathy. His phony pleas were not enough. A jury of his peers took less than ten minutes to find him guilty.

"She was askin' for it," were his last words before they led him out of the courtroom.

Having no relatives to take him in, Luca became just another number in the system. He was too young when his mother died; he couldn't even remember what his mother and father looked like. He learned years later what had happened to them from a foster parent and never talked about it again.

That was, until he met Elana.

***

The two were inseparable friends and told each other anything and everything. Even at school, they chose to hang out with each other during recess as opposed to kids in their own grade. Because of their past circumstances, they shared a special bond that kids who had families just couldn't understand.

Two souls cut from the same cloth.

One of their favorite spots to visit together was the Whelks' summer home in the wild woods of upstate New York. Far away from the noise and smog of the city, the Whelks would visit the family cabin with the children in Brayton, at least five times a year, to go fishing and hunting. Sometimes Mrs. Whelk, who suffered from chronic joint and back pain, would stay behind in the city. Although she missed the kids, she never stopped or guilted them out of going and tried to enjoy the solitude and rest as much as she could.

"Be careful out there," she'd always caution as she saw them out the door and to the waiting station wagon packed full of supplies for the trip. "There are wild animals up in those woods, so keep a close eye on each other."

"Yes, Mom," they would say in unison. Their spontaneous response warmed her heart. Finally, after so many years trying to have children of her own and the heartache and disappointments, children called her Mom.

Once Mrs. Whelk was satisfied that she'd given and received enough hugs and kisses, the three were on the road. Within three hours or so, the concrete jungle they were so used to being surrounded by would be replaced by open countryside.

As soon as they reached the cabin, a quiet little place on Lake George just outside of town, Mr. Whelk would always hurry the kids to help him unpack. Not bothering to hide his enthusiasm, he was overly anxious to get out on the boat and catch some fish. It may have been this enthusiasm that made him forget the agony of progressive arthritis.

"Guy at the tackle shop down the way says there's a big ol' trout in these waters. A whoppin' twenty-five pounder, or so the legend goes." The twinkle in his eye told them that he intended to catch the epic beast all by himself. Not a very good fisherman, Mr. Whelk was usually lucky to catch a few small fish for dinner, let alone a record setter. But with a vigor that could have rivaled a twenty-year-old man's, Mr. Whelk clapped his hands and said, "Now, who wants to come with me and be a part of history?!"

Both Luca and Elana politely declined, offering instead to go swimming by the cabin.

"Ah, shucks," Mr. Whelk said, pretending to be disappointed. "Alright, but be safe, you two. Don't go too far into the lake. She gets deep out there." The two kids agreed and waited on the shoreline until Mr. Whelk was in his boat, paddling toward the middle of the lake.

"He's such a kid at heart. He's so eager to catch the big fish," Luca said jokingly to Elana as they sat together with their toes dipped in the lapping waters.

Elana laughed. "Fat chance. He lets nine out of ten fish slip off the hook."

"Yes, he does," Luca chuckled. "Remember the *big fish* last year? It weighed about half a pound, but by the time we got home, and he told his friend, it became a ten pounder."

"Yeah, and he gave us the evil eye to keep quiet," Elana snickered.

After a good laugh at Mr. Whelk's expense, they enjoyed sitting on the warm sand and the lapping of the waves at their feet for a little longer, before going inside the cabin to change into their swimsuits. Back out at the shoreline, they took turns taking steps into the icy water.

"Ahh! It's too cold!" Elana squealed, only standing waist deep in the water, her skin getting tight as goosebumps rose all over her body. Her teeth chattered, clicking together loudly like pearl castanets. Luca, always the courageous one, stood resiliently by her side, but was also shivering in the cold water.

"Pffft, ddd—don't be a wimp." His voice was wiry and stuttering, and he held his arms like rigid sticks at his sides. "Hey… watch this."

Before Elana could react, Luca dove headfirst into the freezing water, splashing her entire right side. This prompted a quick splash fight, and soon they didn't think the water was cold at all. About twenty minutes later, Elana and Luca stepped back out onto the shore. Both were soaked from head to toe, but happily laughing and chasing each other.

"Ehh! I think I got that yucky water up my nose!" Luca teased Elana as they sat on a blanket, sunbathing on the beach, and waited for Mr. Whelk to return. He was nothing but a tiny dot on the water's edge from where they were, wavering in the mirage of heat that drifted off the lake's surface. The two talked for a while about this and that, mostly kids at school they couldn't stand, until approaching footsteps from behind halted their lively conversation.

"Well, well," a brutish voice said as the couple pivoted on the blanket. Looming over them like tombstones, were three rough-looking boys in cutoff t-shirts. Lined up like a white trash pyramid, the tallest boy was flanked by two significantly shorter boys. Clothes dirty and faces sunburned, these were undoubtedly locals from the small town just down the road. "What we got 'ere? A couple'ah city folk?"

Sensing trouble, Luca quickly tried to stand up, but was shoved hard to the ground by the biggest boy. "Sit down, city boy," he growled with hatred in his tone. Falling hard on his back in the sand, Luca clutched his side in pain as he releveled himself to a sitting position.

"Don't touch him!" Elana yelled, shooting up to her feet. Her eyes were full of fire and worry as she stood protectively over Luca, scowling at the three locals. The boy farthest to her left was quick to react, shoving her hard to the ground next to where Luca sat.

"Shut yer fuck'n mouth, bitch! You speak when spoken to!"

Moving faster than she'd ever seen him move, Luca jumped to his feet and lunged at the boy who had pushed Elana. He got a couple of good hits in before the other two pulled him off and roughly pinned him to the ground.

"This city maggot needs to learn a lesson 'bout r'spect," the bigger boy said while pinning Luca down by the chest with his battered, muddy boot. Before Luca could say anything, one of the smaller boys gave a swift kick to the side of Luca's head, instantly knocking him out cold. The three locals shared a good laugh about this, frightened a few birds from the nearby trees, then turned their attention back on Elana.

"Ethan, you grab 'er arms. Noah, grab 'er legs," the big one said as he inched closer to where Elana tried to crawl backwards in the sand. Like trained monkeys, Ethan and Noah pounced on Elana and did as they were told by their leader.

"Get off me! Help!" she screamed, kicking and flailing her arms against their tight grip.

With Luca unconscious and Mr. Whelk all the way across the lake, it was up to Elana to defend herself. As she was dragged from the shoreline toward the forest's edge, one of her arms—sweat mingling with the remaining moisture from the swim—slipped free. She managed to grab a jagged rock from the sand and, swinging her arm, hit the boy named Ethan in the face, cutting a deep gash on his right cheek. The blood started to flow down his neck.

"Fuck'n bitch!!" Ethan screamed, dropping her other arm and cupping the deep wound at his face.

The other boys stopped to observe the explosion of blood flowing down the boy's hairless chest. The bigger boy stepped in and pushed Ethan to the side, grabbing Elana's wrists so tightly that she thought they might snap like twigs.

"Try dat shit wit me n' I'll kill ya," he growled as he dragged her to the edge of the forest. Elana was forced to drop the jagged rock as he flung her body hard against an old oak tree. Crumpling to the ground from the force of the blow, the three boys stood over her with their backs to the lake.

"Al'ight, who gets first turn?" Noah said, smiling like a vulture with a mouth full of crooked, rotting teeth. The big one slapped him behind the ears, forcing the twisted smile to retreat.

"I get first crack at 'er. I's the one that seen 'er in the first place."

Ethan, despite his low position on the food chain, stomped his feet in defiance. "Gawd dammit, Earl! The bitch cut my face! I should get first turn!"

Earl turned slowly and pushed Ethan's chest, sending him stumbling backwards. Still holding a hand to his bleeding cheek, Ethan immediately bowed his shoulder and fell back in line.

"I gets to go first. That's the rules," Earl shouted, pounding on his chest.

As Earl bent down to touch Elana's exposed leg, she uncurled herself and gave him a swift, strong kick to his groin. Falling onto his back, he grunted and spit obscenities to the sky while the other boys stood over her and watched in silence. As Elana tried again to stand up and run away, Ethan gave her a sweeping kick to her chest, pushing the air out of her lungs. Unable to catch her breath, she fell back down to her side in the dirt.

"You were askin' for it," Ethan said, one hand painted red with his own blood. As he raised his bloody fist high into the air, ready to strike Elana again, a booming voice stopped him.

"Let her go, you animals!"

Standing several feet away, with a softball-sized rock curled in his right hand, was Luca. Blood ran from a small gash in his temple, but his eyes looked cold-steel blue with focused rage.

The three boys turned and ran full force at Luca. He stood his ground and did his best to fight back. He managed to get a couple good hits in with the rock but was outnumbered. Earl managed to knock the rock out of Luca's hand as he pummeled him into the sand with his fists. Ethan held down Luca's legs as Noah began stomping on his chest.

Knowing she couldn't help Luca, Elana saw an opportunity to escape and get help. She jumped to her feet and ran as fast as she could through the brush until she stumbled onto a dirt road. Barefoot and scared, she ran the length of that dirt road until she came across two men riding an old farm tractor. Seeing the frightened young girl, feet bleeding and eyes watering, they stopped and listened to her.

Hearing that young Luca might be severely hurt, the farmers lifted Elana into the cab of the tractor and raced up to the Whelks' summer house. When they arrived at the shoreline, the three boys were gone. All that remained was a crumpled body lying motionless on the glittery yellow sand.

Elana's heart sank. She feared the worst and, jumping off the tractor, ran to Luca, dropping to her knees beside him.

The men wasted no time. One drove the tractor back into town to call for an ambulance while the other stayed at the shore with the two frightened and injured kids. Severely beaten, Luca's face looked like a chewed-up piece of meat. Seeing her best friend broken and left to die in the sand, Elana screamed at the open sky in agony. Feeling her entire body quiver and shake with unbearable sadness, she knelt in the blood-stained sand next to Luca and prayed. Head resting gently against his chest, she listened to his faint heartbeat as her tears mixed with the coppery fluid of his blood.

When the ambulance arrived, the paramedics were quick to check Luca's vitals before moving his body. They did not want to aggravate his injuries or cause more damage than there already was.

"He's breathing, but his pulse is weak," one said before gesturing for the other to bring out the stretcher.

They loaded him into the back of the ambulance. The man from the tractor laid a dirty hand over Elana's shoulder and said, "Pray for him, darlin'. He's gonna need it."

Mr. Whelk saw the ambulance close to the house and paddled back to shore as fast as he could. In complete shock, he peeked into the back of the ambulance and saw Luca's battered body, crumpled and bloody on the stretcher. Mr. Whelk and Elana followed the ambulance in the station wagon all the way up to the E.R. entrance. Forced to stay in the waiting room while the doctors stitched Luca up and ran tests, the two paced endlessly, waiting for any news.

After the x-rays were taken, doctors informed them that Luca had four broken ribs, a fractured jaw, and a deep gash in his head that required ten stitches. The local police came down to the hospital and took a statement from Luca once he was conscious. Elana never left his side.

Mr. Whelk never heard from the police during the three weeks' stay Luca was forced to take at the hospital. Months later, Luca and Elana testified in court, and the three local boys were sent to juvenile detention until they turned eighteen.

Nine Years Ago

Just before Elana's thirteenth birthday, the unthinkable happened. It was late November when Elana and Luca came home from school one day and noticed that Mrs. Whelk wasn't there to greet them. Instead of seeing her in the kitchen baking or cooking like she always was, there was only Mr. Whelk. He sat alone at the kitchen table; his usually strong shoulders slumped forward like the petals of a wilting rose.

"Sit down, kids," he said, slowly lifting his sad gaze to them as they cautiously entered the kitchen. "I have something to tell you both. Please, sit down."

Feeling more confused than concerned, Luca and Elana joined him at the table and waited. Wiping his eyes with one wrinkled hand while the other trembled on the surface of the table, Mr. Whelk took several moments to compose himself before saying, "My wife... she's..."

When the gravity of the situation finally started to register with the two kids, Elana reached out and laid her hand softly over Mr. Whelk's. "What's wrong? Did something happen? Is she okay?"

Taking her small hand into his, Mr. Whelk looked up at Elana, his eyes red and wet. "She... was taken to the hospital this morning. She's very sick."

"Sick? How sick?" Luca blurted out. The sincere level of concern he felt inside was projected all over his face. Deep lines creased his forehead.

Mr. Whelk, letting his tears flow freely now, reached out to Luca and hugged him tightly. "You remember when she started feeling poorly two weeks ago and went to see the doctor? This morning she collapsed and couldn't breathe. It's bone cancer, and it caused an embolism in her lung. They gave her medicine and she's breathing

159

better, but the doctors told me that the cancer is stage four and she doesn't have much time left. She... she refuses treatment."

Both Luca and Elana gasped simultaneously. "What?! Why? Doesn't she want to get better?"

Mr. Whelk gripped their hands a little tighter, speaking soft and slow to calm them. "Kids, she's old. The treatment would be intense, and Mrs. Whelk doesn't want to go through the agony that goes with it. It's hard to accept. Trust me, I know. I want her here more than anything. But, it's her choice, kids." Lips trembling as he coped with the circumstances, Mr. Whelk swallowed his sadness and added, "There's... one last thing that I know she would want. More than anything."

"What is it?" both kids asked, willing to put their own lives on the line to save the kind old woman who had loved them in ways neither of their mothers had a chance to. "We'll do anything."

***

Two weeks later, on Christmas day, Mr. Whelk packed up the station wagon with a wheelchair, oxygen tank, and blankets. They helped the frail old woman into the back of the car and headed into the city. For hours, the elderly couple held each other tight, watching Elana and Luca ice-skate in the gigantic rink at Rockefeller Center. This place was special to them; it was the very place where their relationship began over fifty years ago to the day.

"I wanted to see them happy one more time," Mrs. Whelk whispered to her husband. "Promise me you will take care of them when I'm gone."

"I promise," the old man sobbed, holding his wife's hand. "I'll do my best, promise." He bent down to adjust the blankets on his wife's lap to hide his tears.

Luca and Elana laughed and chased each other on the ice. The Whelks watched them, hearts warm with the sight of their youthful frolic. Even at death's door, Mrs. Whelk wanted nothing more than to watch the happiness of her children. She wanted to relish the feeling for as long as she could.

Later that night on the ride back home, Luca and Elana tenderly held hands in the back seat. "Merry Christmas, Elana," Luca whispered, digging a tiny box out of his pocket and handing it to

Elana. Wrapped not so perfectly in the Sunday comics section of the newspaper, Elana opened the box and had to keep herself from gasping out loud. Inside the box was a necklace. It was a half of a carved wooden heart attached to a leather thong. Luca pulled the other half of the heart out of his shirt and said, "I don't have money to buy you a proper gift. I carved this pendant from rosewood and cut it in half, so even when we're apart, we'll always be together. Two halves of one whole."

"Thank you," Elana mouthed to Luca. She let go of his hand, bending over across the seat and kissing him lightly on the lips. Luca was stunned at first, eyes wide and mouth slack, and froze in his seat. Even under the dim light of the passing streetlights, his cheeks flared crimson against the paleness of his skin.

Elana didn't know it at the time, but this would be the last Christmas that she would spend with this loving family. Mrs. Whelk died in her sleep two weeks later.

***

Mr. Whelk tried to do his best for months, but without his wife, he lost his will to carry on. The once warm and loving home had turned into a place of sadness and sorrow. Elana and Luca tried everything to cheer up the only father they'd known. They let him know how much they loved him, but Mr. Whelk slowly slipped into deep depression. The children tried to hide it from the social worker during her regular visits, but a day arrived when Mr. Whelk's deepening depression and poor physical health became too obvious. He neglected household chores and some days he didn't even get out of bed. He lost interest in everything and stopped talking. He sat staring out the window, humming to himself, and rarely ate the food Elana and Luca cooked for him.

The social worker had to make a tough decision. Due to his deteriorating health, Mr. Whelk was placed in a nursing home and they returned Elana and Luca back to the state. They had no choice in the matter.

"A dark cloud is following me, all my life," Elana cried, supported by Luca's shoulder when they were forced to say a quick goodbye to each other. "I've been thrown from one place to the next and when finally, my life seems stable and happy, the cloud is above

161

me, again. What will happen to us, Luca? If they separate us, will you find me?"

"I will! I promise," Luca sobbed.

With all the stability ripped out of her life once again, Elana was cast back out into the world with nowhere to call home. No more family, no more structure. But, worst of all, she lost Luca. They were separated and sent to different foster homes.

Christmas Tradition

Feeling the sway of the cab nearing the slushy streets of her apartment forced Elana to reemerge from the dark waters of the past. She clutched the wooden heart Luca gave her all those years ago, eyes filling with tears. Since the wonderful night he gave her the half heart pendant, she carried it with her always.

"Fare's gonna be $13.50, ma'am," the cabbie said as he pulled up to the front of Elana's apartment building. Carefully, she slipped the necklace back under her blouse before exiting the cab. Elana paid the cabbie and ascended the icy steps. Once inside, she stripped her winter clothes off and sat down on her black leather couch.

Continuing to reminisce about old times, Elana stared at the framed painting that hung on the wall. Admiring the swooping edges and rich palate of colors, Elana lost herself in the formless depths of abstract art. It was her favorite oil painting she'd inherited from her adoptive parents.

A well-known couple in the art community—New York painter Stuart Speer and his wife/manager Donna Speer—adopted Elana a few months after she was forced to leave Mr. Whelk's home. The Speers were a much younger couple than the Whelks, and a lucky break for Elana, they were happy to adopt a fourteen-year-old teenager.

Elana lived happily in the Speers' swanky uptown Manhattan apartment throughout high school and her freshman year at NYU. The Speers enjoyed spoiling Elana, filling her life with not only affection, but material goods as well. Elana got to go on several vacations to Hawaii and Europe, and even received a brand-new convertible on her sixteenth birthday.

But every year since her adoption, she only ever asked for one thing. She asked to spend Christmas day at Rockefeller Plaza, ice skating. The Speers always agreed, never questioning the request, and soon it became a family tradition. Secretly, Elana held onto a small sliver of hope that she'd see Luca there, waiting for her. But she never did. Nevertheless, she kept the tradition alive. Not just for herself and Luca, but for the memory of Mr. and Mrs. Whelk. It was the least she could do to carry on the memory of the love they had given her when no one else would.

Then, in her second year of college, tragedy reared its ugly head again.

Both Stuart and Donna Speer were killed in a horrific car crash in the Lincoln Tunnel. Had Elana decided to go with them to visit friends instead of burying her head in her anatomy book, she would've surely been in that fatal accident with them. She was alone, again. Grieving her parents, Elana had a strong feeling that she somehow brought bad luck upon those who loved her. Perhaps, it all started with her mother all those years ago.

Leaving everything they owned to Elana, the Speers' last will and testament gave her the opportunity to live her life with ease. Inheriting the Stuart Speer art studio and classy Manhattan apartment, the retro payments from the paintings alone would pay for her college tuition and provide her with a comfortable life.

Yet, Elana couldn't enjoy the wealth. A cavernous void, especially during the holidays, consumed her entire capacity for happiness. How could she be happy when everyone she ever cared about wasn't there to enjoy it with her? The universe was a cruel mistress, and Elana was getting tired of her selfish games.

***

She'd been staring at the painting so long that its curves and lines were burned into her retina when she closed her eyes. Eyes still shut, she watched as the ghostly impression faded into the darkness, like everything else she ever loved in her life. She thought of Luca with deep sadness in her heart. *He promised, but he forgot about me.* Her love for Luca, instead of fading, grew stronger as the years went by. Her teenage years' awkwardness gone, she'd bloomed into a beautiful woman. Plenty of men asked her out and she went on a few dates, but she couldn't forget Luca and hadn't made a connection with anyone.

Slowly, Elana lay down on the couch and did the only thing that she could think to do in that moment of overwhelming sadness. She allowed her body and mind to drift into untethered sleep.

***

Elana spent the next several days before Christmas doing nothing. Aside from occasionally bathing and eating, she did little other than think about all those things that never were. For hours, she stared at that painting, letting the colors and brushstrokes burn tiny holes in the thick veil of her tortured psyche. Elana painfully counted down the days until she could put on her skates and go to the only place that made her feel somewhat happy. Only then could she find any kind of inner peace, even if only momentarily.

Finally, the day came. Elana woke up and, for the first time all week, smiled.

It was officially Christmas.

No matter the weather, Elana felt obligated to be at Rockefeller Plaza. So, after cleaning herself up and getting a bite to eat, she grabbed her ice skates out of the closet and left the apartment for the first time since winter vacation started.

"Rockefeller Center, please," she said as she climbed into the back of the cab, worn out skates dangling by her side.

Without looking back or saying a word, the cabbie started the meter and merged into traffic.

***

Skates strapped to her feet, Elana carefully tiptoed onto the ice. Surprisingly, only a few people were skating in the rink, giving Elana the entire space to move in any way she chose. Letting the inertia leave her body and glide her effortlessly on the polished sheet of ice, her thoughts once again became lost in the past. Back and forth, round and round, small tears leaked from her swollen eyes and mixed with melting snowflakes on her cheeks. Elana relived all those Christmas pasts, her mind racing and tears flowing. Wind blowing gentle kisses through her hair, she closed her eyes and let the pull of the ice lull her grieving mind. If only the wind could carry away her loneliness…

Suddenly, she felt her legs bumping into something soft and heard a painful yelp. Taken completely off guard, Elana let out a high-pitched scream as her legs became twisted, pitching her forward and slamming her onto the ice. Wincing in pain, she looked up in time to see a large black dog skid its way across the ice and out the entrance. Shaken, Elana tried to stand, but when she put weight on her foot, immense pain in her leg pulled her back down to the ice. The sharp pain in her ankle and the numbness of her foot told her that her ankle might have broken in the fall. *Apparently, bad luck is not yet finished with me and rubbing its invisible hands with glee.*

"Oh my God! Are you okay?" a man's voice emanated from over her shoulder. The stranger's voice sounded familiar and sent a shockwave of déjà vu through Elana, but when she turned to look at the man skating across the ice towards her, she did not recognize him. He was a young man in his early twenties with short dark brown hair and narrow cheek bones balanced delicately on his clean-shaven face. His expression was one of intense worry as he shuffled towards her, trying not to fall and hurt himself as well.

Finally reaching Elana, the man knelt to her. "I'm so sorry. That stray dog got in the rink somehow. Are you okay?"

Elana rubbed her ankle, hissing in pain at her own touch. "No, I'm not alright. Pretty sure my ankle is broken."

Scooping Elana up into his strong arms, the man carried her to a bench and carefully sat her down. Pulling out his phone, he quickly dialed 9-1-1 and arranged for an ambulance.

"Do you want me to call your family or...?" he asked, trailing the sentence.

"No, thanks. I'll be fine on my own." She bowed her head sadly and touched her eye, trying to stop a teardrop from sliding down her cheek.

"I'll come with you to the hospital and keep you company."

"You don't need to... and I don't have a family. Not anymore. I'm alone." A painful sob broke free from deep inside her chest.

"I insist," the young man said, touching her hand. His heart ached with sympathy and compassion, watching her crying. He slid closer to her and offered his shoulder to lean on.

Elana rested her head against his chest and couldn't stop herself. Letting all her repressed painful memories out in an inconsolable sob, she forgot about the physical pain. The pain in her tortured soul was stronger.

By the time the paramedics arrived and loaded her into the back of the ambulance, Elana's sobbing calmed. She recalled the summer day, so long ago in her childhood, when Luca was loaded into an ambulance, beaten and broken.

"You really don't have to come with me," Elana assured the young man. "Sorry you had to see me falling apart. I'll be fine. It's just… too many bad memories catching up with me."

The man smiled and took Elana's hand in his. "It's Christmas. My life hadn't been all sunshine either. I understand and I want to make sure you're okay."

At the hospital, Elana and the man waited in a tiny room for a doctor to examine her ankle. They made light small talk, mostly about the weather and the Yankees, while Elana filled out insurance forms.

She felt an unusual attraction to the man. Not only because of his good looks, fit physique, and charming aura, but there was something deeper that Elana couldn't quite explain. As she tried to focus her thoughts back on filling out forms, the doctor entered the room.

"I'm Dr. Nelson," the tall man in a short white coat said, checking the portable computer screen. Taking a seat on a stool by the bed, Dr. Nelson studied Elana's ankle. Swelling had begun to set in, and her skin was already starting to become puffy and bruised from the impact of the fall. "How did you fall?" he asked.

"I was skating at Rockefeller center and tripped over a dog. I closed my eyes for a moment and didn't see the dog until my legs bumped into it. I hope the poor animal is okay," Elana explained as she watched a stocky man in a housekeeper uniform pushing his cleaning cart into the room.

"Couldn't you wait until I'm finished?" Dr. Nelson looked up at the man from the stool, annoyed.

"X'suse me!" the stocky man grumbled. "Just doin' me job," he said indignantly with anger showing on his wide face.

"Never mind, I'm almost done, anyway." He turned back to Elana. "Well, it looks like you hit the ice hard; you might have some broken bones. I'll order an X-ray and we'll go from there."

"Hey, folks. Doctors, eye? Them actin' all mighty," the cleaner cackled, watching the doctor hurrying out of the room. "Looks like clumsy skatin'." He laughed heartily at his own lame joke while wiping the sink, but neither Elana nor the young man found it funny at all.

Sensing their coldness to his sense of humor, the housekeeper cleared his throat. "Well, that'll be a first!" he cackled. "Trippin' over a dog," He again cackled, then looked at Elana with a smirk on his face. "Skatin' with yer eyes closed is askin' for it, I'd say."

The phrase echoed in Elana's mind. Something cruelly familiar tugged at the forefront of her memory at his words.

You were asking for it... were asking for it... asking for it...

She stared at the ragged scar on his left cheek and realized what her unconscious mind was trying to tell her. His badge displayed his name: Ethan Wilson.

Bile rose into her throat and she asked in a shaky voice, "Are you... are you from a town called Brayton? Brayton, New York?" When the housekeeper said nothing, scanning Elana's face for any sense of recognition, she added, "Right next to Lake George?"

"I... yeah, why? How'd ya know me?"

"When I was twelve, you and your friends..." Elana began to say, her words choked with emotion, "you beat up my best friend and tried... tried to... hurt me."

Opening his mouth, the brutish looking man suddenly realized where Elana knew him from. All at once, she could see that he remembered too. His left hand began to rub absently at the dark, raised crescent scar on his cheek.

"Whatd'ya know? The bitch who gave me dis," he murmured under his breath, rubbing his scar.

"Yes, I did!" Elana suddenly screamed, inflamed with rage. "You and your hick buddies almost killed my best friend!"

Realizing that there was no use in arguing or lying to Elana, the man sighed in annoyance and said, "Look 'ere... It was long ago... and ya know... boys will be boys... and we paid fo' it! Juvi been hell, ya know."

Elana's anger and pain erupted, and she jumped off the bed, hobbling on her uninjured foot and screamed in the man's scarred face, "Get out! GET OUT!"

The young man stood up, pushed the housekeeper aside, and rushed to Elana. The housekeeper stumbled and quickly retreated as the nurses came in and helped her back on the bed. Ethan rushed out of the room without saying a word and Elana turned to the nurses. "Please, don't let that man near me!" she sobbed. "Him and his buddies tried to rape me when I was twelve."

Seeing how distraught she was, they kept their questions to themselves, but exchanged disgusted glances. "Don't you worry, darling. He won't be back; I'll make sure of it, and I'll talk to his supervisor," the older nurse said as she helped to elevate Elana's leg with a pillow.

After the nurses left the room, Elana felt a light touch on her arm. The young man put his arm around Elana's shoulder and cried out, "Elana, it's..." the man started to say before his voice faded away. In one motion, he reached with his other hand into the top of his shirt and pulled out a necklace. On the end of the short leather thong that hung around his neck was the other half of Elana's carved pendant. "It's me... Luca."

She couldn't believe it. She was looking for the boy's features in his face; the curl of his upper lip as he smiled and the twinkle in his eyes told her it was the boy she was in love with as a teenager. Unable to control the onslaught of emotions that flooded through her, Elana lunged herself into Luca's arms and wept great tears of joy.

"Luca! Is it really you? You've changed so much, I didn't recognize you," she spoke into his neck as she pressed against him, unwilling to let him go.

The older nurse walked into the room and her eyes misted over, remembering the beautiful feeling of first love.

"Yes, love. It's really me. You have changed a lot too. The lanky teenager I knew became a stunningly beautiful woman. Somehow, fate has brought us back together."

The nurse reached into her pocket and pulled out a mistletoe branch tied with red ribbon. She held it over their heads and, teary-eyed, said in a cheerful voice, "You're under the mistletoe."

And, just as Elana had done on their last Christmas night together, this time, it was Luca who leaned over slowly and kissed her lips, tasting the warm saltiness of tears as they cascaded down her rosy cheeks. Elana looked up at the same blue eyes she'd gotten lost in all those years ago, as the nurse tiptoed out of the room.

"I've been waiting for this kiss for all those years since the last beautiful Christmas we spent together," Luca whispered, his voice choking up.

"I lost faith I'd ever see you again, years ago," Elana admitted. "I thought you'd forgotten about me and I'd never see you again."

"I've been searching for you since the day we were separated, but I couldn't find you," he said with tears in his eyes. "The social worker wasn't allowed to tell me details; the only thing she said was that you were adopted only a few days after I saw you the last time."

"Yes, I was adopted by a wonderful couple. The process was quick because they wanted a teenager," Elana said smiling, and then her smile faded. "They were wonderful parents until… they died in a car accident."

Sitting on the bed with his arms wrapped around Elana's slender frame, Luca exclaimed, "I'm so sorry! But at least you had a loving family for a while. I've searched on every social media site and talked to kids in foster homes, but nobody knew anything about you."

"Oh." Elana's eyes lit up. "My parents were strict about internet; they blocked social media sites and I was only allowed to do research for schoolwork. My last name had been changed when the adoption went through. When I created a profile on social media sites, I was Elana Speer by then. Did you really look for me?"

"I did and I felt devastated when I couldn't find anything. Now I know why. I stayed in the shelter for a couple months before I was adopted by a wealthy British couple."

Elana had all but forgotten about the pain in her ankle, utterly absorbed in everything Luca had to say. "Tell me everything," she prompted.

Luca sighed and continued. "Fairly new to the States, they were amazing parents and saw potential in me that I never knew I had. By that time in my life, I thought only you could ever love me. I literally felt like a piece of discarded garbage when I lost you."

Elana kissed Luca's cheek, but said nothing as he continued his story.

"We moved from New York to San Francisco shortly after I was adopted. They wanted to surround me with the kind of art and culture they loved. I went to art school and I became a sought-after artist. Well, that's what my agent tells me anyway."

"My father was a great artist, too." Elana smiled.

"Well, I'm just trying to be." Luca laughed at his own sense of ironic hubris before continuing. "I love San Francisco, but this year something drew me back to New York. Back to the ice rink at Rockefeller Center. In my mind, over the years we were apart, that place held so much significance to me. It was the place where I went with my one and only love. My soulmate."

Elana looked longingly into Luca's steely blue eyes, soaking in their magnetic pulse. "I felt it too. I've been going back there to skate every year since that magical night, hoping against hope that someday you would be there. Waiting for me."

"And I would've been too," Luca said, a guilty look washing over his handsome face, "Had I known you never left New York, I'd have crawled on my knees if I had to, to see you. But a kid I knew from living in a foster family together before I met you, told me that you were adopted and moved to France."

"No, I've been right here ever since. Why would that kid lie to you?"

"I don't know. Maybe he just assumed. We were young and every kid's dream in the foster system was to be adopted. But when my agent told me that one of my paintings was going to be featured in an art gallery in New York, I felt that something was drawing me back. He said I didn't need to be here for the showing of one painting, but I wanted to be here."

"I'm glad you did."

Kissing each other with the fiery passion of a dying sun, their two bodies melded into one under the intense flare of their rekindled love.

"Excuse me," a young man interrupted, pushing a potable X-ray machine. "I'm going to take a picture of your ankle."

He did the X-ray, and a short time later the doctor entered the room. "No broken bones." He smiled. "Luckily, it's just a sprain.

You'll need to wear a brace for a few weeks and start physical therapy next week."

The nurse came in and fitted the brace on Elana's ankle. "How's the pain?" she asked.

Fingers interwoven into Luca's and heart swelling with happiness, Elana smiled and said, "The physical pain is unimportant. What is more important, I don't feel any pain in my soul. Not anymore."

Epilogue

Within a month, Luca sold his studio in San Francisco and moved to New York. He rented an apartment in Elana's building. His parents, happy for him and wanting to be close to them, sold their home and bought a co-op apartment in Manhattan a few weeks later. They welcomed Elana into their home and hearts.

Taking over the unused art studio of Elana's father, Luca had no trouble with the transition. Elana, conscience cleared and heart reset, continued medical school. Leaving the painful past behind, there was nowhere else to go but forward, and Elana felt the dark cloud that followed her since the day she was born, finally lifting.

On Valentine's day the following year, their long-awaited dream came true. They declared their undying love and were married by the priest who had found Elana on the steps of St. Patrick's Cathedral all those years ago.

They held the two halves of the carved wooden heart together as the priest announced them husband and wife.

Fate had finally realigned their paths and put their hearts where they belonged. Together.

SMALL TOWN MYSTERY

The Worthless Painting

THE WORTHLESS PAINTING

An art expert's lie
To arrogant socialite
Help worthless painting
Make past wrongs right
When actual value
Is brought to light

~Cindy J. Smith

Chapter One

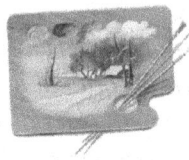

Danielle Clearwater, a tall, slender woman in her late twenties tried to fish out the key to her small antique store from her handbag. She held a large canvas to her body with her elbow while balancing a paper tray with coffee and a bagel in her hand. When she reached into the bag that was hanging by a long strap off her shoulder, the canvas started to slip. She tightened her hold on it, which made the tray flip. The coffee cup lid flew off spraying her lilac dress with dark brown spots. *Just great! Now I'll have to wear jeans and a t-shirt all day.* She was grateful for the spare clothes she kept in the backroom.

She didn't have any customers waiting and didn't expect anyone until Mrs. Castle's usual visit at 10 am sharp. The old lady was a regular and always on time, never a minute late. Danielle had always been an introvert when interacting with people her own age and was more comfortable with older people. She loved the stories they told when they came into her store to buy and sell items.

***

Danielle lost her father when she was only a toddler and didn't really remember him. She could only recall moments and sometimes in her dreams, she felt his presence. Her mother made sure she was well cared for but didn't pay much attention to her. Busy with work and in and out of fleeting relationships, Danielle spent most of her time with babysitters.

Danielle's passion for art paid off, she applied to art school without telling her mother and was accepted. Her mom was furious and forbade her to go to art school. She enrolled Danielle at a local college to become an accountant. "You can't make any money from art. I'm moving to England with Luke soon and you need a job that provides you with a decent living. I'm not going to support you anymore, and I'm not paying for a hobby you could never make enough money to live on."

Danielle accepted her mother's decision and after she got her accountant certification, she started a job at a local tax office. She hated it so much that some mornings her emotional state made her physically ill. She kept pushing herself but after a few months of misery, she couldn't take it anymore. "I can't do this, Sarah," she cried to her best friend since elementary school. "I can't live my life dragging myself out of bed and hating every minute I spend doing a job I loathe."

Sarah, who was a nurse at the local hospital, knew that antiques were Danielle's next passion after art and books. "No, you can't. You're miserable! In this digital age, bookstores are a dying business. You should open a store and sell antiques and stuff."

Danielle liked the idea and when a large store space became available on Main Street, she rented it. She painted a sign, Antiques & Stuff, and slowly filled the store with items she'd found in estate sales and flea markets. As she sold pieces, she bought more, and the following year she bought some quality antique furniture, household items, and paintings as well.

***

After changing in the backroom and making coffee to replace the one she spilled, Danielle stood by the wide window warming her fingers on the mug. She glanced at the bookstore that had a constant stream of people coming and going. Sometimes she wondered if she made the right decision by taking Sarah's advice. Although her store was slow, she had a lot of customers on weekends. So much so that Danielle changed her hours and closed the shop on Mondays and Tuesdays. The lull between customers, and the two days off, did give her time to do what she loved most, restoring antique art and paintings. Overall, it was a good decision. She was glad she had listened to Sarah.

When she finished her coffee, she walked to the well-lit corner of the store and pulled her long auburn hair into a ponytail. She put on her painting apron and sat down on the stool in front of her easel. She enjoyed painting landscapes as an amateur artist, and sometimes people bought her paintings when she displayed them in the store, which brought her a lot of joy. The painting was starting to come together but it was still missing something. The composition was off, and Danielle couldn't figure out why. She stared at the canvas for a minute, sighed, and dipped her brush into the paint. Squinting her blue eyes in concentration she started to add details to the weathered oak tree, which was the focal point of her painting.

Sometime later the doorbell tinkled, and Danielle looked up from the canvas feeling disoriented. *Is it ten o'clock already? Then I've been painting for two hours.* "Good morning Mrs. Castle," she greeted her faithful customer with a smile.

"Good morning, dear. Did you get the furniture from the Couture house?"

"Yes, I did. There are some nice pieces, now I just need customers to buy them. Thank you for recommending me to the Couture family."

"Don't mention it, dear," Mrs. Castle waved her hand. "I stopped by after the funeral and talked to Gloria's daughter-in-law." She paused for a second and continued. "I never understood why that nice boy married such a persnickety person. His first wife, Elizabeth, was such an angel. Everyone loved her." She sighed. "Well, I heard from the real estate agent that she put the house on the market as it is, and I knew there was some nice furniture there, so I told her that if she doesn't want them, you might be able to sell some pieces."

"Her secretary called me, and I went up to the house on Sunday. I put everything in the storage room for now. Yes, I met her too." Danielle rolled her eyes. "When I told her that I couldn't pay her in advance, only as I sell things one by one and I keep thirty percent of the selling price, she said she didn't want any money. She just wants to get rid of the 'junk' before the new owners move in."

"Gloria, may she rest in peace, had some very valuable antique furniture and lots of paintings of the family. I guess her daughter-in-law packed up the valuable pieces to ship to France because I saw the truck up there." Mrs. Castle speculated.

"I'm glad they're not moving here, though." Danielle offered. "Everyone liked Gloria and her son, but this woman he married… stuck-up people don't survive long in this town. I wonder who bought the house? We'll see," Danielle said and turned back to her painting.

The elderly woman nodded and started wandering up and down the crowded aisles of Danielle's store, as she did every week. Most of the merchandise was the same, but Mrs. Castle loved to browse while she chatted about her everyday life.

Danielle continued to paint and listened to Mrs. Castle's calming voice as she talked about the neighbor's cat leaving a dead mouse on her doormat. "I guess she was thanking me for the liver pate I made for her the other day," Mrs. Castle announced. "Betty always feeds her that awful store-bought cat food. The poor kitty was grateful, you should've seen her enjoying the liver pate. That reminds me, I'll stop at the butcher shop on the way home and make some more."

After she finished browsing and informed Danielle about her granddaughter's ballet recital in detail, just like every week, she handed Danielle a box of homemade cookies and headed toward the door. "See you next week," she said on her way out. Although she rarely bought anything, Mrs. Castle always told her friends about the treasures she'd seen in the store.

Danielle returned to her canvas enjoying the cranberry cookies. *These are delicious! I wish I had her talent for baking.* She stared at her painting feeling exasperated. The half-finished forest was giving her more trouble than her paintings normally did. She wasn't sure why the composition felt off. Briefly, she debated setting it aside and starting a new painting. *No. I'm not going to give up on it.* When she started the painting, she had a vision, and she was determined to put the vision on the canvas.

The chime of the doorbell broke her concentration. "I'll be right there," she called out. It was the mail carrier, Mr. Jones. He was an older gentleman with dark leathery skin from years of delivering mail in all kinds of weather. His mustache kicked up at the sides of his mouth when he talked, and it always made Danielle smile. Mail in hand he leaned on Danielle's counter. She knew he was ready to share some juicy gossip.

"Did you hear?" Mr. Jones asked with an excited twinkle in his eyes. "Some rich folks bought the old Couture mansion already. The house is haunted, I tell you. Since the old lady died, people hear weird noises coming from the house at night."

"Nah, there's no such thing as a haunted house, you know that."

"I'm telling you, it's haunted. The family put it on the market the day after the funeral and some rich people from the city bought it already. I saw the wife in the driveway this morning."

"They live in France," Danielle tried to trail the old postman's thoughts. "I don't think anyone in the family wants to move to a speck on the map town in New York from their mansions on the coast of the Riviera."

"Is that so? How do you know?"

"Mrs. Castle told me. When Mrs. Couture's son remarried, they moved to France, but Mrs. Couture refused to give up the house she lived all her life and stayed here."

The doorbell chimed again, and they saw a middle-aged woman walking in. Danielle hadn't seen her in the shop before. Her straight blond hair cut in a bob grazed her shoulders. Her designer handbag, shoes, and clothes all screamed of money. Danielle couldn't imagine why she came to her small shop. Although she didn't have too rare or expensive items, Danielle doubted a woman of her possible status would be interested in any pieces in her store.

"She's the rich woman I was talking about," Mr. Jones whispered as he leaned closer to Danielle. "The one who bought the Couture house."

Standing by the door the woman pulled her designer looking sunglasses down her nose and peered around. "Are you the owner?" she called out looking at Danielle.

"Yes, I am." Danielle smiled wondering what the rich-looking woman could be interested in a shop like hers.

"I'm Mrs. Van Bramer. I was told you're the one who cleaned the junk out of my house. The builders found a painting, but it's too pretty to throw it in the trash, so it's yours if you want it."

"Would you like me to sell it for you?" she hesitantly asked.

"Oh," the woman brightened. "This painting doesn't have any value; I just want to get rid of it." She went out the door without waiting for Danielle's reply. She returned a few minutes later holding a large painting in a weathered, gilded frame.

When the woman turned the painting around, Danielle held her breath feeling stunned. A young man in a blue Musketeer uniform stared at her from the painting. His hair and beard were dark, and his eyes were chocolate brown. The painter managed to make them look so real that it made Danielle wonder how he did it. The tall, handsome man in the painting had a self-assured look about him. The feathers on his hat and the hilt of his sword were painted with incredible detail and the painting itself was in amazing shape.

"Magnificent," Danielle whispered scanning every tiny detail of the man's face. "The painter captured the playful, lingering smile in the corner of his lips, and even depicted the twinkle in his warm eyes with a speck of gold paint." She marveled and took a step closer. "It seems like... it looks like the face and hair were painted over. I have to take a closer look to be sure, but the paint and brushstrokes seem to be different and the face area doesn't seem as aged as the rest of the painting."

"I don't see it, but I'm no artist," replied the woman seemingly uncomfortable. "Anyway, this was left in an upstairs closet. The painter found it when he removed the old wallpaper that covered the door. My husband had an expert authenticate it and he said it's totally worthless because an unknown artist did it and it was painted over. He said he'd take it and use the frame. I thought because you have the rest of the stuff from the house, I'd bring it to you."

"This portrait is amazing! I can't believe the amount of detail, but to find the real value of paintings is difficult. You should find an antique dealer or auctioneer to take a look at it."

"Nah, the expert says it's worthless; do what you want with it. I don't want worthless junk in my new house."

"Well, I can hang it up, and see if I can find a buyer."

The woman scanned the room with pity in her eyes. "I don't care what you do with it. If you can get a few bucks for it, sell it and keep the money. It's yours. You don't make a lot of money by selling these..." her voice trailed as she waved her hand pointing at the items on the shelves and tables with her freshly manicured fingers.

"I don't have a lot of customers, but I get by," Danielle said, feeling hurt by the woman's callous words.

"I can't imagine what you like about that painting, though. It nice, but it makes the little hairs stand up on the back of my neck every time I look at it. It's just too lifelike. I keep waiting for him to move or say something. It's really creepy how his eyes seem to follow me." The woman shook her head.

Danielle marveled at the painting. "The composition and details of the original art are magnificent, but the expert is correct. Someone had painted over parts of it not too long ago and ruined it."

The blonde woman gave her a half smile. "You're an artist, I see you appreciate the artistry of this painting. Do as you wish. Portraits of long-dead people creep me out; I want paintings with flowers in my house."

After Mrs. Van Bramer left, Danielle propped the portrait up on the shelf behind the counter. Mr. Jones straightened up huffing with anger. "What a rude woman, I'd say! I can see already; she's not going to be a popular person in town."

Danielle sighed, "Well, she's probably used to ordering people around."

"Rich or not, she doesn't need to be rude. Your shop is nice, and you have a lot of great things here."

"Thank you, Mr. Jones. I know I can't compete with the antique dealers in the city, but I like this little town."

"And everyone loves you here too." Mr. Jones hugged Danielle. "Oh, I've got to run!" he wrinkled his forehead looking at the clock and hurried toward the door. "See you tomorrow."

Danielle sat down on her stool staring at the painting. She took in all the details. The fine wisps of hair that stood up and away from his wavy shoulder-length hair. The fine lines near his eyes and lips. *How in the world had the painter accomplished this?* The composition and colors are striking, but the face is so different from the rest of the painting. *I'd love to meet the artist who'd painted the most beautiful man I've ever seen.* She searched the painting for the signature of the artist, but it seemed to be painted over as well.

Time flew by fast when surprisingly, a group of people walked into the store. They walked around and gathered bedside lamps with silk shades, Chinese vases, small collectible statuettes and teapots in their arms. *I really should get shopping baskets.* Danielle thought. *But I never felt the need for them before.*

The customers kept bringing their treasures to the counter and by the time they were ready to pay, the counter was covered with all the sold items. Danielle wrapped and bagged everything and sighed when

182

the group finally left. When she added up the purchases, it came to close to three thousand dollars. She turned and looked at the man in the painting. "Well, Monsieur Musketeer, it seems like you've brought me luck."

The bell to the shop rang dragging Danielle out of her happy mood, but not before she noticed the tiniest fraction of movement in the corner of the man's lips in the painting. *He smiled at me... Oh, for Pete's sake, it's a painting! It was just a reflection of the sun on the shiny seal of the oil paint.* She shook her head and turned toward the door.

It was Sarah, her best friend. The short-statured woman Danielle's age with fiery-red curly hair and freckles stormed through the door. "You forgot our dinner plans, didn't you?" she laughed as she dropped her purse on the counter.

Danielle looked at her watch and couldn't believe it was nearly six o'clock. "It's going to be my treat," she announced, with a huge smile. "I made three thousand dollars today."

"Awesome!" Sarah cried out and hugged Danielle. "I knew your store would be a success one day." As Sarah let Danielle go, she noticed the painting of the Musketeer leaning against the wall on the shelf. She stared at it for a long moment and shuddered, and then started walking away, always keeping her eyes on the painting.

What are you doing?" Danielle asked.

"Where did you get this? It gives me the creeps how his eyes are following me. And that look on his face... as if he's mocking me or laughing at me."

"Don't be silly. It's just a painting. The new owner of the Couture house gave it to me."

Sarah shook her head. "I'm telling you. It gives me the heebie-jeebies. Sell the damned thing as soon as you can. But he's handsome, though."

"I don't want to sell it, at least not yet. It's been painted over and I want to study it because the original artist has an unusual style." *I'll find a place for it tomorrow.* Then it dawned on her as she turned to Sarah. "I'm not dressed for dinner. Can I have a raincheck?"

"Are you kidding? There's no dress code at Dino's place; you're fine in jeans and t-shirt. Let's go."

Chapter Two

The Musketeer's painting was waiting for Danielle when she opened the store the next morning. It sat leaning against the wall on the shelf, just where she left it. She needed to hang it, but where? Danielle scanned the walls. There was a spot on the far wall where customers would see it as they walked in and she could see it from her painting corner as well.

It took Danielle a few minutes to find the appropriate nails and picture hook in her stash under the counter. As she climbed to the top of the stepladder, she suddenly regretted wearing a short skirt. She had no idea why, though. She just felt exposed. Like someone was peering up her skirt. Danielle shook off the odd feeling as she hammered the nail and picture hook into the wall. She stepped off and with the painting in hand, climbed the stepladder again.

The bell on the door chimed as Danielle hung the wire on the back of the painting to the picture hook and shifted the painting left and right to find the best position.

"I'll be right there," she called out. It was her mail carrier, Mr. Jones. Danielle took the three steps down to reach the floor.

"It looks nice on that wall," Mr. Jones observed. "Are you going to keep it or sell it?" Mr. Jones scratched his beard staring at the painting. "He's one handsome looking Musketeer," he exclaimed.

"He is, indeed," Danielle sighed.

I wonder why the face was painted over? Danielle pondered as she gazed at the portrait and folded up her stepladder. "I don't have cookies today; the bakery was closed this morning." She trailed the conversation. "I hope Nancy is okay. She always opens the shop early."

"Oh, her niece went into labor last night and she's staying with her in the hospital. Didn't she put a sign in the window?"

"I didn't see any signs. Maybe she forgot."

"I'm heading that way; I'll tape a note to the door." He adjusted the carrier bag on his shoulder, flashed a warm smile at Danielle and walked out the door.

Danielle took a longing glance at her abandoned canvas in the corner. She wanted to paint but it was Thursday, bookkeeping day. The padded barstool scraped on the floor as she pulled it out from under the counter. Her ancient computer always booted up painfully slowly, which gave Danielle a chance to make coffee. By the time she came back with a cup, the program was ready. Danielle sat down by the computer with a sigh. She knew it might even take her the entire day of entering receipts into a spreadsheet and paying bills.

It was dark by the time Danielle finished sorting through receipts and organizing everything. She had enough money to pay all her bills and had a nice sum leftover too, thanks to the huge flow of sales the day before. She was too tired to walk the two miles home in the dark, so she ordered takeout and after finishing the meal, she settled in to sleep in the back room on the comfortable couch she kept from an estate sale.

Chapter Three

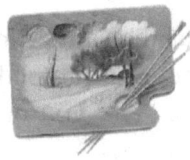

Danielle fell asleep as soon as her head hit the pillow. In her jumbled dream, she was running in a dense forest and her shoes kept sticking in mud slowing her down. She tried to scream but couldn't make a sound. Someone or something was chasing her, and she knew she had to get away. Suddenly, a beautiful man appeared and embraced her. She felt the warmth of the sun on her face and all her fears disappeared. She held onto his strong arms and looked into his passionate eyes. He started talking in a soft voice and Danielle struggled to hear his words but couldn't. He caressed her shoulder and when their lips met in a sensuous kiss, she felt a pleasant tingle deep inside her body.

A sudden crashing sound yanked her out of the sweet dream. 'Bloody Hell' she heard a man's muffled voice. *What the— someone's in the store!* Fear coursed through Danielle as she stood up and reached for the handgun she kept by the couch, just in case. She felt safer when she occasionally slept in the store after a long day.

Gun in hand, she tiptoed from the backroom and turned the light on. "I have a gun, and I'm a good shot," she warned, cocking the gun, trying to sound confident.

"Don't shoot!" The man yelled and Danielle saw him running toward the door. He yanked the door open and heard his footsteps as he was running down the street. A minute later she heard a car engine and then the car speeding away.

Danielle took a deep breath and put the gun on the counter. Her hands were shaking as she dialed the police. "A man broke into my store! He's gone but I'm afraid he might come back!" she cried.

"The dispatcher instructed her in a calming voice, "Hide in a room where you can lock the door. I'm sending a patrol car right away."

Danielle was afraid to stay alone and called Sarah. Her best friend didn't need a long explanation. "I'll be there in a minute, don't hang up," she said, in a sleepy voice and Danielle heard the jingle of keys and Sarah starting her car engine a few seconds later.

The police car arrived at the same time as Sarah's car screeched to a halt in front of the store. She jumped out and ran into the store barefoot, still in her pajamas. "Are you okay?" she cried out running to Danielle and hugged her.

"I'm fine," Danielle assured her and looking at the two officers entering the store with guns in hand, continued. "He ran out of the store when I put the lights on, and I heard him driving away."

"Did you see his face?" the taller officer asked, putting his gun in the holster.

"No, he stood here in front of the counter," Danielle recalled. "But he turned his back to me so fast that I couldn't see his face. All I saw was his dark overcoat, and he had gray, neatly trimmed hair."

"Please look around to see if anything is missing."

Danielle scanned the shelves and looked at the register. "Nothing seems to be missing."

"The lock is busted," the officer observed. "We'll park in front of the store for a while. I advise you to go home."

"No, I want to stay here," Danielle replied. "I'll call the locksmith in the morning."

"Then I'm staying with you." Sarah decided.

"I have spare clothes in the backroom. Go, change."

"Okay." Sarah turned and walked by the counter suddenly becoming upset. "Put that gun away, Danielle! I hate guns."

"I will, don't worry." Danielle smiled and put the gun on the shelf under the counter.

After the officers walked out to the patrol car, Danielle closed the door behind them and secured a sturdy chair under the doorknob to hold the door closed. She left the lights on and legs still shaky, walked to the backroom to make coffee.

"Who could it be and what did he want?" Sarah questioned, putting the sweater on she found in the closet.

Danielle spooned the coffee into the filter and filled the machine with water. "I have no idea. Nothing is worth a lot of money in the store."

Sarah cocked her head and pulled her thick, curly hair into a ponytail with a scrunchie. "Maybe he thought he'd find cash, or perhaps he knew exactly what he wanted."

"He didn't seem like a bum or addict who would steal anything to get his next fix. He looked well-groomed and wore Italian loafers. I recognized it because the lawyer down the street wears those kinds of shoes and he makes sure everyone knows that they're Italian leather."

"Yeah, he's a pompous fool." Sarah giggled and then her voice changed to a serious tone. "But if this man wasn't just an average burglar who steals anything, he could get his hands on and wanted something specific, why didn't he just come to the store and buy it?"

"I have no idea. I'm sorry I woke you up, but I was really scared. Thank you for coming over so fast, even in your PJs," Danielle hugged Sarah.

"Of course, what are besties for?" Sarah patted Danielle's back.

"I'm too wired to sleep, but you need rest. You're working today, right? It's 2 a.m. so you can still sleep for a few hours."

"Nope, I'm off today, and I'm not going anywhere until I know you're safe."

Danielle held up the coffee pot. "Do you want some?"

"No, it always gives me heartburn in the middle of the night. Why don't you lie down to sleep a little? I'll stay up."

Danielle filled her cup. "I'm too wired to sleep. I'm going to paint for a while."

"Okay, then I'll rest my eyes on that comfy couch." Sarah yawned.

Danielle walked to her painting corner and after taking the cover off the half-done painting, she changed her mind. *I'm going to clean the portrait of the Musketeer. Let's see what's hiding under that new coat of paint.*

189

Chapter Four

Danielle heard a knock on the window and looked up startled. She saw Mr. Jones straining to peek into the store through the window. Sitting on her stool in front of the easel with a brush in hand, she glanced at the clock. *Oh, my! Is it nine o'clock already?* She stood up and hurried to the front door. Pulling the chair from under the doorknob, she opened the door.

"Thank God you're okay!" Mr. Jones pushed through the half-open door and hugged her. "I just heard from the butcher. Do you know who it was? Did they take anything? Did they try to hurt you? Why were you in the store so late?" his questions came as he was trying to catch his breath.

"I'm fine," Danielle assured the worried mailman, smiling. "I haven't the faintest idea who it was and what he wanted. He ran away when I yelled out and cocked my gun."

"Oh, good! You should've shot him in the leg. He deserved it."

"I don't think he's from around here," Danielle speculated. "Only the lawyer down the street wears that brand of expensive loafers."

"You don't think…"

"No, he has brown hair and the burglar had silvery gray hair."

"Now wait a minute!" the mailman grabbed Danielle's arm in his excitement. "I might have seen that man at the Couture mansion. Mrs. Van Bramer's secretary said he's an art expert."

"What's going on?" Danielle heard Sarah's sleepy voice behind her. "Oh, good morning Mr. Jones."

"Mr. Jones just told me he saw the man who broke into the store," Danielle explained to her best friend.

The mailman yanked his carrier bag higher on his shoulder. "I'll stop at the police station and report this." He started walking away but turned back. "Oh, I almost forgot. The bakery is open. Lucy's niece had a baby boy. I got you fresh croissants." He smiled and handed a paper bag to Danielle.

"Thank you, Mr. Jones! It was very nice of you," Danielle called after the mailman as he hurried away down the sidewalk, and then turned to Sarah. "You're not going to believe what I've found! Come, let me show you." She reached for Sarah's hand and led her to the corner in the store.

"Phew, it smells like turpentine over here." Sarah crinkled her nose.

"I've been working on taking off the new layer of paint and now the signature of the artist is visible. He was a much sought-after painter in 17th century France."

"Let's search it," Sarah perked up. "Maybe this painting is worth a lot of money!"

"I'll boot up the computer, but first, I'm going to call the locksmith. While the computer is warming up, we'll eat the croissants Mr. Jones brought." Danielle decided and covered the painting.

"Your ancient computer takes forever. You have to get a new one."

"I know." Danielle sighed. "I never had the money for it, but after the surge of customers, now I do."

The locksmith said he'll stop by before lunch and by the time the women finished breakfast, the ancient computer was ready for search. Danielle Googled the name of the artist and her jaw dropped when she clicked on the first website which popped up on her screen.

Sarah peeked over Danielle's shoulder. "What? No way!" she shrieked and read the headline out loud. "The portrait of a noblewoman of the famous 17th century artist was sold to a well know American art collector for ten million dollars."

Danielle, not believing her eyes, backspaced and clicked on the next link. It was the auction website where the price of the painting was confirmed. She kept searching and found fifteen more paintings from the same artist that had been sold for similar amounts in the past ten years. "I have to tell Mrs. Van Bramer about this. She gave me the painting not knowing the possible value of it."

"Wait a minute!" Sarah exclaimed. "What if that so-called expert knew the value of the painting and lied to Mrs. Van Bramer? I think he broke into the store. And what if she wants the painting back after she finds out how much it's worth?"

"I'll give it back to her, of course. She bought the house and found the painting in the hidden room; it belongs to her."

"Nah-uh!" Sarah announced. "That's not right. It belongs to the Couture family. I bet the old lady didn't tell her relatives about the hidden room."

"Or, maybe she didn't even know about it. But you're right; it had to be a member of the family who hid the painting in the secret room. It belongs to them. I'm going to finish cleaning the signature part to be sure, and then I'll call Mrs. Van Bramer."

"Sounds like a plan." Sarah decided. "I'm gonna go home to change but I'll come back around one o'clock to bring you lunch."

Chapter Five

Danielle didn't have any customers all morning and the locksmith finished changing the lock within a few minutes, giving her plenty of time to work. She finished cleaning the signature part and the full name was visible and matched the signature she found on numerous paintings from the artist on the auctioneers' websites. This confirmed that the artist was indeed who she thought he was. She covered the painting on the easel and was ready to turn the "out to lunch" sign on the door when Mr. Jones rushed in exasperated.

"I came as fast as I could. Did Mrs. Van Bramer get here yet?" he asked out of breath.

"No, why?"

"Because... because I kinda told her about the silver-haired man and she was convinced that he was going to steal her painting from your store because he lied..." The mailman blurted out trying to catch his breath and continued. "And she's convinced that the portrait is worth a lot of money, and she said she wouldn't let him, or you, steal it from her."

"Me? Stealing? How could she say that?"

"Oh, you should've seen her! Under that fancy looking exterior hides a very mean woman." He turned toward the door as they heard a car stopping in front of the store. "Here she comes," warned the mailman as Mrs. Van Bramer stormed through the door.

"I want my painting back!" the elegantly dressed woman shouted, her face distorted with anger. "I knew it! That scoundrel was lying to me. He called me yesterday and said he might be able to sell the painting for a few hundred, but I told him that I gave it to you. But now that he tried to steal it, I'm sure it's worth a lot more and he knew it. I want it back, right now!"

"Uhm…" Danielle took a small step back. "I do think it's worth a lot of money, too."

"I knew it! Give it to me. I'll have it authenticated and sell it." The blonde woman pushing Danielle aside scanning the walls. "Where is it?"

"It belongs to the Couture family, you should give it back to them," Danielle protested.

"What do you mean?" the woman snapped. "They left it in the house and the house is now mine with everything in it."

Mr. Jones cleared his throat and said in a shaky voice, "By the law, it might be so, but you gave it to Danielle yesterday when you brought it to the store, remember? You told her to sell it or keep it—it's hers."

"What?" the angry woman shrieked. "Because I thought it was a piece of junk. Had I known it's worth something…"

Mr. Jones raised his voice. "Your word is your word, and I'm a witness to it. You gave it to Danielle, and you said so. Not once but at least three times."

Danielle tried to ease the tension. "You gave it to me, so I'm going to keep the painting until I can talk to the Couture family."

"So that's where we stand, young lady! You're a thief just like that weasel expert. You'll hear from my lawyer, today!" Mrs. Van Bramer shouted and hurried out the store pushing Sarah aside who was about to enter with takeout bags in her hands.

"Who is that? What's going on?" Sarah turned her head looking after the seething woman who yanked the door of her Bentley open and barked at the driver to take her back to Manhattan as fast as he could.

Danielle explained everything as Sarah stared at her astounded. "What are you going to do?"

"First, let's eat, I'm starving. I'll call the real estate office later; they might have the phone number or at least the address of Mrs. Couture's son in France. I'll contact him and tell him about the painting."

"Sounds like a good plan." Sarah nodded and looked at the old mailman. "Would you like to join us for lunch? I brought plenty."

"I would love to!" Mr. Jones smiled. "Thank you very much."

After lunch, Danielle took the portrait to her bank with Sarah and rented a vault. She knew Mrs. Van Bramer would file a lawsuit claiming rightful ownership and she wanted to keep the painting safe until the court made the decision.

When she got back to the store, she felt like her unfinished painting was calling her. She worked on in until late that night. "You're done. Now I'm satisfied. All you needed was a friend to hold hands with," she told the oak tree in the painting.

Chapter Six

The next few weeks were uneventful yet filled with anxiety. The Van Bramers filed a lawsuit and claimed rightful ownership of the painting, and the court date was set.

One morning Sarah burst into the store feeling excited about her first date with a Respiratory Therapist from the hospital. "I was surprised when he asked me out. We're going to have dinner tonight at Dinos," she announced happily. "He's new and every nurse in the hospital has been drooling over him for weeks. He's so handsome and so nice to everyone. And he asked *me* out!"

"I'm so happy for you." Danielle hugged her friend. "But what did you do to your hair?"

"I straightened it. You don't like it?"

"Honestly? No. It's not you and it makes your face look drawn."

"Thanks a lot!" Sarah exclaimed, trying to make her face look angry. "You're such a killjoy!"

"What are best friends for?" Danielle laughed. "But seriously. Your natural curls are so beautiful. This straight hair is not you."

"Okay. Two hours wasted. Now I'm going home to wash my hair again." She turned and ran out the door.

Shortly thereafter Mrs. Castle stopped by and this time she didn't start browsing. She was furious. "Did you hear, Danielle? I'm outraged!"

"What happened?" Danielle asked, feeling alarmed.

"The cat is out of the bag!" Mrs. Castle fumed.

The door opened and Mr. Jones rushed in, his face red with anger. "I can't believe it!" he shouted. "We must start a petition to stop them."

Mrs. Castle nodded in agreement. "Yes, we must."

Danielle stood between them totally confused. "Would somebody please tell me what's going on?"

"Well," Mrs. Castle took the lead. "Those no-good people who bought the Couture estate. I'm so angry, I can't even... Tell her Mr. Jones."

The mailman dropped his carrier bag on the floor. "We just heard that the Van Bramers got the permit to build a leather factory on the Couture estate, even before they bought the mansion with the hundred fifty acres land. They will destroy wildlife and poison the river with chemicals."

"Not to mention the rotting smell of leather that would make life miserable for everyone in town." Mr. Jones added seething with anger.

Danielle stood there astounded. "They can't do that—can they?"

Mr. Jones huffed angrily. "We don't know who they paid off, but the Mayor's office said there's nothing they can do to stop them. So, we started a petition and I'm collecting signatures. When everyone in town signs it, we'll file the complaint. Would you sign it?"

"Of course!" Danielle took the clipboard from the mailman and signed the paper.

"Let's get busy," Mr. Castle headed toward the door. "I'm going from door to door with Mr. Jones and we'll tell everyone in town to protest against this atrocity."

"Let me know what I can do," Danielle called after the pair hurried out the door.

***

The court date finally arrived. Danielle sat nervously by her lawyer in the packed courtroom. When Mrs. Van Bramer arrived with her lawyer, she had a smug expression on her face as she glanced at Danielle.

"We're calling Mr. Jones as our first witness." Mrs. Van Bramer's lawyer announced.

Danielle was stunned and looked at her lawyer questioningly. He stood up and shouted, "Objection your Honor! Mr. Jones is our witness."

"Not anymore." Mrs. Van Bramer's lawyer announced.

The mailman walked to the witness stand. He was sworn in and was seated.

"Mr. Jones," the lawyer started his questioning. "Please tell the court what happened when Mrs. Van Bramer commissioned the antique store owner *to sell* her painting."

Danielle felt nauseated. *Why is he doing this? He's testifying on her behalf! It can't be happening. This is not the kind and righteous man I know.*

"I'll tell you exactly what happened," Mr. Jones started talking and placed a thick envelope on the stand and pointed his finger at Mrs. Van Bramer. "This is the bribe Mrs. Van Bramer gave me to lie to the court in her favor."

The courtroom erupted and everyone started shouting. Danielle sighed with relief.

The judge's gavel silenced the crowd enough for him to speak. "Please continue, Mr. Jones."

The mailman cleared his throat and continued his testimony. "I was in Ms. Clearwater's shop when this woman came in. She gave the painting to Danielle, and when she offered to sell it for her, Mrs. Van Bramer said this word for word, 'I don't care what you do with it. If you can get a few bucks for it, sell it and keep the money, it's yours' and this is the truth. She gave me this money this morning to testify that she never gave the painting to Danielle; she wanted her to restore it and sell it for her."

The judge thanked Mr. Jones and announced his verdict, "Case closed. The painting belongs to Ms. Danielle Clearwater." The Judge looked at Mrs. Van Bramer and continued. "Tampering with a witness in the fourth degree is a class A misdemeanor. I will turn your case over to the District Attorney's office."

Chapter Seven

The next morning Danielle called the real estate office and got the phone number of Mrs. Couture's son in France. Ready to dial the number, she heard the door chime and looked up. Danielle froze and dropped the phone when she saw the young man stepping into the store. His dark, wavy hair slid off his shoulder as he turned his head looking around. His neatly trimmed goatee made his face look chiseled and masculine while his warm brown eyes gave him a softer appearance. He took a few steps forward looking at Danielle and gave her a friendly smile. "Are you Danielle?" he inquired.

"Ye… yes, I am she," Danielle stammered.

"Hello, I'm Louis Couture, Gloria's grandson," he said stepping closer and extended his hand over the counter. "Nice to meet you."

"It's… nice to meet you too." Danielle accepted the handshake.

"I went to visit my grandmother this morning. I didn't know she passed away because I haven't been in contact with my father for over ten years," he bowed his head with a sad expression on his face. "The construction people told me that the new owner gave you everything my stepmother left in my grandmother's house."

"Yes, she did. Everything is in the storage room."

"Please don't get me wrong, I don't want any of it," Louis assured her. "But there was a painting in the house which has sentimental value to me. The man told me they discovered the closet behind the wallpaper in my old room. You see, when I was fourteen, I was fantasizing about being a musketeer and painted my face, well the way I imagined I would look like as a grown man, over one of my ancestor's portrait." He let out a slight laugh. "My stepmother hated the idea of me becoming an artist, so I had to paint in secret."

"I have your painting." Danielle offered, trying to drag her eyes away from his mesmerizing stare. "I picked it up from the bank this morning and planned to work on it to restore it to its original state."

The young man looked at the covered easel and his eyes jumped over to Danielle's painting next to it. He took a sharp breath and called out, "That painting... it's amazing!" He took a few steps toward the easel. "The composition, the colors, and the way the trees are holding onto each other, it's magnificent! I can see the paint is not dry yet. Are you the artist?" He asked with excited sparkles in his eyes.

The man's spontaneous compliment warmed her heart. "Yes, I am." Danielle offered, blushing.

"This is amazing! I wish I could paint like you," he gushed but Danielle didn't detect any jealousy in his tone, only admiration.

"Thank you. You're too kind. But let's look at your painting." She pulled the cover off the Musketeer's portrait.

"Oh." Louis smiled as he scanned the painting. "I think my imagination was correct. I forgot about the beard I painted on it, and now I have it." He laughed touching his face.

And you're wearing it so well. Danielle thought, feeling the heat rising to her face and collected herself quickly. "I was just about to call your family in France when you walked in. I wanted to inform them that under the recent overpaint the original painting is very valuable. I discovered the original artist's name when I cleaned the corner. If the portrait is fully restored, it might be worth over ten million dollars."

"Wow! I was a stupid kid when I ruined it," he frowned. "I had no idea it was valuable. My parents refused to buy me canvases, so I just took a painting off the wall and painted over it."

"Let's sit there. You can help me decide what you want to do with it." Danielle motioned to the comfortable armchairs in the corner. "Would you like a cup of coffee? I have some cookies, too."

"Yes, please. That would be nice." Louis sat down and Danielle walked to the backroom to make coffee.

Danielle came back with a tray in her hand and sat down. Louis reached for the steaming mug with a concerned look. "Don't call my parents. They have plenty of money and the painting is clearly yours. You don't have to give it to the family."

"I know, but it doesn't feel right. It feels like I'm cheating your family out of a valuable inheritance. Yes, the new owner gave it to me, but it belongs to your family, not me. I accepted the court's decision only because I didn't want that snobbish Van Bramer family to have it. Moreover, had your parents knew about it, they wouldn't have left it in the house. If you don't want me to give it to your parents, then you keep it and do whatever you want with it."

"Oh, I don't want it. I just wanted to see it as a reminder of my childhood." He smiled warmly. "I don't need money. My father disowned me when I turned eighteen, and I told him that I wanted to follow my dreams to become an artist. I worked my way through college, and I was lucky to be discovered by an art dealer in New York. During the past ten years, I've made enough from the sales of my paintings to fulfill my dream of building a retreat for talented young artists who haven't had the support of their families."

Danielle wrinkled her forehead in concentration. "I'm pretty much up to date on famous artists of our time, but I never heard of you."

Louis gave out a nervous laugh. "That's because I don't use my *precious* family name. According to my father and stepmother, being a painter is a disgrace. I adopted my great grandmother's last name, St. Claire."

"Oh. My. God!" Danielle cried out. "I've been to every single exhibit of your paintings in Manhattan. Of course, I could never afford your art, but I always admired your talent."

"Now you can afford anything you like." Louis reached for her hand over the coffee table. "I'm planning to stay in town for a few days. I'm staying at a Bed and Breakfast by the lake. Would you let me help with the restoration of the painting? I'm sure my agent could find a private collector to buy it."

"I'd like that." Danielle lifted her cup to hide her blushing cheeks.

Chapter Eight

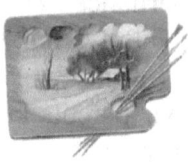

Danielle and Louis spent the following week together in the shop. Customers were scarce, as usual, so they had plenty of time to work on the musketeer painting and getting to know each other.

After they finished the restoration Danielle took a few steps back to admire the portrait. "You know," she said cocking her head and looking at Louis. "I liked it more with your painting over it. You must teach me how you made the eyes twinkle and follow the viewer."

"It's just a speck of gold paint at the right place." He laughed reaching into his pocket for his cellphone. "It's my agent. I'll call him later."

"Yes, but still. I taught myself to paint but I don't have your talent."

"Your talent is powerful, believe me." Louis took a step closer to Danielle and reaching for her hand looked into her eyes. "I took the liberty of taking pictures of your paintings in the storage room yesterday and sent them to my agent. That's probably why he called. Let me call him back."

He pushed the speed dial button and the agent picked up at the first ring. Louis put the phone on loudspeaker, and they heard a man's excited, raspy voice. "Louis! Why didn't you pick up? Where did you find her? These paintings are absolutely superb. She has an amazing talent. When can I meet her and look at the paintings?"

"Henry, calm down. She's right here listening to you."

"Hi," Danielle managed to croak out. "I'm Danielle and I'm honored. I can show you my paintings any time."

"How's tomorrow sound?" Henry asked with urgency in his voice.

"Tomorrow sounds fine."

"Louis text me the address," Henry said hurriedly and hung up.

Danielle watched Louis typing the store address with tears in her eyes. "I can't believe it! He likes my work."

"He loves them, believe me! He's a stoic person and a man of few words. I've never heard him being this excited since I've shown him my first painting.

"I'm so happy and I'm a little scared too. I'm..." Danielle admitted and was interrupted by the chime of the doorbell.

Mr. Jones burst into the store. "I have such great news!" he shouted dropping his carrier bag to the floor. He took a deep breath and continued. "I just heard from the Mayor's secretary that the Couture estate sale is off. The Van Bramers will not move here, and they can't build the factory. I don't know the details, but isn't this exciting?"

"That's great news, indeed!" Danielle exclaimed. "But how did this happen? Did they change their minds?"

"I don't know," the mailman said looking at Louis. "I think it's because of your father. The secretary said that he and his lawyers are still in a meeting with the Mayor and the real estate agent, but she overheard them saying that the deal is off."

"My father's in town? I haven't seen him or spoken to him in ten years." Louis cried out, with a sad expression on his face.

"Let's go to meet him." Danielle grabbed his hand and, taking not taking no for an answer, pulled Louis toward the door.

"Find out the details," Mr. Jones begged picking up his bag and hurrying after them.

Danielle and Louis walked to the Town Hall building and saw a handsome white-haired man in his late fifties walking down the steps trailed by a woman and two men in suits.

"That's my father," Louis whispered.

Mr. Couture stopped in his tracks and stared at his son for a second. A warm smile spread on his face then quickened his steps to reach Louis and Danielle. "Louis!" he shouted and embraced his son in a tight hug.

"Dad," Louis managed to say and swallowed hard.

"I missed all those years because I listened to that wretched woman. It was my fault. I should've paid attention to what she's been doing behind my back."

"What happened?" Louis took a step back staring at his father.

"Let's have lunch and I'll tell you everything. But first, introduce me to this lovely lady." He smiled at Danielle.

"Where are my manners?" Louis flashed an apologetic smile at Danielle. "Dad, this is Danielle Clearwater. She owns an antique shop on Main Street and she's an amazing artist as well."

Danielle curtsied as Mr. Couture extended his hand. "Nice to meet you, Ms. Clearwater," he smiled, lifted her hand to his lips and exchanged approving looks with his son.

Mr. Couture turned to his companions. "I'm going to spend time with my son today, I'll meet you all tomorrow at ten at my hotel." He then dismissed them.

Epilogue

"I'm so sorry for all those years we missed together, Louis," Mr. Couture began in a shaky voice putting his napkin on the table and pushing the plate to the side. "I didn't know, and I've been a fool letting her poison our relationship. You see, when your mother died, you were only five years old. I missed her so much. I was overwhelmed and lonely. I was still blinded by grief a year later and clung to the beautiful woman I met at a fundraiser when she showed interest in me. I was an imbecile not to see who she really was."

"It's okay, dad."

"No! I shouldn't have listen to her when she accused you of trying to force yourself on her. I was furious and blinded by jealousy. In my rage, I immediately severed ties with you and didn't even ask you if it was true or not. I simply believed her."

"Dad, I would never... how could she say that?" Louis gasped.

"I know now. She's a conniving, cruel woman. All these years she's been lying, cheating, and robbing me..." he bowed his head in shame.

"What happened?" Louis inquired. "What were you doing in the Mayor's office?"

"Okay, let me start from the beginning. A few days ago, I got home earlier than usual. Clarice was in the bathroom. Her laptop was open, and I saw a bank account in her maiden name. The account had a half a million transferred from the Van Bramers. I wrote down the account number and left the house. I went straight to see my detective friend and he opened an investigation."

Louis clung to every word with such pain in his eyes that it made Danielle choke with tears. She squeezed his hand under the tablecloth and rested her forehead on his shoulder for a second.

Mr. Couture cleared his throat and continued. "It turns out she had embezzled over nine million from my company in cahoots with my trusted accountant. The police arrested both and froze the numerous bank accounts that were opened in her name. They traced the half a million transfer which was done after she sold my mother's estate illegally."

Louis stared at his father wide-eyed. "So, you didn't even know about it?"

"No." He bowed his head. "Per our prenuptial agreement, thank God I listened to my mother when she insisted, she couldn't make any large purchases or sell anything without my approval and signature. She made the hushed deal with the Van Bramers, but now the sale agreement is null and void. The accountant admitted to the police that they were having an affair for years and planned to move to the Caribbean after they got the money and transferred everything to a Swiss account. My lawyer had drawn up the divorce papers and she'll be prosecuted. I wish I had found out sooner."

"Let me get this straight." Louis wrinkled his nose in concentration. "So, the Van Bramers can't have any claim to grandmother's estate, and they can't build the leather factory they planned."

"That's right, son. I had my lawyers transfer the ownership to you, and you can do whatever you want with it."

"Mr. Couture," Danielle interrupted, getting the man's attention. "There's an antique painting Mrs. Van Bramer found in the house and she gave it to me. When she found out that it's worth around ten million dollars, she demanded to get it back, but the court decided that it's mine. Now it's clear that she didn't have the right to give it to me, therefore, the painting belongs to your family and I'd like to return it to you with all the furniture your wife gave me from the estate."

"Dear girl, don't even think about giving anything back. Despite my wife's embezzling, I'm still a very rich man. You could put that money into much better use than I ever could."

Louis's eyes lit up. "Dad, I've made enough money to build an artist retreat for disadvantaged, talented artists. Do you mind if I build it on grandmother's estate?"

"By all means, son! I've been such an idiot. I just found out that you became a successful artist and went to see your gallery yesterday. Your paintings are amazing!" he cried out, with tears in his eyes. "I'm so proud of you."

Louis turned to Danielle. "Would you be my partner in building the retreat?"

"Yes, I'll be happy to, but only if you let me invest the money your agent will get from the sale of the musketeer painting."

"I have more than enough money now because I don't have to buy the property. Let's do it, together," Louis suggested and placed a gentle kiss on Danielle's hand. *"DaniLou Artist Retreat.* How's that sound?"

"It sounds wonderful," Danielle agreed.

Alone

Prologue

Being a fiction writer, anything can trigger a story followed by an avalanche of stringing words. When I read about the theory of Parallel Universes, I started thinking. *What if...*

It triggered a thought-provoking short, easy-to-read story about love, loss, and... Nah, I'm not going to spoil it for you. Enjoy the story!

"A parallel universe, also known as an alternate universe or alternate reality, is a hypothetical, self-contained reality co-existing with one's own. A specific group of parallel universes is called a "multiverse," although, this term can also be used to describe the possible parallel universes that constitute reality.

The world as we know it has three dimensions of space—length, width and depth—and, one dimension of time. But there's the mind-bending possibility that many more dimensions exist out there. According to string theory, one of the leading physics model of the last half-century, the universe operates with 10 dimensions.

The multiverse, also known as an omniverse, is a hypothetical group of multiple universes, including the universe in which we live. Together, these universes comprise everything that exists: the entirety of space, time, matter, energy, and the physical laws and constants that describe them."

~Wikipedia

Tears in the Wind

Valerie's Universe

The bright Spring sun bathed the budding trees with warm sunshine and tickled the grassroots to life. Petals fallen from the magnolia tree covered the ground, but the slight breeze sent chills through Valerie. The young, slender woman with long, brown hair wrapped herself inside a warm sweater.

When she reached her destination in the secluded corner of the cemetery, tears welled up in her eyes as she ran her fingers over the name, Caleb Winston, carved into the marble gravestone. *Everyone keeps telling me I should be over the mourning period by now.* She thought, sighing deeply. As she sat down on the bench by the side of the grave, she let the tears fall for the first time in a week.

She allowed herself to cry only when she'd made her weekly walk to the cemetery. She hid her sadness and tears from her family and friends. They kept telling her she was only eighteen and had her whole life ahead of her, so there was no reason for her to hold on to the boy she once loved.

They aren't the ones who lost the only person they could ever imagine loving. Such was her thought as she ran her tongue over her upper lip, tasting the salty tears. She fished a handful of tissues from her purse, wiped her face and blew her nose, whispering under her breath, "None of them believe in soulmates, Cal, and I can't get them to listen to me when I try to tell them what it was like between us. Not even my sisters understand. Mom and Dad keep telling me there's someone else out there for me, and I know they're saying it in the belief it should help, but it doesn't. It just makes me think of you more, and of the future, we planned together before it all fell apart."

***

Valerie closed her eyes and remembered standing by Caleb's hospital bed four years ago. Most cystic fibrosis patients could live close to their forties or even longer with good medical care, but there were always those who were not going to make it. Those who, like Caleb, would develop fatal complications after an infection their body just couldn't fight, even with the best medicine and care. He'd been in the hospital for over a month and on the lung transplant list for years, but because of his rare blood type, his chances to find a suitable donor were slim.

Her best friend and soulmate was dying. The pain Valerie felt was unbearable, but she put on a brave face and hid her agony from everyone. All she could do was be there, holding his hand and hoping that he'd get better as he did before. She could tell he was tired. Deep down she knew his body was losing the battle before a donor could be found, but she refused to let that thought surface and desperately held onto hope. A tear trickled down her cheek, and she couldn't stop it before it dripped down onto his hand. His eyes slowly opened, and he looked up at her. The emotion in his eyes was almost too much to bear.

"I'm sorry." She squeezed his hand. "I didn't mean to wake you."

"You didn't. I wasn't sleeping. I was resting because I don't really seem to sleep now. Not for a long time. Every time I feel I'm drifting into sleep; I'm scared I won't wake up." He sighed. "I... Val, I don't think I can hold on too much longer..."

There were so many things she could have said, but Valerie nodded. "I know, I don't want to accept it, but I feel it..." She blinked away more tears that were threatening to fall. "I love you, Cal, and I can't imagine my life without you, but this is too much for you to bare." With her free hand, she swept away a strand of hair matted with sweat from his forehead. "You don't need to fight anymore; it's hurting you too much."

"I must fight. For us, for our future."

Unable to stop the tears, she rested her forehead on his. "Maybe we need to accept that our time together is up, and our future is not going to happen." She swallowed the lump of emotion that constricted her throat. "I hate this. I hate seeing you suffer and struggle for each breath you take. And, I hate knowing that you're fighting to stay with me. Please, I know you're tired... nothing I say seems like it's going to be right, but I want you to know I'm going to love you no matter what happens."

"No matter... Where I am... I'm going to... Love you too." He rested his hand on hers, struggling with every word. "You're my life. You're my soulmate. Forever."

***

As she opened her eyes again, Valerie sobbed, and there was nothing she could do to stop her flowing tears. Caleb had died that night, as though her words had been what he needed for him to be able to move on.

"We were so happy, Cal!" She sobbed. "We'd spent almost every waking moment together since we were toddlers. I remember Mom telling Grandma how lucky we were to be born a month apart and live next door to each other because Helga, your nanny, was happy to babysit me. Then you got sick and spent a lot of time in the hospital... but when you felt better, we did everything together. I will never forget our first and only romantic kiss... when we were thirteen. It was so beautiful and felt so natural... That's when we knew we were soulmates. Then you got sick, and a series of infections made you weaker with every passing day. I wish you were still here, healthy and happy." She couldn't continue her monologue. The deep, powerful sob overwhelmed her and erupted from her chest.

After she cried herself out Valerie whispered, "I miss you, more than I can put into words." Wrapping her arms around herself, she leaned back on the bench, feeling the hardwood pressing against her upper back. "I didn't want to, but I had to let you go. I couldn't be selfish. I couldn't ask you to fight when I knew how much you were hurting. I just... sometimes I wish something could have happened to me too, so we could be together. I don't know how I'm meant to live this life without you, Cal. I keep on doing what I'm supposed to be doing, but my world is empty and colorless without you."

A sudden gust of wind blew her hair and showered her with pink petals from the nearby magnolia tree. "Cal?" She whispered, but then shook her head. "It can't be. I wish, but it's just the wind."

TEARS IN THE WIND

He's gone
The world is so much colder
His name etched upon the granite
So final, so impersonal
Tears I've been holding back now free
They fall in rivers down my cheek
A soft breeze begins to blow
Magnolia petals float by
My tears join them in a dance
A dance of loss
A dance of remembrance
Listening, I hear his voice
Floating on the wind
~Cindy J. Smith

Alone

Caleb's Universe

"How could I do this alone, Val?" Caleb reached out and gently traced the name, *Valerie Taylor*, carved into the white marble headstone, with his fingers. "We were meant to be together until we grew old."

As he had done every week since she passed, he sat down in front of the gravestone. Leukemia had taken her from him, moving so much faster than either of them could ever have imagined possible. All the plans they'd had for what was going to come meant nothing. She was gone.

Caleb sighed to ease the heaviness in his chest and looked up at the tree covered with flowers, close to the grave. "We had studied here when we were young. But always loved this magnolia tree. That's why your parents chose this secluded spot to… Oh, Val. I miss you so much!"

More than once, over the past four years, he'd been told he was young and there would be someone else in his life. He'd love someone, to fill the void, but nobody understood what it was like to find a true soulmate. "I miss you, every day, and I keep trying to push myself to keep going, but there have been so many times when I've thought about just ending it all. I know I shouldn't. You would never forgive me if I'd throw my life away, but you were my life, and…" He took a deep breath. "I'm sorry. I know every time I come here it seems like I say the same thing. I want things to be different, but without you here, there's no happiness in my heart."

***

Closing his eyes, Caleb remembered sitting at Valerie's bedside on that dreadful day. He still remembered the two of them walking into the doctor's office together to get her test results, just a few weeks before. She'd been feeling tired and sick for days, but neither of them had even thought it was possible she might be dealing with something as complicated as leukemia.

She was fading fast, and the treatments wiped all her energy. She had to stay in the hospital because she no longer could keep fluids and food down. She was more tired than she ever had been before, but he could tell she was fighting, for him and for the future they'd always talked about. As she coughed, he reached over to get water for her, and she looked at him. The pain in her pale, thin face was impossible to ignore. Gently, he stroked stands of hair off her face, wishing there was something he could to take the pain away and make her well.

"I'm okay." She smiled at him with dry, cracked lips, but it was impossible for her to hide how sick she was. "You shouldn't spend so much of your time here."

"Of course, I should." He smiled back, hoping she didn't see how much he was hurting, and yet he knew she could tell. The way her smile faded was a telltale sign. "Spending as much time as I can with you is the most important thing." He ran his tongue over his own dry lips. "I know what the prognosis is. I was there when you were told, and your parents understand me wanting to be here."

"Don't put your life on hold for me, Cal." She reached out to take his hand. "You're the one who'll have to keep going when I'm gone."

He swallowed, feeling the knot of emotion in his throat, and he squeezed her hand. "I hate the thought of you not being here, but I hate this more. I hate you being stuck in this hospital, fighting a battle we both know you aren't going to win, and I... I don't even know if I should be saying this, but I don't want you to be fighting for me. If you're too tired..." One of the tears he'd been trying desperately to hold back trickled down his cheek. "I love you, no matter what. Nothing's going to change that."

"Nothing's going to change how I feel about you either. I love you, more than I can put into words, and I'm so sorry."

***

Caleb opened his eyes, thinking about how quickly her death had come. It was as though him telling her she didn't need to fight for him had been what she needed. "Val," he spoke to the cold headstone. "I know what you'd want, and I'm trying. I'm trying harder than I think I've ever tried before, but I don't know how I'm supposed to do this without you, especially when everyone keeps telling me I should be over this by now. I should be over you. They have no idea how much it still hurts, and I just… I'm going to keep trying, for you, but my life is so different now. When I said I'd love you no matter what, I meant it. I still love you, and that just makes this all that much harder."

Life Must Go On

Valerie's Universe

Valerie stood up and stroked the granite stone with trembling fingers. "I have to go, my love, I must study for the finals. I'll be back next week."

She drove home and walked into the apartment to the sound of laughter. It was a nice thing to hear, even if it felt like it had been years since she'd last laughed like that. Probably since before Caleb got sick. She made her way into the kitchen, where her younger twin sisters, Alice and Lianne, were working together on what appeared to be homemade pizza.

"Hey, Val." Alice smiled at her. "We didn't think you'd be back so early."

"It's chilly out there." Valerie avoided answering the question and tried to smile back, but she didn't think it worked all that well. "I'll leave you two to finish cooking."

"Join us." Lianne stepped around the table, hands covered in flour, and stopped in just the right place to prevent Valerie from leaving the kitchen. "I know that look! You went to the cemetery, didn't you?"

"Yes, I did."

"You should stop going there because it always makes you sad. The best thing you could do is spend more time with us. It's about time you made some friends to take your mind off everything."

"Maybe." Valerie sighed. "I just can't help thinking that all I'm going to end up doing is bringing the two of you down."

"Val, you're our sister. We were there when Cal died. We know how much it affected you, how much it still affects you, and how little you want to move on, but eventually, you must. He wouldn't want you to be living like this. He'd have wanted you to find a way to move on."

Biting her lip, Valerie looked between the two of them. "Only he's not the one who's still here, is he? He doesn't know what it's like to be here without him." She shook her head. "You don't understand what it's like, and I don't think you ever could." Gently, because she wasn't truly angry, she brushed past Lianne. "I know you're doing what you think is best, but it's not helping. I'm never going to get over him, no matter how much you may want me to, because he was, and forever will be, my soulmate."

Behind her, she could hear Alice make a sound, and Valerie knew that was because neither of them believed in true love between soulmates. "Val..."

"I don't want to hear it. I don't want to have to argue about the same thing every week. The two of you can think what you want. I don't care. All I want is to be left alone."

Valerie didn't look back as she made her way to her room, but she didn't need to know she'd destroyed their happiness for the night, the way she always did. As she closed her door behind her, she slid down to the floor, tears streaming down her cheeks again. *Maybe it will be easier when I start college in the fall. I'll rent a small apartment where I won't have to pretend and wear a happy face for other people.*

Hope

Caleb's Universe

As always, Caleb's dad was in his lab. He resigned from the research company after he got a large sum for one of his inventions and spent every free minute on his own research. He built the lab eighteen years ago after his beloved Claire passed away giving birth to Caleb. He felt devastated and hired Hilda, an au pair from Poland, to raise Caleb.

Instead of going down to see his dad, only to be told that he was still nowhere near finished with his work, Caleb sat in the kitchen, eating cold potato salad and ham, leftover from the night before.

***

Ever since Caleb's mother died, his dad had been working on something that was meant to break the barrier, so it would be possible for him to find out if his soulmate existed in the parallel universe. He accelerated his work after Caleb had lost Valerie and felt devastated his son had to go through the heartache he did. Only, it had more setbacks than he expected it would. The longer it took to try and try again, the more it seemed like breaking the barrier would never be possible. He worried he'd never be able to be with his wife again, and that his son would never find happiness again.

***

Sighing, Caleb dropped his fork on the plate, wishing things were different. Wishing she hadn't died. Even if his father succeeds, how were they to know they'd even be able to find a Valerie in a parallel timeline who'd lost her Caleb? The more he thought about it, the more this idea sounded like an unreachable dream. Unable to sit any longer, Caleb stood and paced from one side of the kitchen to the other, telling himself it was probably better if the machine never worked. That way he wouldn't need to worry about stepping into a world where Valerie lived a happy life without him.

Blinking, not wanting to cry, he turned to make his way up to his room, in the hope he'd be able to find something he could do to distract himself.

He heard the front door open and Hilda walked in with shopping bags. The middle-aged woman with high cheekbones scanned his face while dropping the bags on the chair. "You've been in the cemetery again," she commented with a sad tone in her voice.

"Yes. Do you have a problem with that?" Caleb snapped.

"Of course not!" Hilda protested weakly. "It's just... I hate to see you sad."

***

Caleb loved Hilda, until he was about thirteen, and saw her coming out of his father's room in the middle of the night. "My dad loves my mom. How could he cheat on her like that?" he fumed to Valerie the next morning in childish anger.

Of course, later, he understood and accepted the relationship between his dad and the faithful nanny, who stayed with them as an unofficial housekeeper after her contract ended. But, he couldn't help feeling a slight resentment sometimes ever since that night.

He was also jealous of the time his dad spent with Hilda, discussing theories that he didn't understand as a child. Hilda was a science major in her country, but knew there was no future for her in Poland as a female scientist. Caleb's father, Frank, acknowledging her brilliant mind, encouraged her to go back to school, but she refused. "I'm happy here. I want to live a quiet life and I'm not interested in working for a company, but I'm happy to work with you," she'd said.

***

Caleb immediately felt remorse for snapping at Hilda. He apologized, and Hilda gave him a hug. "I understand. Don't worry about it." She dropped her arms and turned away. Picking up the shopping bags loaded with bathroom supplies, she headed upstairs.

Caleb heard his dad's loud footsteps as he rushed up the stairs from his basement lab.

Their eyes met for a moment. And, then, slowly, his dad's face broke into a huge smile. Caleb was taken aback by what he saw. Ever since he could remember, he rarely saw his father cracking a short-lived smile.

"The machine is finished, son!" He could hardly contain his excitement. "It works!" He hugged the fluffy, black cat with white whiskers in his arms to his chest and planted a kiss on the hissing animal's head. "Look!" he grabbed the cat's white paw and showed it to Cal. "I sent Midnight through the portal, and I brought him back unhurt with muddy paws, an hour later. It must be raining in the parallel universe. We'll find your Valerie—promise."

Caleb's face lit up with excitement and he rapidly fired questions at his father. "How? When? What happened? You've been working on that damned machine for eighteen years."

"I've found a miscalculation in the original base program a few hours ago. Hilda and I've been through it a thousand times, but we've never seen it before. Did Hilda get home yet? I can hardly wait to show it to her."

"She's not home yet." Caleb lied. "I want to go, Dad! I want to go now!" Caleb grabbed his father's hand and started pulling him toward the basement door."

"Wait! We must do more tests. This was the first step and I don't know where Midnight had been exactly. I must go over everything again and look at the coordinates carefully. If you go now, and something goes wrong, you might end up trapped in the wrong parallel universe that doesn't have a Valerie in it, for the rest of your life. We both know that's not what you want."

For a moment Caleb thought about arguing, but then he nodded. "You're right. I don't want to get trapped anywhere." He sighed. "I'll have to wait, but at least I have hope now. Thank you, Dad!"

"This is a huge step, Son. I must work out how we can be sure where exactly Midnight was, and I must send him through the barrier again before we try it ourselves." He spotted Hilda coming down the steps. "I've found the error in our calculation. The machine is working!"

"I'm happy to hear that," she replied, but the tone of her voice told a different story. She walked to the table, picked up a bag and opened the fridge door with a head of lettuce in her hand.

Frank gave her a disappointed look. Hugging) Midnight, he rushed toward the basement door and disappeared into the lab. Hilda stared after him with deep sadness in her eyes.

Caleb found it odd the way both his father and Hilda behaved. *My dad doesn't love her, I know that. But, the poor woman... she loves him. That's why she stayed with us.*

Weeks went by, and every morning Caleb watched as his dad disappeared into the lab. Caleb joined him as soon as he got home from school. They spent endless hours checking calculations and meticulously going through every detail, step by step, and emerged from the lab only at mealtimes.

Frank noticed, with concern, that Hilda grew quieter and barely said a word as the days went by. When he asked her to join them in the lab, she always found excuses.

"Are you okay, Hilda?" he'd ask between hurried bites, eager to get back to the lab.

"I'm fine. I... I don't want to break up the much-needed bond between you too, but I'm just a little lonely." She sighed and turned away.

"Sorry, I'm so close to a breakthrough... I could really use your help," Frank mumbled.

"You're very capable of doing it without me. I've been only a mere helper, and mostly just keeping you company. It's your work, Frank, finish it." Hilda stood up to clear the table.

The next day, when Caleb joined his father, his dad was about to open the glass cubicle of the machine to let Midnight out. "He's been acting strange the past few days," Frank mumbled, scratching the stubbles on his chin. "I send him over for a few hours and as soon as he comes back, he curls up on the couch and goes right to sleep. He didn't touch his food for days, but he seems healthy. I'll ask Hilda to take him to the vet."

"Maybe someone is feeding him on the other side," Caleb speculated.

"That's it! You're a genius, Son! Why didn't I think of that?"

"Does it mean that..."

"Yes, oh, yes!" Frank shouted, grabbing Caleb by the waist, and jumping up and down, pulling Caleb with him. "I'm going to try. Right now!"

"Dad, it's best if I go first, in case something goes wrong. Then you can bring me back, somehow. If you go, I wouldn't know what to do with the machine and you'd be stuck there."

"Yes, you're right. Let me go over everything one more time, and I'll explain everything as we check the machine."

***

They spent half the night in the lab. Dragging himself up the stairs Caleb felt exhausted, but when he fell into bed, he couldn't fall asleep. He was too excited about the possibility of finding Valerie in a parallel dimension. He heard Hilda's door open and her steps going down the stairs. *Probably she's thirsty* he thought and drifted into sleep.

A few hours later, as Caleb opened his eyes, the first thought which came to his mind made him jump out of bed. *We're doing it, today!* He pulled his jeans up, stepped into his sneakers and rushed down the steps. He found his father in the lab.

"You're up early," Frank greeted his son. "Let's eat and then we'll check one more time before I send Midnight through. I have a good feeling about this, Son."

"Me too, Dad."

Hilda was quiet and looked nervous while serving breakfast, but Frank and Caleb were occupied discussing last-minute details. They didn't pay attention to her.

"Where is Midnight?" Frank stood up and looked around. "There you are!" He spotted the cat sleeping on a pillow Hilda placed for him under the corner table. Frank gently woke the cat and cuddled him in his arms. "You're going for a ride, kitty."

They walked down to the lab and Frank went through his checklist one more time.

"Dad, I want to go. Now. You've checked everything, and Midnight is okay after being through the portal so many times. I don't want to waste another minute."

Frank hesitated, but thought it over, and nodded. "Okay. Everything is ready and the machine seems to be in perfect order." He gave Caleb a locating device similar to a wristwatch and fastened a collar to the cat's neck.

Caleb put the locator on his wrist. "Ready as I'll ever be."

Frank opened the door of the glass bubble and Caleb stepped in with Midnight in his arms. The cat seemed calm and started purring.

"Okay, so remember, I don't know where you'll end up. I'm not even sure it's the right parallel universe. But, we'll never find out if we don't try. I wish Midnight could tell us. Anyway, when you cross the portal, technically, you should feel dizzy for a moment. When your vision clears, everything is supposed to look normal. Don't forget, exactly an hour later, I'll open the portal when I detect signals emitting from both locators.)

"Got it, Dad. I'm ready."

Frank closed the door on the bubble with trembling fingers, sitting himself down in front of the monitors and control panel. The machine started humming. When) he pushed the *engage* button, his son and the fluffy black cat disappeared from inside the glass bubble.

A Ghost from the Past

Valerie's Universe

Caleb felt slight dizziness for a moment and shook his head to clear his vision. He found himself in a cemetery looking down at the gravestone with his name on it. *It must be the right universe. I'm dead here.* He rejoiced and felt Midnight squirm in his arms and jump to the ground. "Where did you disappear so fast?" he mumbled looking around but didn't see the cat, only a slight shimmer as if the air was thicker at the small area where he stepped through the portal. He touched the small locator fastened to his wrist.

Feeling great anticipation and hope, he started walking in the direction where his and Valerie's house was supposed to be, side by side. It took him only a few minutes to reach the street, where he found both houses exactly the same as in his universe. Then he heard Midnight's loud meow from Valerie's garden, but he didn't see the cat anywhere.

The front door opened, and Valerie stepped out holding a small bowl. "Here Whiskers, I have a special treat for you."

Caleb's heart skipped a beat seeing Valerie all grown up. *She was a lanky teenager when I saw her last. She's more beautiful than I'd ever imagined she would be.*

He heard a meow again and watched as Valerie looked around, confused. "Where are you, kitty?"

The cat meowed again, sounding close by, but was nowhere to be seen.

Caleb didn't ponder the fact that he didn't see the cat, or Valerie didn't notice him standing only a few feet away. "Val," he called out.

She froze and looked in his direction. "Caleb?"

"It's me, but from a parallel dimension."

"Who said that?" she cried out and started trembling. "Nobody is here. I'm hallucinating!"

"You're not. I'm here! Look at me. I came from a parallel universe to find you. Please, look at me!" Caleb begged.

Valerie broke out in sobs and turned to go back into the house. "Either I'm going batshit crazy, or I'm schizophrenic. I read about that. I'm about the right age when the first symptoms appear. That must be it," she mumbled between sobs.

"Val, I'm here."

She slowly turned and took a step closer. "It's Cal's voice but nobody is here. I must be having auditory hallucinations."

Shaking her head, she turned toward the door again. Caleb moved toward her. He reached out and touched Valerie's shoulder. Her body shook as she turned and took a step back. "Is this a sick joke? Who's there?"

Caleb knew something was terribly wrong. "You can't see me." When he looked down, he couldn't see his own body. "I can't see me either! Val, I'm here but I seem to be invisible."

Valerie scrubbed the tears off her cheeks. "That's impossible! I... I can hear you, but I can't see you. This can only mean two things. One is schizophrenia, and two, you're a ghost."

He shook his head. "No! There is nothing wrong with you and I'm not a ghost. I'm from another dimension." Caleb reached out to touch her, but she pulled back as soon as she felt his touch. "You're scaring me. What is happening to me? Who are you? It's Caleb's voice, but he's dead."

"My dad built a machine, and I came through a portal from a parallel universe to find you. My Valerie... my soulmate, she died in the universe I live in and I saw the grave of your Caleb in the cemetery."

"Are you sure I'm not hallucinating? Are you really here?" Breathing in deeply, doing her best to stay calm, Valerie pinched her arm. "Ouch!" she cried out. "At least I know it's not a dream. Are you supposed to be invisible?"

"No, this is not how it's supposed to be. Dad said everything is supposed to look and feel normal once I came through the portal, so I'm sure something went wrong."

They heard a meow again, and Valerie jumped when she felt something soft brushing against her leg. "What is it?"

"It must be Midnight, my cat. He came through the portal with me like he'd gone through many times before." Caleb rationalized

"Midnight? Is he a black cat with white whiskers?" Valerie asked, feeling a little relieved. "He's been around for weeks, but he comes only for short visits."

Caleb chuckled. "So, you've been feeding him. He's been getting a little porky, and he's never hungry after his trip through the portal."

The front door opened a crack, and a young girl poked her head out. "Val, who are you talking to?"

"Nobody," Valerie replied quickly. "Just Whiskers—you know, the black cat that's been hanging around."

"I don't see any cat." Lianne stepped out and scanned the garden and driveway. "Come in. Alice made chocolate pudding, your favorite."

"In a minute."

"Okay." Lianne turned, walked in, and then closed the door behind her.

"I have to go, Cal," Valerie whispered. "Will I see… or rather, hear you again?"

"I'll come back, promise. As soon as my dad fixes the machine. Now that I've found you, nothing could keep me away."

Valerie smiled with hope in her heart and went inside.

Caleb started walking toward the cemetery. "Midnight are you coming?" he called out. He heard the cat's quick footsteps behind him and felt him brush against his leg. He reached down and picked up the cat. Just in time, because he felt a slight dizziness. When his vision cleared, he was back at his dad's lab.

Despair

Caleb's Universe

"That was not supposed to happen." Caleb watched as his dad scratched his stubbles and stared at the controls. "When you went through you should have been flesh and bone. Not invisible!" He raked a hand through his hair. "Valerie should have been able to see you just like she saw Midnight, before, and not just hear you. Going through the portal and being invisible in the parallel dimension is a sign of a malfunction, so it's likely to take at least a couple of days to work out what happened. Maybe longer. The poor girl, no wonder she thought you were a ghost."

Nodding, Caleb slowly moved away from the machine. "I am going to be able to go back, aren't I?"

"Hopefully. I'm not going to make any promises, Cal. This is more than anyone has done before, and it's uncharted territory for any scientist."

Emotion swept through him and there was nothing he could do to stop feeling despair creeping up on him. Breathing deeply in a weak attempt to stay calm, he looked down, not sure whether he was about to scream or cry. "I know you will do whatever you can. But I want to see her again, visible or not. Dad, it was so good to see her. Thank you for making it possible." Caleb reached out and hugged his father.

"I know, Son." Frank hugged Caleb tightly and sniffed back the tears. "Okay, let me get to work." He pulled out of their embrace and patted his son's shoulder.

As they parted, they heard Hilda walking down the steps. "Is everything all right? Did the machine work? Where is Midnight?" she called out.

"It malfunctioned." Caleb offered. "Dad's going to try to fix it."

"You've always been eager to help, Hilda. But, the past few weeks you've been staying out of the lab." Frank said quietly, looking at Hilda.

"I hate it and I'm sick of it! You've been working on that damn machine for eighteen years since I came to live with you."

Frank stood there, stunned. "Why didn't you ever say something?"

"I was waiting... I waited for you to forget Claire and to feel something for me."

"I do, Hilda. I like you—a lot!"

"Yes, you like me enough to come to my bed, but you never loved me. That's what I was waiting for," she said sobbing.

"But you knew all along that Claire was the love of my life and my soulmate. How could I fall in love with someone else?"

Hilda started crying and Caleb felt sad for her. "Dad, I guess the Winston men are destined to find and lose their soulmates. We weren't meant to live a happy life."

Hilda put her hand on Caleb's shoulder and looked at Frank. "They're gone and you both must move on. There is happiness in life, for both of you."

Caleb shook her hand off his shoulder and took a step back. "The only woman I want to spend the rest of my life with is Valerie. There's no one else for me. She was my soulmate since we were babies. And, seeing her just now, even if she's not the Valerie I lost... no matter how long it takes, I'm going to find a way back to her."

Hilda inhaled sharply and the color drained from her face. "You saw her? You mean you went through the portal?" she shouted. With a couple of long strides, she reached Frank and started pounding his chest with her fists. "How could you be so irresponsible? Putting your own son's life in danger because of your impossible dream? How could you?" she cried.

Frank stood there, stunned. "He wasn't in any danger. I checked the calculations a thousand times."

"But, I made some changes last night hoping that when you couldn't bring Midnight back, you'd finally give up and abandon your research."

Frank couldn't believe his ears. "You did what?"

"I didn't know you'd planned to send Caleb through, today! You said it very clearly that you'll do one more test with Midnight!"

"How dare you?"

"I would never want to put Caleb in danger."

Caleb called out, "That's enough you two! It's done and I'm okay."

Hilda sobbed and ran over to hug Caleb. "I'm so sorry! Luckily the changes I made didn't prevent the locator from detecting you, and you could come back. Tell me what happened."

"I could see Valerie, but she couldn't see me. I was invisible." Tears trickled down his cheeks. "All I wanted was to hold her, but I couldn't."

Biting down hard on her lip Hilda looked over at the machine, and then back at Caleb. "You don't think you're ever going to be able to move on, do you? You plan on going back there!)

"Valerie was and is everything to me. Her not being here isn't so much of a problem now, because I know she's alone there, but if Dad can't fix that machine…"

"Okay." She breathed in deeply and stepped over to the controls. "I know why it didn't work properly." She glanced over at Frank. "I'm sorry. I just thought if you saw that the machine keeps malfunctioning, then you'd give up and move on. But, I never thought you'd send Caleb through the portal, only the cat."

Frank shouted. "You could have killed Caleb! You better tell me what you did!" Frank demanded with angry sparks in his eyes.

"I can fix it. I know now that this is your chance to truly be happy, and I can't take that away from either of you. I can't be selfish and stand in your way any longer. You'll never love me the way I… Never mind." She sobbed.

Frank felt deep remorse as he watched Hilda break down and admit her feelings for him. "I'm so sorry, Hilda. All those years I never really thought about how you must feel. I've been so obsessed with the idea of finding my Claire again that I took you for granted. But, it never occurred to me to ask you how you feel. I'm sorry."

"It's okay. I know I'll never be the woman you love, but I've been happy my own way."

"There's someone out there who can love you the way you deserve to be loved, Hilda, but that person isn't me."

"No, it's not, and I can see that now." She turned to the machine. "I'll fix the code and promise to never interfere again."

Love

Valerie's Universe

Caleb stepped through the portal and saw Valerie standing by her Caleb's gravestone. Her sad demeanor in the way she rested her forehead on the cold stone broke his heart.

"Val."

She heard his voice from behind her. For a few seconds, maybe longer, she couldn't bring herself to turn around, but then she did. She expected him to be invisible just like when he first visited her, but instead, she was looking at a handsome young man. Her Cal in this universe was a thin and sickly boy, but the Cal from the alternate universe was healthy, rosy-cheeked, and all grown up.

Tear welled up in her eyes, and then with a long leap, she was in his arms. She could touch him. She could smell him. She could feel his heartbeat. She reached up to touch his face. She felt his body tremble and she tightened her arms around him.

"I'm here. I'm really here." He kissed the top of her head, the way he had kissed his Valerie so many times before. "Even though Dad told me he believed he could make this happen, I couldn't let myself truly believe it was possible. Now I'm here, and you're here, and this... I've dreamt of this so many times. You and me together, the way we were always supposed to be."

Valerie stepped out of his embrace and motioned for Caleb to sit on the bench. "How is this possible? We're different people from different dimensions, but it feels like an instant connection between us. Do you feel it too?"

"Yes, I do! The way Dad explained it to me is that parallel dimensions are the same, but some things are different as well. He said, for example, that I'm the same person in both universes, but circumstances and actions might take a different turn. Just like when I was sick in your world and you were sick in mine. Although our personalities might have developed a little differently, we're still the same people in both worlds."

"It's a little too much to wrap my head around."

Caleb held her hand and kissed the tip of her fingers. "I can't express with words how happy it makes me to see you and touch you. You feel and smell exactly the same as my Val before she got sick."

"Strange as it is, you smell the same as my Cal, too."

His eyes wandered to the gravestone. Turning back to Valerie, he said with excitement in his voice, "Cal died the fifteenth of June in your world, and Val, in my world, passed away the same day. I remember the puppy I gave her a few days before, and the nurses turned a blind eye when I smuggled the little furball into hospice. He was crying his little heart out on her bed when she took her last breath. She named her Muffin."

"No! It couldn't be!" Valerie cried out. "On the way home from the hospital when my Cal passed away, my dad almost hit a golden lab puppy that appeared to be wandering the streets, lost. She's been my comfort ever since. And, you're not going to believe this, but her name is Muffin too."

"No way! This is way too much for coincidences, don't you think? My Val's parents took the puppy home from hospice and they still have her."

Valerie smiled and sighed. "If all this is true and we can be together, how are we going to explain everything?"

"I don't know." He tightened his arms around her. "And I don't really care, as long as I can spend the rest of my life with you."

"We need to explain to a lot of people what happened and how it's possible that you're here. You, being back here, is going to change everything. Maybe it'll help your dad to find his way again because he was more lost without you than without your mom. Or, it seemed that way because she left him shortly after you were born."

Caleb was taken aback. "Wait! Are you saying that in this world both my... uhm... your Cal's dad and mom are alive?"

"Yes, my mom told me that everyone knew their marriage was failing shortly after she got pregnant, but it was still a shock when she just packed up and left. Mom said she moved to another state with her lover, and she has two kids not much younger than us."

"She left your Cal—and, his dad too!" How could she?" Caleb cried out.

"I don't know. But when my Cal's dad hired a nanny, things got better. I think Helga was a better mother to Cal than his real mother ever would have been. After my Cal passed… Helga and his father got married. What happened to your parents in your world?"

"My mom died of complications when I was born, and Dad buried himself in his work. Hilda, my nanny, raised me, and she… she's been my dad's lover for a long time."

Valerie was in deep thoughts for a few minutes. "Maybe your parents and my Cal's parents weren't meant to be together in either universe."

Caleb sadly bowed his head. "Maybe they weren't, but I'm sure we did."

"Could it be possible for us to live a normal life, Cal?" Valerie sighed. "Everyone who knew you was at your funeral. If you want to live here… I don't know if it's possible." She bit down hard on her lower lip, wishing she could stop being logical, but she knew better than to think his traveling from one universe to another was normal. "I'm not saying I don't want you here, because I really do! More) than anything!"

"Maybe we can move to another state, or to my universe. I can…" He gave out a nervous laugh. "I never thought I'd say something like this, but if I'd stay here, I could steal documentation from my father here, so we can travel far away, where nobody knows either of us, so we can start a new life, together. It's been four long years since I lost my Val, and now that I found you, I don't want to live another minute without you. Losing her… I didn't know how it was going to be, but I can't give up on this chance for us to be together, even it is going to be hard to make it happen." His eyes met hers. "Give us a chance. Give the future that I'm sure we were meant to spend together, a chance."

"You don't even know for certain if you're going to be able to live in my universe, Cal. And, I don't know if you're the person my

Cal was. I don't know if I could be the person your Valerie was. This is way too complicated!"

"I admit it's complicated and unbelievable, but not impossible."

Valerie rested her head on Caleb's shoulder, enjoying the lost closeness. "Let's take it slow. For now, come visit me once a week, and let's keep it a secret. We need to get to know each other and see where the future will lead us."

Caleb shifted on the bench to face Valerie and looked into her eyes. "I'll do anything to be with you. My Val was my soulmate in my universe, and I feel it in every fiber of my body that you're my soulmate in this dimension."

Valerie reached up to touch his face, looking into his eyes. "I feel so close to you, just as close as I felt to my Cal."

Caleb ever so slowly leaned closer. The world disappeared around them as their lips touched in a soft kiss. Her body trembled as she kissed him back gently before their faces slowly parted.

Epilogue

As soon as Caleb stepped out of the portal bubble, he told his dad and Hilda everything he learned.

"Dad, I'm sorry your wish didn't come through."

"I know it now, Son." He put his arms around Hilda's waist and looked into her eyes. "All my adult life I've been chasing a dream to reunite with the love of my life while I never realized she was right beside me all along."

Caleb visited Valerie's world every week throughout the summer in their secluded spot of the cemetery. Although they kept it a secret, Valerie's family and friends noticed a positive change in her. They thought, with relief, that Valerie had found a way to move on.

In the fall, Valerie and Caleb enrolled in college together in a different state. A few years later they married and started a family. And they lived happily ever after.

"In all the world, there is no heart for me like yours. In all the world, there is no love for you like mine."
~ Maya Angelou

LOVE CONQUERS FEAR

Fake It Till You Make It

Prologue

Nancy arrives home from a long day at work. She kicks off her high heels and walks into the kitchen. Bruce lights the candles on the dinner table and embraces her in a warm hug. Her two girls, ages five and six, are running from the playroom to greet her. Their handsome seventeen-year-old boy looks up from his computer and smiles at her.

"Welcome home, honey. Dinner is ready, go wash up," Bruce announces, smiling. Nancy is happy; she counts her blessings to have found a man like Bruce.

They eat dinner and talk about their day. Nancy works at a law firm; she tells him about the long and boring meetings, and that she had to bring some work home. He assures her that it's okay because he has some laundry to finish. He winks at her playfully, hinting and promising a pleasure-filled evening before they go to sleep.

The children are chatting about their day.

"Mommy," Dayna announces with sparkly eyes. "We made a new pillow for Muffin. Isabelle sewed it together and I stuffed it. Muffin loves it!"

Isabelle stands up and grabs her father's phone. "Look, mommy," she shows the picture of a sleeping puppy to her mother. "Look, he's hugging Teddy."

"You gave him your favorite Teddy?" Nancy asks. "You never let anyone touch Teddy before."

"I did because Muffin is a baby. He needs Teddy more than I do."

"I'm so proud of you, my beautiful girls!" Nancy says with tears in her eyes. "What have you been doing all day, Liam?" she turns to her son.

"I drove to the store and picked up the dry-cleaning." Liam says feeling proud of his brand-new driver's license. And after lunch I drove when we went to take a walk in the woods. We saw a baby deer; it was so cute."

A beautiful picture, isn't it? The man plays the role of the happy househusband and the wife is the breadwinner. Nothing is wrong with that. But, let's just see how they got to this ideal picture of a happy home.

The Clock Is Ticking

They were in their early thirties when they met, and after a short courtship, Bruce proposed. They decided to get married and start a family. Nancy adored good looking Bruce who was five years her junior.

Cathy—Nancy's best friend—had a strong feeling and voiced it many times, "Bruce doesn't love you; he admires your business talent and your fat paychecks." Her woman's intuition warned her about his lack of romantic emotions.

"I know, Cathy, and I'm okay with it. I'm thirty-six. I've spent most of my younger years building up my career. Besides fleeting relationships that were based on short-lived lust and physical needs rather than finding love, I've always been alone. I gave up on my *prince on the white horse* and *earth-shattering love story* a long time ago, because he never came. At thirty-six I can't ignore the ticking clock any longer, and I want a steady relationship and a family."

"That's a mistake! You'll see!" Cathy warned.

Nancy didn't listen. "I'm done with waiting and trying to find Mr. Right. Bruce is a good man; he comes from a large Italian family. He will make a good father to my children."

Nancy defended her position. "Nancy, this is crazy. He has a roving eye. I heard stories about him you won't believe. He can't keep a job for more than a few weeks. He's a loudmouth, lazy bum who will suck the life out of you!" Cathy reasoned.

"Then what? What do you want me to do? Wait until I am too old to find someone by the time I'll be too old to have kids? If you didn't notice, there is nobody else lined up begging to be my husband and nobody is eager to father my children I desperately want."

"But he goes from one failed relationship to the next. He will cheat on you!"

Nancy bowed her head biting her lower lip. "I know he's a lady's man. He's good looking, and I am attracted to him just like others," she sighed and continued. "But I'm sure he will settle down once he's in a steady, happy home. I can give him that. He told me that his father had many girlfriends, but his mother never loved his father. He had to find love and affection somewhere else. His mother is a cold, bitter woman. She treats her husband badly. She puts him down all the time with her constant nagging and criticism, so the poor guy is unhappy."

Cathy shook her head in frustration. "But Nancy, he is a lazy bum like his son. My mother told me that he always finds an excuse not to work. He gets a job and two weeks later he gets himself fired. It's always someone else's fault, and then it takes him months to find another job. She puts up with it for the sake of the kids, but you're better than that."

Nancy's sad, submissive manner change to anger and shouted at her best friend, "You're just like my mother! Nobody is good enough for you. Leave me alone, Cathy! I love him, and that's that."

Cathy held her tongue and tried to respect Nancy's wishes. She left her alone and she didn't mention her doubts again, but she was anxious and worried.

Painful Past

Nancy was an only child and her father left them when she was three. She barely remembered him.

As a small child, Nancy's mom always told her what to do. It seemed natural. However, Nancy's memories of her childhood as she grew older were painful. Living under her mother's thumb, her whole existence was controlled. Although she started rebelling in high school, she couldn't escape the strong emotional hold of her mother.

In school, she was desperate to be accepted and popular. But in her naïve mind, she mistook popularity with being popular with boys.

She didn't like to think back at her promiscuous years in junior high; she buried that period of her life deeply. She became pregnant, and she had no idea of who the father was. Her mother, Joan, confronted her after noticing the sanitary pads were untouched in the bathroom for two months. She had to admit that her periods had stopped, and she was pregnant.

Her mother freaked out. "You stupid slut! How could you do this to me?" she shouted in frustration.

"I didn't do this to you, Mother!" Nancy cried. "I'm the one who's pregnant."

"You did this to hurt me!" she shrieked. "Your father can't find out. Let me think!" Deep down she was still hoping her husband would come back to her one day if she could prove to him that she had raised their daughter properly. Her dream had been shattered.

Joan came up with a plan to take Nancy to her sister after she was in the fifth month of her pregnancy, and her increasing roundness couldn't be explained by just having a healthy appetite. Nancy did everything her mother told her to do, and she gave birth to the baby in secret. Her aunt arranged the adoption. Nancy wasn't allowed to look at the baby. It was just fine with her back then, but later she was thinking about her baby more and more.

Her aunt and mother refused to give her details. They said it was a part of her life that was closed. She thought about the abandoned child with much sadness, and she promised to herself that she would find him or her someday.

Her mother kept her busy and planned her day; she told her what to do and how to behave every minute of the day. She was scared leaving her comfortable and secure home when she enrolled in college. She called her mother for advice on what to wear, how to do her hair and even what to have for breakfast.

Later, she gained some confidence and she learned to decide small things for herself. However, as her phone calls grew less and less, her mother's phone calls became more and more frequent. Nancy became annoyed with the constant advice from her mother, and Joan became more and more desperate to stay in control of Nancy's life.

When Nancy was in her early twenties, her mother kept badgering her to find a man, settle down, and start a family. Nancy tried, but whenever she introduced a man to her mother, she found something wrong right away. She began planting doubts in Nancy's mind and the relationship ended up in a breakup.

When she met Bruce, she didn't introduce him to her mother until he proposed. She was desperate to have a relationship; she felt her clock ticking. She knew her mother would find something to discourage her and she could end up being alone again.

Her hunch was right. Two days after their dinner together, Joan called her and began her campaign against Bruce. Nancy wasn't strong enough to stop her, but she listened. Surprisingly, her mother's negativity had an opposite effect on her. The more her mother tried to put Bruce down, the higher he rose on Nancy's mental pedestal. Nancy became annoyed, they eloped, and a week later she announced to her mother that she was a married woman.

Joan felt devastated and left out. She shouted, and then begged. Nancy didn't budge; she had Bruce to lean on for strength. After months of trying to fight her way back in control, Joan resigned or seemed to. Her tactics became less obvious, but she didn't give up.

She realized that if she stayed pushy, Nancy could shut her out completely. She learned to push her more gently than before, but she couldn't let go of the times when she had total control of Nancy. She decided to wait and work hard to rebuild the relationship she so desperately needed.

The Ropes are Breaking

Nancy wanted to bury the bad memories and didn't want to listen to anyone's advice when Bruce proposed, and they eloped. They were happy, at least Nancy was.

Bruce was between jobs; he said his main priority was to take good care of Nancy. She gave him access to her bank account, and he began shopping. Big screen TV, Play Station, smartphone: he bought all the gadgets he wanted. In return, he waited for her with a delicious dinner every night. He cooked all the Italian dishes he learned from his mother and learned to cook Nancy's favorite foods.

He was attentive in the bedroom and was always ready to satisfy her needs. She was happy, although in the back of her mind she had doubts, she tried to ignore them. She got pregnant within months. She was elated. Finally, she could have the wonderful husband and family she always wanted.

She steadily gained weight as was expected, up to her second trimester. He became less and less attentive. He went up to their bedroom a little later every day as her pregnancy progressed. She protested at first under the influence of her hormone surges, but she accepted his explanations of 'you know how intense I get, I'm afraid that I'm gonna hurt the baby' and such.

She was even happy that he was so thoughtful. They attended Lamaze classes and they practiced the exercises together. She wanted him to be her birth coach, and of course, she wanted him to be in the delivery room during the birth.

He argued at first that his father never saw any of his children born and he wanted to do the same.

She argued that because her father wasn't present in the delivery room either, he never really formed a close bond with her. She was very adamant about this subject, so he reluctantly caved in.

"You're right! I will be there," he promised.

Fake It 'Till You Make It

Bruce remembered a conversation he had with his father a long time ago. They were sitting at the kitchen table having a beer when he was just a teenager. He felt so grown up and important because his father let him drink a beer. He asked his father if he ever loved his mother. He had watched their relationship since he was a small child, and he couldn't sense any devotion on his father's part.

"She's a dumb bitch. What's there to love? But she's a good mother and a good provider. I find my love elsewhere, son. The home is for security and comfort while I'm looking for a job," he said, winking at Bruce. "She's well trained if you know what I mean," he continued.

Bruce wanted his father's approval desperately. He was the role model for absentee fathers, but occasionally they had a moment together when he felt some closeness to him. All his life he believed that his mother and, as a matter of fact, every woman was just a meal ticket to an easy life. That's what he saw, and that's what he learned. He thought about relationships rationally: have fun with a girl but marry a steady woman on whom you can depend, as his father said. He had many girls to have fun with, and when he was in his early twenties, he began looking for a wife. He moved in and out of fleeting relationships, and he was surprised in the beginning that after four or five months, the women threw him out. They saw right through him and they refused to be used. He asked his father about it.

"Son, you have to be smart. You can't just sit at home watching movies all day. Of course, they will find out you have no intention to work. You must 'fake it till you make it' Take a job, do it for a couple of weeks, and then get yourself fired. Find a way that makes it look like it wasn't your fault. Then you're okay for a couple of months;

they will leave you in peace to look for another job," his father advised him.

It worked for years, and he could stay in a relationship longer and longer.

Then he met Nancy. She was the first woman in his life who was successful, compared to the waitresses and hairdressers he'd lived with before. Nancy was sophisticated and well-spoken, and she had a high paying job at a law firm. She was soon to be made partner. Bruce could never even dream of the money she made. She decided that Nancy was his dream woman. He thought that if he played his cards right, he could be set for life. He was excited; he worked very hard at wooing her. He learned the little things she liked; he lavished her with white roses and foot massages while they were courting. She let him move in. Her house was a mansion. He settled in quickly, and he began his campaign of seducing her to trust him completely.

It worked, although it was touch and go after he met her mother. Joan was suspicious and she had almost total control of Nancy. He succeeded in keeping Joan somewhat out of Nancy's mind, keeping her comfortable and happy. While he was 'looking for work,' he managed to cook delicious meals that, luckily, he'd learned from his mother when he was a young boy. He always loved to cook and bake and set the table beautifully. It made Nancy happy to come home after a hard day to a home-cooked meal. The laundry was done, her clothes were all pressed and hanging on the rack, and her house was spotlessly clean. After a glass of wine and a soothing foot massage, he led her up to the candlelit bedroom. He learned quickly what made her squeal with delight, and what made her happy. He thought they could live happily ever after.

She wanted kids. He didn't, but he was afraid to tell her. He tried to leave the options open. He told her it was too soon, so she reluctantly agreed to wait. He knew he would have to give in sooner or later, because she seemed eager to become pregnant and that's all she wanted to talk about. She went to see her mother, and after the visit, she became somewhat distant. She started questioning him about his job hunt, and she didn't seem to be satisfied with his lame excuses anymore. She told him she could use her influence to find him something.

He became desperate, and he told her on a whim that it was very degrading to use her as a jumping board; he wanted to do it on his own. She wasn't convinced, so he told her he was ready for a baby. He was secretly hoping she wouldn't even conceive, but he had to take that chance. He didn't want her being unhappy, because he knew she would focus more on the job hunt. It had worked for a while; Nancy was happy with the pregnancy.

Later on, she became worried, because she was used to the lifestyle which her paychecks provided. She began talking about staying home with the baby and started mentioning to Bruce that he had to take it seriously and start looking for a job with more force.

Confessions

Bruce was sweating under this pressure. After a long debate, he decided to tell her the truth. He slowly awoke Nancy's sympathy by telling her about his traumatic experience at his first job. He told her he was raped by his uncle when he was twelve and he worked in his store. He was too ashamed to tell anyone, and he was begging his mother not to make him work there anymore. She was angry and called him a lazy bum just like his father, and she ordered him to go to work every day after school.

He came so close to telling her the truth a couple of times, but he didn't. His mother adored her brother, and Bruce thought that she would take his side. He obeyed and worked there for two years, enduring his uncle's sexual advances. After his fourteenth birthday, he couldn't take it anymore. He pushed his uncle one day and told him that it must stop. His uncle wouldn't listen. He tried to kiss him. Bruce became angry; he pushed him so hard that his uncle fell backward and hit his head on one of the shelves. He slumped to the floor, bleeding profusely. He was unconscious.

Bruce became frantic; he didn't know what to do. He sat down on the floor, watching his uncle taking shallow breaths. *The bastard! He deserves to die,* he thought, but then the better part of him kicked in. He couldn't just leave him there bleeding to death, no matter how deeply he hated him, so he reluctantly called the ambulance.

His uncle never regained consciousness, and he died weeks later. His nasty doings never surfaced. Bruce buried it deeply and he tried to forget, but it was very hard. In his mind he was gay. He had nobody to talk to, he was too ashamed. He was sure his uncle had made him gay, although when he tried to have a relationship with boys, he got disgusted. He realized he preferred girls, and he jumped into many feverish affairs as if he were trying to prove to himself that he was 'normal' despite what happened to him.

"Nancy, I've found you. I want to spend the rest of my life with you, just give me some time. I'm trying very hard to find and keep a job, but something always triggers bad memories. Can you understand that? I never told anyone, ever. You're the first person I feel close enough to share this dirty secret with. Can you keep this secret with me?" he asked Nancy.

She was in tears by the time he finished. Her heart went out to him. She was sobbing so hard. "Of course I can. I'm so sorry you had to go through something like that when you were so young. You should have talked about this to your parents and go to therapy. They can help you to deal with this."

"No therapy. I'm sorry now that I told you about it. I thought that you would understand."

"I do, I really do, but you should get help. You can't carry this burden with you, and it is holding you back from living a normal life."

"No, I'm not doing it. If you don't want to help me then forget I ever told you." He clammed up.

"I can't forget, and I promise this will be our secret. I will help you the best I can to deal with it," Nancy promised.

She stopped badgering him about finding a job, and she resigned herself to taking the role of the breadwinner. She reasoned that she made good money. She had to work long hours, so instead of losing the money she would pay for a housekeeper, he could stay home and be happy and take care of everything around the house.

The truth was, she loved to go home to a cooked meal and clean house; those were never her favorite chores. This arrangement made them both happy. Nancy was worried about Bruce suppressing his bad memories, but she didn't dwell on it for long. *So, what if my marriage is somewhat unconventional? He is a good man, he loves me, and I love him. That's nobody's business how we live!* Nancy reasoned.

He's Scared

When Nancy started having contractions, Bruce drove her to the hospital. He looked very nervous and complained that the hospital smell was making him nauseous. She ignored his silent plea. He put up a brave face and stayed. Squirmed in his chair, sighed or paced the room, but he stayed.

Isabelle was born after long hours of hard labor. She was red, wrinkled, and she cried ferociously. Bruce threw up in the sink, his stomach turned seeing the bloody mess of birth and forced himself to cut the umbilical cord as everyone expected him to do.

Nancy was happy; she'd never felt more happiness in her whole life. When the nurse placed Isabelle on her chest and she connected with her flesh and blood the first time, she felt like her heart could burst with love. She touched the baby's tiny fingers. Isabelle wrapped her hand around her finger; Nancy knew that instant she was meant to be a mother. She looked up to her husband adoringly. He was pale, and he seemed shaken up, but he smiled at her. He touched the tiny baby's head with trembling fingers. She thought he was just nervous and worried; she was proud of her man.

Bruce could hardly wait to get out of there. The doctor was sewing Nancy up, she was exposed, and the smell of blood filled his nose making him gag. *This is disgusting! That kid is going to squeal like that all the time. Nancy looks like a beached whale on that bed. Even if she lost the weight, I'm never gonna erase this picture from my mind,* he screamed inside but then his calculating side took over. *Maybe I'll get used to it. My father did, and he had four of us to deal with. Yeah, he was lucky. He didn't have to see how his kids came out of there!* he thought and tried with all his might to keep it together.

Doubts

Finally, Bruce could go home, but he couldn't sleep. The picture of his daughter's birth was haunting him. He wished he'd never had to see it, but it was done. He had to learn to deal with it. He had a daughter, a flesh and blood human being, and he couldn't comprehend the thought that he was a father.

"What am I gonna do?" he mumbled. "My comfortable life seems to be over. What if she's expecting me to change diapers and feed the baby? Moreover, what if she wants to stay home and is expecting me to be the breadwinner?"

He sat up in, his bed heart racing. "I hate working. I can't stand it when I must be there on time and do what others tell me to do every minute. She makes good money, she should work, and I could be the stay at home dad. But then I'd have to deal with this screaming and pooping little monster."

He got out of bed and stumbled towards the bathroom. After he splashed cold water on his face his racing mind calmed down enough so he could weigh his options. "Which one is better? Go to a job that I hate eight hours a day, or stay home and do what I want all day? How bad can it be? If I feed the kid and keep her clean, she will sleep most of the time and I could do whatever I want. Now, talking her into going back to work right away could be a challenging job. It must look like it was her idea and not mine."

After a few hours restless sleep, he spent the better part of the day thinking when he had a few minutes between answering the congratulatory phone calls and getting the nursery ready. He washed and pressed the tiny baby clothes and organized the changing table. Doing the small chores around the house calmed him, and he realized that the activity made him happy. He read the 'Welcome your brand-new baby' book again and realized that he forgot to pick up a thermometer.

He stopped at the drugstore on his way to visiting Nancy in the hospital. He lied to her saying that he stopped by the nursery and Isabelle was beautiful. He couldn't make himself do it; he was thinking he had one more free day without the screaming bundle. He forced himself to kiss Nancy while the picture in his mind was her bloody, exposed female parts. He smelled her sweat and he almost gagged, but he forced a nervous smile.

He's scared out of his mind! Nancy thought, alarmed. "It's going to be alright, honey. I know you're scared; a child is a big responsibility. Mom said she will stay with us for a couple of weeks to help."

Bruce got scared for real hearing that. He was thinking frantically, trying to come up with something. "No honey, we don't need her to stay. We're totally capable of taking care of Isabelle. I'm here. Don't worry. I'll take care of her," he protested quickly.

The Plan

Bruce hated Nancy's nosy and controlling mother because she could see right through him. He knew Nancy would listen to her mother and that would make it much harder to convince her. He knew he had to learn quickly and show her he could be the best person to take care of the baby.

"Okay, but are you sure? We could use any help we can get. I'm pretty weak. I'm not sure if I can care of her for a while," Nancy worried.

"I'm sure, honey. I've been studying the books, and I will ask the nurses to show me everything. We're family; we can take care of our own baby. How hard can it be?" He smiled at her showing confidence, while inside he was making a compromise.

I'll learn everything, and I'll show her that I'm the best father there is. Otherwise, I can say goodbye to freedom. I can go and look for another boring job and be miserable. I can't leave her either, then I'd have to work anyway until I find another woman to take care of my needs. What if she's disgustingly fat? She could lose the weight, or I could close my eyes and picture someone else while...oh crap! I'm never gonna lose that picture of her bottom all bloody and split. No, get a hold of yourself, idiot! She's your ticket to a comfortable life, deal with it, he decided while stroking his wife's hand.

"But Mom will be devastated. You know how desperate she gets when I don't answer her phone call. She imagines the worst right away. How can I tell her not to come when she's so looking forward to meeting her first granddaughter?" Nancy protested weakly.

Bruce thought about it for a minute and decided that it was too soon to sever the toxic but strong ties Nancy had with her mother. It had to be done gradually if he wanted to keep Joan out of their business.

"Okay, you're right. We need a little help at the beginning, but I don't want her running our lives. She can stay for a week."

"You're the best. I will tell her, and I will stick to my guns. I won't let her stay a minute longer," Nancy promised happily.

She adored him for being so sure of himself. *He's gonna be a good father,* she thought. She called her mother to tell her their decision. Joan protested and tried to put her foot down, but Nancy was firm. She had never said no to her mother before, but Bruce gave her confidence. She told her mother she could come to stay for a week and that Bruce was very capable of helping her and taking care of everything. She was proud of herself. This was the first time in her entire life that she had the courage to say no to her bullying mother.

The nurse came in and asked them if they would like to bathe Isabelle. Nancy agreed happily, looking at Bruce.

"Of course, I'll do it, honey." He turned to Nancy, displaying excitement. "You need your rest; you did such a great job last night. You brought a new person into this life. Let me do it," he begged, knowing that with sweet words that appealed to her, he could influence her.

"Okay, but I'll come too."

"Of course! Let me help you." He jumped up eagerly.

He was scared shitless. *What if I drop the baby? What if I squeeze her hard enough that it could hurt her? She looks so fragile. Okay, okay, deep breaths. If other fathers could do it, so could I. Father! Holy crap! I'm a father.* It dawned on him suddenly. *That kid out there is my flesh and blood.*

She's Happy, He's Petrified

Bruce pushed her wheelchair into the nursery. This was the second time he laid eyes on his daughter. He was nervous and scared, but he put on his brave face. He remembered his father's favorite saying: 'When you fake it long enough, it will come.' His father applied this philosophy to everything in his life, from his loathing toward his wife to his indifference toward his children.

Bruce looked at Isabelle, and his heart skipped. The tiny baby was beautiful. Her skin looked smooth as velvet. She opened her eyes and looked up at Bruce. She had this old soul look about her, as if she knew that her parents were there to take care of her. Nancy cried softly, caressing Isabelle's hand.

"Our beautiful little angel. Isn't she beautiful, Bruce?" She looked up. Something stirred deep down inside Bruce. It was a painful yet beautiful feeling. A deep sob choked him.

"She is very beautiful," he managed to croak out, barely seeing his daughter through a veil of tears.

"Are you ready to hold your daughter?" The nurse surprised him.

"Let me sit down. I'm afraid that I'm going to drop her," he answered nervously.

He sat down in the rocking chair and he took a deep breath. *I can do this,* he thought, and he held out his arms to receive the beautiful little bundle. He was shaky and nervous, but as soon as the baby nestled into his arms, all his doubts and fears disappeared. *My baby! My beautiful baby,* he thought, and a teardrop rolled down his cheek.

Nancy caressed Isabelle's little tummy and looked up at her husband with adoration shining in her eyes.

Bruce looked into her eyes and felt the warmth spreading in his chest. *I love her! I truly love my wife. I never really noticed how beautiful she was, until just now. I don't care if she's fat, and I don't care about that picture that is stuck in my mind when Isabelle was born. All forgotten, it was all just a part of getting this beautiful new life in my arms. My father was perhaps right, if you fake it long enough, it will come. I don't care what was in the past; my future is here with my wife and my daughter.* Bruce sobbed softly and felt true happiness for the first time in his life. He leaned over to share a loving kiss with his wife.

Epilogue

Bruce adapted to the role of being a househusband and devoted father. Nancy went back to work just two weeks after their baby was born. She was happy with their arrangement and realized that she wasn't meant to be a stay-at-home mom after all. She loved the excitement and accomplishments of her job, and she loved to come home to a clean house, attentive husband and a happy, well cared for child. She decided to open up the last baggage she came into the marriage with. She told Bruce about her baby when she was a teenager. Bruce hugged her, and he promised they would find the child together.

They did find him a year later, thanks to Bruce's thorough research. He was a teenager by then and he'd lived in foster homes all his life. Nancy found out that her aunt and mother had lied to her. They said that the baby was adopted by a loving couple; instead, her aunt left the baby on a church's steps. Bruce insisted on visiting him and after blood tests and long paperwork, Nancy was reunited with her long-lost boy.

Bruce happily embraced Liam and treated him as if he was his own son, and Liam adapted to the new family life quickly. He forgave his mother for leaving him, and he understood that what Nancy did was a teenager's mistake. She had trusted the adults in her life to take care of things for her. Nancy's mother denied any knowledge of the mistreatment of her grandson, and although Nancy didn't believe her, she forgave her. She allowed her to visit her grandkids, but only after her second daughter Dayna was born. She never let her mother influence her again in any way. She developed a strong bond with Bruce and her three children, and she didn't allow anyone to break her family apart.

Special Thanks

Thank you, <u>Cindy J. Smith</u>, author of amazing poetry books, for the wonderful poems you wrote for this book.

The Author

http://www.authorerikamszabo.com/

"The writing bug bit me on a rainy afternoon when I couldn't find any new book to read. My daughter had enough of my moping around and snapped at me, "Mom, stop whining! If you haven't a book to read, then write one." Her challenge shocked me, but I started playing with the idea and I've been writing stories, that I like to read, ever since."

Erika loves to dance to her own tunes and follow her dreams, introduces her story writing skills and her books that are based on creative imagination with themes such as alternate history, urban fantasy, cozy mystery, sweet romance and supernatural stories. Her children's stories are informative, educational, and deliver moral values in a non-preachy way.

"I followed my dream to become a writer. As an artist, I paint pretty pictures with my brushes, and as a writer, I paint vivid pictures with my words."

Books by the Author

Fiction novels & novellas by Erika M Szabo

Children's books & audiobooks by Erika M Szabo

www.authorerikamszabo.com

Contents